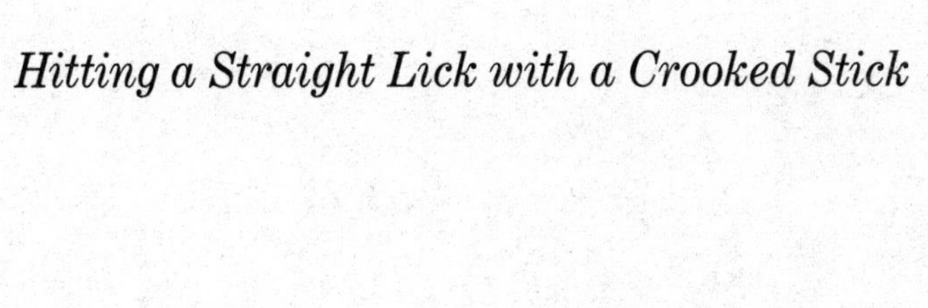

Hitting a Straight Lick with a Crooked Stick

ALSO BY ZORA NEALE HURSTON

Jonah's Gourd Vine

Mules and Men

Their Eyes Were Watching God

Tell My Horse

Moses, Man of the Mountain

Dust Tracks on a Road

Seraph on the Suwanee

Mule Bone

The Complete Stories

Every Tongue Got to Confess

Barracoon

Hitting a Straight Lick with a Crooked Stick

STORIES FROM THE HARLEM RENAISSANCE

Zora Neale Hurston

Foreword by Tayari Jones

Introduction by Genevieve West

AMISTAD

An Imprint of HarperCollins*Publishers*

This is a work of fiction. Names, characters, places, and incidents are products of the author's imagination or are used fictitiously and are not to be construed as real. Any resemblance to actual events, locales, organizations, or persons, living or dead, is entirely coincidental.

HarperCollins books may be purchased for educational, business, or sales promotional use. For information, please email the Special Markets Department at SPsales@harpercollins.com.

FIRST EDITION

Designed by Michelle Crowe

Library of Congress Cataloging-in-Publication Data has been applied for.

ISBN 978-0-06-291579-5

20 21 22 23 24 LSC 10 9 8 7 6 5 4 3 2 1

Contents

EDITOR'S NOTE

This volume constitutes an entirely new edition of Hurston's short fiction. Each story here has been transcribed anew using, whenever possible, the first documented publication of the story as the copy text. When a first publication was not available, typescripts served as the foundation. I respectfully corrected errors that likely occurred during the typesetting process, such as missing end punctuation, missing opening *or* closing quotation marks, obvious spelling errors, and idiosyncratic capitalization. Hurston's punctuation—particularly her use of commas, dashes and commas together, and punctuation of contractions and dialogue—evolved considerably over the course of the Harlem Renaissance. Consequently, rather than impose a single standard on the volume, I have looked to the stories themselves for guidance. Each story has been treated as a discrete text with its own conventions. For instance, when *ain't* appears five times in a story with the apostrophe and once without it, I have replaced the missing apostrophe in that story only. In later stories, readers will then see words spelled and punctuated differently in the various stories as Hurston's distinctive voice matured. I have preserved her punctuation and spelling to ensure fidelity to her vision at the time the story first appeared.

* * *

Concerning the discovery of the stories, in 2005 I documented four that were found in the *Pittsburgh Courier* in *Zora Neale Hurston and American Literary Culture*. I uncovered them in the landmark microfiche collection *Black Literature 1827–1940* as I searched for reviews of Hurston's books. Edited by Henry Louis Gates Jr., *Black Literature 1827–1940* collects the poetry, fiction, and reviews that appeared in 110 significant—but rare—black magazines and newspapers from the period. Although the work of developing the microfiche collection began in the early 1980s, the Hurston stories contained therein waited—undocumented—until 2005.

In 2010, Glenda S. Carpio and Werner Sollors working collaboratively also chanced upon the *Pittsburgh Courier* stories while perusing microfilm of the newspaper. Through their efforts, the *Courier* stories became front-page news in the *Chronicle Review*.[1] A short time later, Carpio and Sollors gathered all five of the *Courier* stories as the centerpiece of a special issue of an academic journal, *Amerikastudien / American Studies*.

FOREWORD

Love Letter and Testimony

Zora Neale Hurston is in that rare category of writer who reached the type of notoriety that gives her one-name status. This isn't terribly uncommon—think Faulkner, Hemingway, and Fitzgerald. However, there are precious few whose one name is their first name, and fewer still who are easily known by their given names and/or their family names. I can think of only three—Toni Morrison, Maya Angelou, and the great Zora Neale Hurston, who predated them both.

Whenever I think of Zora, by this single name, I have the urge to go wild with punctuation: Zora!!! Part of this is motivated by the audacity of the name itself. There is something brazen about the letter *Z*, bringing up the rear of the alphabet with three bold slashes. And this is compounded by the fact that the name is perfectly suited to the woman herself. Who hasn't admired the images of her that we see on postcards in bookshops? The most memorable are the portraits taken by Carl Van Vechten in which Zora poses with her felt hat tilted to shade one eye, or she wears a coat that frames her face with a dramatic fur collar. These are black-and-white photos, but my favorite features her against a red background in which she sports a beaded cap that matches her cream-colored dress. Her lips are curved into something between a smirk and a smile, like she knows something that we don't.

Have you ever noticed that Zora Neale Hurston is seldom photographed looking squarely at the camera? I can never decide whether she is being coy, deliberately cultivating the mystery of her persona. Maybe she spares us the intensity of her straightforward gaze because one should never look directly into the sun. Regardless of her motivation, the images we have are captivating and enchanting. She may not meet our eyes, but she leaves us unable to turn away all these years later.

The page of her insightful prose is where Hurston chooses to reveal herself. Gone are the dramatic hats and headdresses, the sidelong glances, and the rouged lips. The stories in this fine collection are the tales of country folks—farmers, factory workers. And through their lives we experience the full range of human emotion. Hurston's sense of humor is legendary. I dare you to read this book in public without releasing at least one leg-slapping guffaw. Although people often suggest that black folks "laugh to keep from crying," these characters show that some laughter is simply the reward for a joke well told. But even the folks who sit on the porch telling lies and playing the dozens still get the blues. After all, they are parents, lovers, children, spouses, and friends; with these connections come vulnerability and even grief. Hurston illuminates the breadth, depth, diameter, and circumference of the lives of those she knows and loves best.

Like Faulkner, Hurston's muse is her hometown, the landscape and culture that formed her. But while Faulkner sets his work in a fictional place, Yoknapatawpha County, Hurston calls

Eatonville by its true name, giving credit where it is due. (She represents for Eatonville harder than Biggie did for Brooklyn and Tupac for LA.) Hurston's writing is both love letter and testimony. For too many years, the American South has been evoked as a shorthand for African American misery and oppression. When Nina Simone said, "Mississippi Goddam," she covered the entire region. But Hurston loved the land that she called home. Eatonville boasted a black mayor, and although Hurston roasts him mercilessly in this book, as well as in *Their Eyes Were Watching God,* there is an empowerment that comes from black self-governance. Although racism and "white folks" present real challenges to the characters that people this collection, oppression is not the center of their lives. This is one of the many intricacies of the southern experience that is on full display in this excellent collection.

Short stories offer us something that novels do not. With a novel, even a masterpiece like *Their Eyes Were Watching God,* our attention is aimed at one or two characters as we take a deep dive into their complicated psychology, actions, and circumstances. With each short story, we encounter the same degree of complexity, but the characters' experiences are distilled into a few defining moments. To use a metaphor of which I hope Hurston would approve: A novel is like a whole watermelon, gorgeous striped rind, white pith, red flesh, and shiny black seeds. It is delicious; it is a work of God's majesty. The short story is more like the watermelon heart. In the country, men stand by the side of the road and throw the watermelon down on the pavement, just so. Upon impact, the melon will break in such a way that the juicy center is separated from the rest. This is the best part of the fruit—ripe, firm, seedless, and sweet. If a man offers a woman the heart of the watermelon, well, things are serious.

Similarly, these stories get right to the heart of the matter.

Hurston, trickster that she is, has chosen comeuppance as her literary specialty. Hers is a world populated by people who are more powerful than they seem. A jilted husband, so timid that he can only gulp when his wife's lover passes by. However, through his own death, he takes the Romeo to his grave. (The wife, on the other hand, lives her best life—free of them both.) The Baptists and the Methodists square off for an epic clash and nobody quite wins, but laughs abound. But in the realm of payback, there is more than fun and games. In tales that feel as ancient as "The Monkey's Paw," characters learn to be careful what they wish for. The delight of this collection is the way the stories feel rooted in a reality that is nearly a century old, yet still manage to achieve timelessness.

On Hurston's tombstone are engraved the words "A Genius of the South." The memorial stone was commissioned by a young Alice Walker who was so moved by *Their Eyes Were Watching God* that she took a pilgrimage to Florida to find out what became of Hurston and to pay her respects. Many people know this part of the story. Hurston died penniless and in obscurity. Walker searched an unkempt cemetery, battling mosquitos and sticker briars until she found the sunken, unmarked grave. At the time, this was a deterrent example and rallying call, admonishing us to take better care of our cultural workers as they age. Hurston became symbolic of the many black women writers who fell into obscurity due to the twin burdens of racism and sexism. Virginia Woolf mused about Shakespeare's hypothetical sister, but Walker championed Zora Neale Huston, an actual person.

I wonder what Hurston would make of this. I do not doubt for a moment that she would have enjoyed the attention. She was the life of the party, after all. Thanks to the advocacy of Walker and other writers and scholars, *Their Eyes Were Watching God* is now regarded as an American classic and has been translated into dozens of languages. Zora Neale Hurston is perhaps the best known of all the Harlem Renaissance writers, surpassing even Langston Hughes. However, I think she would be dismayed at becoming a cautionary tale. In her famous essay "How It Feels to Be Colored Me," she declared, "I am not tragically colored."

In that spirit, I offer a different interpretation of these same events. We can all agree that the end of Hurston's life was difficult. We can all agree that she deserved her laurels while she still walked among us. Yet Zora, being Zora, did not let mere death end her life. Alice Walker found Hurston's grave, but Hurston's work found Alice Walker.

Some readers may not understand the title *Hitting a Straight Lick with a Crooked Stick*. I will explicate it the best I can. Like Hurston, I understand that sometimes the most vibrant language doesn't translate well into the more formal tone of well-meaning documents like this foreword. The expression, one I know from my own southern childhood, means to achieve a goal that seems to be in contradiction to the means by which it was accomplished. (It's amazing, isn't it, how the act of translation boils the life out of the phrase, leaving it as limp as overcooked vegetables? This is why Hurston captured the language of her community phonetically, so that none of the music and magic would be lost in the alchemy from breath to ink.)

I would not do justice to this latest addition to Hurston's oeuvre if I didn't praise the splendor of its language. No writer before, or since, has regarded the language of the African American South with such affection and seriousness. Unfettered by respectability politics, Hurston lets the people speak for themselves. And speak, they do.

I recommend reading this work aloud, enjoying the feel of the words in your mouth, and the sound of English tightened and strummed like the strings of a banjo. Lose yourself in these stories. Laugh when it's funny. Wipe your eyes when the spirit moves you. Remember Hurston in this way—complicated and brilliant. These pages, like their author, contain multitudes.

Tayari Jones
August 19, 2019

INTRODUCTION

Outstanding novelist, skilled folklorist, journalist, and critic, Zora Hurston was for thirty years the most prolific black woman writer in America.[1]

—Mary Helen Washington

For Zora Neale Hurston the Harlem Renaissance began in 1921, when she published her first short story, and it ended in 1937 with the publication of her masterpiece, *Their Eyes Were Watching God.* In the period between, she wrote twenty-one stories, all of which appear here together in a single volume for the first time. Included in *Hitting a Straight Lick with a Crooked Stick* are several "lost" Harlem Renaissance tales, eight of which challenge readers to rethink their assumptions about Hurston's literary interests. An author long associated with the rural, with Eatonville, Florida, she wrote eight stories about northern cities and the Great Migration. She also wrote about Harlem's middle class. Thus, this new Harlem Renaissance volume provides a much-needed correction to Hurston's legacy and better reflects the true breadth of her subject matter.

Presented in the order of their composition, the stories collected here allow readers to track the evolution and maturation of Hurston's skills and interests as a fiction writer, from what her biographer Robert Hemenway describes as her "apprentice" work to her mature, masterful critiques of the politics of race, class, and gender—what we today call the politics of identity.[2] Hurston typically submerged her explorations of such serious topics within plots revolving around romantic relationships between men and women. Literary critics Claudia Tate and Susan Meisenhelder adopted Hurston's own phrase, "hitting a straight lick with a crooked stick," to describe the ways in which she subversively critiques the politics of race and gender, and, I add, the politics of class as well. Zora herself described what it means to "hit a straight lick with a crooked stick" in slightly different ways. In her autobiography, *Dust Tracks on a Road* (1942), she uses the phrase to describe her hometown because "[i]t is a by-product of something else." In the essay "High John de Conquer," she describes it as "making a way out of no-way" or "[w]inning the jack pot with no other stake but a laugh."[3] Hurston's "making a way" to express herself in a racist and masculine publishing industry required subversive strategies for exploring topics, critiquing behaviors and norms, and expressing perspectives that editors and readers might have rather avoided. Across the body of her Harlem Renaissance fiction, again and again Hurston "hit[s] a straight lick with a crooked stick" to address the politics of identity.

Eight of the nine recovered stories that appear here are set in urban environments that reflect the tumult of the Great Migration. More than two million African Americans left the largely rural South between 1910 and 1940 for the industrialized cities of the North.[4] On their journeys to build new lives, migrants faced collective and individual challenges in urban communities as they encountered new expectations for dress, deportment, speech, education, religious practice, and entertainment. So profound were the changes wrought by the Great Migration that it spawned an entire body of what scholar Farah Jasmine Griffin describes as migration narratives—songs, stories, novels, and paintings—that depict the upheaval of migration, the resulting loss of community, confrontations with the new environment, attempts to reestablish community, and even reverse migration, which some undertook when the North failed to fulfill its promise of a better life.[5]

Until the recovery of Hurston's lost stories, it had appeared as though she had opted to limit her treatment of the Great Migration to a single story, "Muttsy," and to the subtle references that appear elsewhere in her fiction, such as in her first novel, *Jonah's Gourd Vine* (1934). Cultural and literary critic Hazel V. Carby had even gone so far as to suggest that Hurston "attempt[ed] to stabilize and displace the social contradictions and disruption of her contemporary moment" by focusing on "a utopian reconstruction of a historical moment of her childhood" in Eatonville.[6] Today—with the recovery of these urban stories—we know that Carby was mistaken. She simply did not have access to Hurston's entire corpus. When Hurston explores urban settings and characters, the Great Migration may be central to the plot, or it might loom in the background. Both strategies, however, expand her treatments of the politics of gender, class, and race to include another layer of complexity produced by regional differences. Migrants were forced to reconcile conflicting norms on matters both secular and sacred—many of which intersected with gender-based norms related to race and class. The choices Hurston's characters face, mundane and momentous alike, illustrate the tumult of the times. Hurston's short stories rarely fail to engage identity politics, and in this way her urban tales are no different from her better-known Eatonville stories and her novels. At the same time, the urban settings do change the nature of the politics her characters must negotiate.

HURSTON "REALLY DID GET BORN"

Zora Neale Hurston claimed, at various times, to have been born in 1901, 1902, and 1903 in Eatonville, Florida, the first "incorporated" black town in the United States.[7] It is probably more accurate to say that Eatonville was *home,* the place that not only inspired her but also shaped her identity. In addition, Zora was also a decade older than she publicly acknowledged, having been born (according to US Census records) in 1891 in Notasulga, Alabama.[8] Her family relocated to Eatonville in 1894. When Zora's mother died and her father remarried to a woman she despised, it initiated a period of wandering. Unable to finish high school because she needed to support herself, she worked in white homes as a maid, bounced among relatives and friends, and then took a position as a lady's maid in a Gilbert and Sullivan troupe traveling the country. When the woman she worked for left the company to marry, Hurston settled in Baltimore, Maryland, where her sister Sarah was, to complete her education.[9]

State law in Maryland guaranteed a free high school education to anyone under the age of twenty. Hurston seized the opportunity that she had longed for and promptly took a decade off her life to begin passing as a teenager rather than the twenty-six-year-old woman she was. Thus Hurston began the masquerade of being born in 1901 rather than 1891. In 1917 Hurston enrolled at Morgan Academy, then the high school division of Morgan College, which we know today as Morgan State University. The following year, she moved to Washington, DC, with the hope of attending

Howard University, which she would later call "the capstone of Negro education in the world." Admitted first through the college preparatory program, Hurston spent close to four years at Howard, in and out of class as her finances and health allowed. There she discovered that she was not only "Howard material," as a friend put it, but also Zeta Phi Beta material.[10]

When Hurston's first story appeared in print in 1921 in the Howard University literary magazine, *The Stylus*, she was still a student trying to make rent and pay tuition by working as a manicurist. Fortunately for Hurston, the literary renaissance was already taking place in Washington, as well as in other cities around the country. A lifelong lover of books, the would-be writer found in the city a lively black literary community, focused on a group known as the Saturday Nighters. Elizabeth McHenry's research has demonstrated that such groups "provid[ed] a network of support for African American intellectuals" and helped shape American literature and modern culture.[11] Weekly gatherings of the Saturday Nighters—at which participants discussed books, plays, and poetry—often took place at the home of Georgia Douglas Johnson, who was already an established poet. For this group of writers, many of whom found the city's racism and narrowness isolating, Johnson's home proved "an assembly of likeable and civilized people." One contemporary recalls that Hurston actually lived at Johnson's home for a period.[12] There, Zora, as an evening's guest or in residence, would have encountered not only faculty members and mentors from Howard University, like Montgomery Gregory and Alain Locke, but also a range of other luminaries from the period, including W. E. B. Du Bois, Charles S. Johnson, Marita Bonner, and Jessie Fauset, as well as native Washingtonian Jean Toomer, whose *Cane* (1923) instantly made him a literary celebrity. It was during these years that Hurston began publishing her fiction and her lesser-known poetry, suggesting that the lively discussions may have helped foster her desire to put pen to paper.

Hurston wrote her first four extant stories during this period. By the fall of 1924 her work had been accepted in one of the period's leading magazines, *Opportunity*. It was her breakthrough. "Drenched in Light" would become her first major publication. The success encouraged her to consider writing as a career. Unable to raise the funds to finish her degree at Howard, Zora packed her bags and migrated to New York, the center of American publishing. She tells us in her autobiography that she arrived in Harlem with only $1.50 in her pocket. Short of funds but full of dreams, she carried "a small suitcase of . . . short stories and plays."[13]

The connections that Hurston established through *Opportunity* proved essential once she arrived in New York. The monthly magazine of the National Urban League served as a major publication venue for New Negro writers. Charles S. Johnson, a young sociologist who acted as the magazine's editor, fostered Zora's career by publishing three of her early stories. The magazine also sponsored a series of literary contests and award dinners in the 1920s to help introduce emerging writers to judges and editors who could open doors to periodical and book publications. At the May 1925 *Opportunity* awards, where the fledgling writer won *four* prizes for her short stories and plays, she wisely made the most of her meetings with the (white) writers Fannie Hurst and Annie Nathan Meyer.[14] Their assistance allowed her to return to college in the fall. Hurst offered the recent transplant a secretarial position while Meyer facilitated admission to Barnard College, then the women's division of Columbia University, where she matriculated that fall and from which she would graduate in 1928. A 1925 letter from Hurston to Meyer reflects the goals the young writer had set for herself: "My typewriter is clicking away till all hours of the night. I am striving desperately for a toe-hold on the world."[15] *Hitting a Straight Lick with a Crooked Stick* demonstrates just how successful she was in attaining her goal.

Zora's short fiction opened doors that allowed her to network with the period's most powerful figures and would help her find a publisher for her books in the 1930s. It was her 1933 short story "The Gilded Six-Bits," included here, that attracted the J. B. Lippincott Company to Hurston and led to her first novel, *Jonah's Gourd Vine,* published in 1934. Four other books followed with Lippincott. In her lifetime only her last novel, *Seraph on the Suwanee* (1948), would be published by another. Without Zora's early success as a Harlem Renaissance writer of short fiction, it seems unlikely that her beloved novel *Their Eyes Were Watching God* (1937) would ever have found an audience.

THE POLITICS OF ART IN THE HARLEM RENAISSANCE

When Hurston arrived in New York, the Harlem Renaissance was in full bloom, but the debates about black art were thorny. At the heart of the matter was the battle over images of African Americans. Alain Locke, in his landmark 1925 essay "The New Negro," describes the race as a butterfly undergoing the transformative process of emerging from "a chrysalis." But who was the "New Negro"—or the "old Negro," for that matter?[16] How was he or she to be depicted? It was hardly a theoretical question. The New Negro movement advocated for art as a means of changing American culture and challenging its racism. To advance the cause of racial equality, writers and other artists battled racist stereotypes of African Americans that had existed since the transatlantic slave trade. Dehumanizing images of Africans had helped make the institution of slavery possible. Those same stereotypes had been deployed in the years following Reconstruction to repress African Americans' political and economic progress. Many of them manifested on the stage and in popular culture through the minstrel tradition. The New Negro movement in the 1920s sought to correct those images and to celebrate "authentic" black culture.[17] One strategy for advancing the race was to establish that there were class differences within the group—that there were educated, refined, intelligent, and properly chaste middle-class black people.[18] Consequently, depictions of middle-class characters were a popular means of challenging stereotypes. Hurston, however, allied herself with the younger writers who were willing to challenge the establishment, including Langston Hughes, Wallace Thurman, and Rudolph Fisher, to explore the lives of the common people. She introduced folk characters who speak in their own voices and typically fail to conform to middle-class New Negro standards.

Perhaps inspired by James Weldon Johnson's 1922 call for African American writers to do "something" for black dialect like John Millington Synge "did for the Irish," Hurston and some of the other, typically younger, writers of the period challenged long-held assumptions about art, language, and politics.[19] Her decision to write in idiom—often described as dialect—was a risky enterprise in the 1920s, particularly when that writing was funny. The history of minstrelsy meant that dialect and idiomatic expression, particularly when coupled with humor, evoked the very stereotypes New Negroes hoped to vanquish. Zora's essays make it clear that she understood the inter- and intraracial politics of her artistic choices, but she persisted in her efforts to break the chains of the past.

Hurston's earliest statement on aesthetics appears in the neglected essay "Race Cannot Become Great Until It Recognizes Its Talent."[20] There she compares African Americans to the English after William the Conqueror's conquest in the year 1066. She credits Chaucer with recognizing the beauty of writing in English (rather than the French or Latin that had been used for centuries) and Shakespeare with incorporating folklore into his plays. Implicitly, we see Hurston following the lead of these canonical figures by devoting herself to writing about the beauty of the folk. She saw African Americans as "physically but not spiritually free, unable as yet to turn our eyes from the distorted looking glass that goes with the iron collar [of slavery]." Imitation of white traditions, she cautions, will do nothing to advance the race, as "pupils never stand on equal footing with the master."[21] In search of something original, she refused to shrink from aspects of black life such as folk traditions and patterns of speech that others found undesirable or shameful. Hurston was proud of the way she depicted the speech of her African American characters on the page. She described this as her use of "the idiom—not the dialect—of the Negro." She wanted to capture the "poetical flow of language," the "thinking in images and figures." She says it provides "verisimilitude to the narrative by stewing the subject in its own juice."[22] Committed to representing those Langston Hughes called "the low-down folks," Hurston resisted the pressure to conform and presented her characters in their full, complex, and contradictory humanity. In a 1938 essay written for the Florida Federal Writers project, the now-established novelist would describe this as her "objectivity." Of course today we recognize that there was nothing neutral or apolitical in her passionate work in a violent Jim Crow culture to reclaim black folk speech and traditions and to establish the full humanity of its creators. She depicted the full range of the human experience in her characters, even when doing so did not suit a New Negro agenda.[23]

Hurston's stories from the Harlem Renaissance typically revolve around courtship and marriage, a trope that scholar Ann duCille describes as "the coupling convention." The convention allowed generations of black women writers a way to critique the inequities and injustices they saw.[24] Zora deployed the convention regularly. Instead of critiquing directly, she used her "crooked stick" to work in subversive, often subtle, ways that challenge the status quo. Through her use of language, characters, and plots, she interrogates and disputes the very stereotypes New Negroes objected to and treats subjects that continue to trouble American culture today. One of the reasons that *Their Eyes Were Watching God* has a current popular readership is that the issues her characters wrestle with continue to be relevant more than eighty years after the book's initial publication. Implicitly, the novel asks, What is the purpose and function of marriage? What does it mean to be a woman, particularly a married woman? How should a man behave? What are his responsibilities? How do couples navigate or share power? What is the community's role in negotiating difficult or abusive relationships? These questions are all posed implicitly by *Their Eyes Were Watching God,* but Hurston was exploring such topics long before writing her masterpiece. Her Harlem Renaissance short fiction also reveals the intersections of race, class, and gender that scholars talk about as intersectionality.[25] In short, the term means that we should not talk about one aspect of identity without talking about others. Hurston was not only a woman; she was a black woman from the rural South. This intersectionality makes it difficult—and shortsighted, if not foolish—to try to separate race, class, and gender in Hurston's life and in her work. Rather, they intersect and intertwine to create complex subjectivities and systems of oppression. She worked within those systems and wrote about them.

Hurston's earliest stories reveal that she was wrestling with the politics of identity from the very beginning of her career, regardless of whether she was focused on rural or urban communities. Her early narrative "A Bit of Our Harlem" implicitly asks what it is that connects people. This recovered story first republished by Tony Curtis appeared in the weekly newspaper *Negro World* in 1922 while Hurston was still pursuing her studies at Howard University. A publication of Marcus Garvey's black nationalist Universal Negro Improvement Association, the paper boasted a weekly circulation of nearly 200,000 and would, undoubtedly, have introduced Hurston's fiction to a large reading audience.[26] Here, in her second published story, class divisions dissolve over the course of a conversation between the unnamed middle-class narrator, who is likely a stand-in for the author, and a child with a disability selling candy. Despite their many differences, the educated narrator finds in the boy "the world of sympathy, understanding, and fellowship" that "seldom had she found" in "her own class." And although these two characters overcome their class differences, in the majority of Hurston's stories class differences serve as a wedge that divides people.

INTERROGATING THE POLITICS OF GENDER AND CLASS

In some of Hurston's earliest stories, she focuses on the ways in which class intersects with masculinity to determine just what it means to be "a man." While Hurston has become known for her depictions of female characters, she began her career exploring *masculine* identities in both the North and the South.

"The Conversion of Sam" (ca. 1922), a recovered story, is one of Hurston's earliest, written before her migration to Harlem. The original story exists only in typescript form at the Schomburg Center for Research in Black Culture. Scrawled across the top margin in Hurston's craggy handwriting are her name, the Washington, DC, address of the barber shop in which she worked as a manicurist, and the phrase "submitted at the usual rate." The library has no record of the story's provenance, so we can only speculate about its history. In the same collection at the Schomburg are letters Hurston wrote to Lawrence Jordan, a 1931 graduate of Columbia University who worked as an assistant to the curator of the Schomburg Collection from 1930 to 1932.[27] Since Jordan clearly knew Hurston and they corresponded in the 1920s, perhaps he is responsible for the story finding its way to the collection. It appears that Adele S. Newson in *Zora Neale Hurston: A Reference Guide* was the first scholar to document the story's existence, while John Lowe in *Jump at the Sun: Zora Neale Hurston's Cosmic Comedy* was the first scholar to comment on it.[28] A published version has not been located, but the phrase "submitted at the usual rate" tantalizingly suggests it may have appeared in a newspaper or magazine. The stilted, nineteenth-century dialect suggests she wrote the story between 1921 and 1923—before her use of African American idiom and vernacular was fully developed.

"The Conversion of Sam" appears in print for contemporary readers for the very first time in this collection. The narrative introduces readers to Sam, who falls for Stella, a recent urban migrant. He has a reputation as a gambler who refuses to work, but his desire to marry Stella prompts Sam to change his lifestyle and become "dickty," or middle class. When a former gambling buddy realizes just how prosperous Sam has become, the man jealously works to undermine the couple's happiness. Faced with different lifestyles, Sam must decide whether he will "be a sensible, steady man" by providing for his wife. This tension between the gambler and the middle-class employed worker is Hurston's first examination of the ways class intersects with and complicates life in the black community. In the story, to be a "steady man" requires that Sam earn a steady living, provide a home for his wife, and "keep her clean," likely meaning that she will not have to work outside the home. Implicitly, then, Stella is a domestic figure, a woman to be cared for and protected, but her character is secondary to Hurston's focus on Sam's journey into manhood.

Sam's story has much in common with the previously anthologized "Muttsy." In this urban migration tale, Hurston's migrant is also a woman. Pinkie has journeyed to Harlem from Eatonville, Florida. Pinkie, like Hurston in 1925, wishes to continue her education and has "no home to which *she* could return." In an unfamiliar city, Pinkie's traditional middle-class notions of femininity and her beauty make her vulnerable to exploitation. Muttsy, a well-respected and successful gambler, pursues Pinkie and even takes "nice," or respectable, work in order to make himself more attractive as a potential husband. In an ironic twist, however, the final lines of the story leave readers to wonder whether Pinkie will find her marriage to Muttsy the refuge from exploitation and the source of respectability she seeks.

Hurston wrote two additional stories that focus on male migrants, only one of which appeared in print in her lifetime. Despite the commonalities of these two recovered stories, "Book of Harlem" and "The Book of Harlem" are distinctly different, with different protagonists and different conclusions. Both, however, work against the grain of her contemporaries' treatments of the Great Migration. While many other Harlem Renaissance stories of migrants end tragically, Zora finds humor in the experience.[29] "The Book of Harlem" (1927) appeared in the *Pittsburgh Courier,* while "Book of Harlem" (ca. 1925) appeared posthumously in *Zora Neale Hurston: Novels and Stories* (1995).[30] Unlike the protagonists from other migration stories from the Harlem Renaissance, Hurston's are not escaping lynching or seeking relief from the economic exploitation of sharecropping. Instead, her male protagonists are pleasure seekers. Loaded with their fathers' "shekels," the young men leave their rural towns for Harlem in pursuit of "Shebas of high voltage." These details challenge the stereotypes of poor southerners and of the migrant escaping persecution. Hurston's humorous versions of the greenhorn story employ mock biblical language to marry the high and the low, the sacred and the secular, with terrific results. The narratives allow readers to see the characters transform themselves from men in "mail-order britches" to Harlem sophisticates. In their southern clothing that marks them as outsiders, they are dismissed by urban women. The characters' transformations require financial resources. Only after the migrants adopt urban clothing and straighten their hair will women interact with them. Here, even in funny stories, the author presents serious issues.

Hurston's focus on masculinity also drives two of her early well-known Eatonville stories, "John Redding Goes to Sea" (1921) and "Spunk" (1925). "John Redding Goes to Sea" has long been accepted as Hurston's first published short story. The "apprentice" effort follows the efforts of John to see the world, a desire his father attributes to his being a man. The women in

John's life, however, want him to stay home, leading to inevitable conflict. While these characters split along the lines of gender in their thinking about masculinity, "Spunk" presents conflicting views held by the men within the Eatonville community. In the first of Hurston's stories to introduce the Eatonville store porch and the men who talk there, readers meet a cuckolded husband who has lost his wife to Spunk, the title character. When the wronged husband seeks revenge—despite being fearful and outmatched—he loses his life. From beyond the grave, however, the husband continues to seek vengeance. Submerged within this ghostly love triangle, almost out of view, lies Hurston's exploration of masculinity. The men on the porch debate whether the betrayed husband is braver—that is, manlier—for having conquered his fears and attacking his rival. Or is Spunk manlier for "go[ing] after *anything* he want[s]"? Even within the same community and among men of the same class, there is no clear consensus. The story exposes conflicting constructions of masculinity within this community, but the narrator avoids drawing a conclusion to allow the reader to decide.

Hurston's recovered story "Under the Bridge" (1926) was first printed in *The X-Ray: The Official Organ of the Zeta Phi Beta Sorority* along with a play and an essay by Hurston. She joined the sorority while still a student at Howard University, but her writing was published in the *X-Ray* after she moved to New York. Wyatt Houston Day, a collector of African American sorority and fraternity memorabilia, bought several items at auction, and among his purchases he uncovered the story, which he reprinted in *American Visions* in 1997.[31]

"Under the Bridge," the story of a May–December love triangle, follows Luke, a widower, who marries Vangie, a woman less than half his age.[32] As fate would have it, Luke has a handsome son the same age as his new wife. While it takes little to imagine the painful outcome, there is nothing tawdry in the tale. Rather, the two young people grow closer emotionally. As Henry Louis Gates Jr. puts it, "The air is thick with temptation in this story, but it is also thick with the young people's love of the old man."[33] Luke feels his age in a growing sense of competition with his beloved son. In an effort to keep his wife, the husband and father resorts to "a hand" from the local conjure man. Hurston's decision to introduce conjure plays a crucial role in the plot, but it also has class implications. Middle-class black readers who saw such practices as ignorant or backward often wanted to distance the race from practices that had so often been yoked to stereotypes. It was a part of African American life in the South that they wanted to leave behind. The story has elicited speculation that it, like much of Hurston's fiction, may be autobiographical. If it were, an early marriage to a much older man might account for the lost decade of Hurston's life—those years between school and the Gilbert and Sullivan troupe—that biographers have been unable to reconstruct.[34]

Hurston's exploration of manhood also introduces extreme behaviors that demonstrate what I call tyrannical masculinity.[35] "Magnolia Flower" and "Sweat" both explore violent tyrants who seek to control the women in their lives. The first introduces colorism or shadeism, while the latter raises questions about the responsibilities of men in the community to deal with abusive husbands. "Magnolia Flower" (1926) opens in the years following emancipation. Bentley's daughter, Magnolia Flower, falls in love with a light-complected African American teacher. Rather than see his daughter marry a man who reminds him of his white oppressors, the father vows to hang the lover. To punish most cruelly, Bentley vows to make the lover watch Magnolia Flower marry one of his lackeys before the hanging. Bentley emerges as a tyrant who exploits, abuses, and exercises complete control of his family and neighbors. In this way and in others, "Magnolia Flower" anticipates themes that would reach their fullest representation twelve years later in *Their Eyes Were Watching God*. Bentley's character prefigures the better-developed one of Joe Starks, Janie's second husband, in the novel. Although Joe Starks is not a would-be murderer, both men build big houses, control the men around them, and verbally and physically abuse their wives. Joe Clarke, a similar figure, also dominates Eatonville in Hurston's 1925 story "The Bone of Contention," in which readers witness Joe's power to banish others from the town he founded.

In "Sweat" (1926), Sykes has been cheating on and beating Delia for fifteen years. Despite his abuse, Delia has built a home for them washing the clothes of white families in a neighboring town. The men on the store porch know that Sykes has subjected Delia to "brutal beating[s]." In fact, they agree that Sykes has beaten Delia "'nough tuh kill three women." At the same time, the larger community becomes a target for criticism when the men continue to turn a blind eye to the violence. They discuss whipping and killing Sykes, but "the heat . . . melt[s] their civic virtue." They opt to cut a watermelon rather than address his abuse. Hurston raises a number of unanswered questions. If Sykes has beaten Delia too much, as the men suggest, readers are left to wonder, How much violence toward a wife *is* acceptable? At what point should other men in the community intervene in domestic violence? If they do so, what form should that intervention take? If the men in the community fail to intervene, have they failed to act as "men"?

As Hurston was exploring masculinity in her fiction, she also began to develop the female characters for which she has become so well known. Although "Drenched in Light" (1924), her third published story, often prompts discussions of race, the author also explores constructions of gender. Isis, the story's eleven-year-old heroine, strains against and even flouts the gender norms her grandmother would impose on her. Perched on the fence post, Isis loves to watch the parade of people and cars on the shell road outside her home. Doing so, however, puts her at odds with traditional femininity, which would describe such behavior as unladylike. The child also likes to whistle, slouch in her chair, and sit with her knees apart, which her grandmother describes as "settin' brazen."[36] Isis clearly does not care and would much rather be on horseback herding cattle and cracking the whip (a masculine, phallic symbol) than washing dishes for her family, a chore that falls to her as the only female child. Hurston cleverly turns this traditional construction of ladylike womanhood on the grandmother when Isis and her brother try to shave the woman's chin whiskers as she snores loudly through her afternoon nap. While Hurston doesn't tackle constructions of femininity directly, she reveals a girl resisting traditional gender roles and the grandmother's hypocrisy in imposing them.

"The Back Room" (1927) is one of the four stories I discovered in the *Pittsburgh Courier,* a weekly black newspaper.[37] It is unique among Hurston's fiction, as it focuses on an educated and evidently prosperous migrant. It is Hurston's only work of fiction to plumb New Negro life in the Harlem Renaissance. The thirty-eight-year-old Lilya Barkman is living, in the words of Glenda R. Carpio and Werner Sollors, the "upper-crust party life" of Harlem's elite. She is approaching the age of forty but has by choice remained unmarried. She has remained "on the battlefield" and "had her fun" in the belief that marriage "ages a woman so—worrying with a house and husband at the same time." Lilya's home includes a large portrait of her painted years earlier, when her beauty and her marriage prospects were at their peak. Unwittingly, she has constructed herself as an object of the male gaze, both in art and in life, but in order to land on her feet at the end of the story, she must reclaim her agency.

The narrative names Porter David as the artist who created the painting that captures Lilya at her best. His name, as Carpio and Sollors astutely point out, evokes the painter James A. Porter, a 1927 Howard graduate.[38] While Carpio and Sollors suggest "the world in a jug" reference in the story constitutes an "uncanny anticipation" of Porter's award-winning painting *Woman Holding a Jug*, it seems more likely that both Hurston and Porter allude to the blues song "Down Hearted Blues," which made Bessie Smith famous in 1923.[39] Like so many blues songs, this one chronicles a broken relationship. Smith, however, puts her own stamp on the song by reorganizing the lyrics to emphasize the blues singer's resilience. Although Smith's man has left her, she still believes that she has "got the world in a jug—the stopper's in my hand."[40] In Hurston's story, the line "the world in a jug" appears in the opening paragraphs, foreshadowing the ending, in which the male characters leave Lilya behind.

"Monkey Junk" (1927), another recovered story, also evokes an element of Harlem life that is unlike anything else in Hurston's work. Although funny, it is perhaps the author's most cynical look at relationships between men and women. The narrative juxtaposes the high and low in mock biblical chapters, much like "Book of Harlem" and "The Book of Harlem." "[M]ixed up proverbial wisdoms" like "He that laughest last is worth two in the bush," Carpio and Sollors note, provide much of the humor.[41] Beneath this humor, however, Hurston takes her "crooked stick" to both genders. The plot unfolds as an unnamed man journeys out of the South to Harlem. He believes he "knoweth all about women," and by story's end that overconfidence has cost him dearly. He is trapped by a woman infatuated with his checkbook. As a consequence of underestimating the power of feminine wiles and overestimating his own skills, the exploited and outmatched husband finds himself responsible for a hefty alimony payment. It is easy to laugh as the unnamed woman takes advantage of his arrogance. At the same time, however, Hurston also interrogates the way the woman exercises her agency. In divorce court the judge and jury view her as a woman in need of rescue when nothing could be further from the truth. As readers watch the woman lie and manipulate, her performance becomes central. Admittedly, as Carpio and Sollors point out, she is hardly a feminist role model. And yet, she uses what she has—her appearance—to achieve her ends in a patriarchal culture. Through the introduction of the woman's lawyer, Hurston "hit[s] a straight lick." He is the only man who sees through the woman's performance. Through his character, Hurston cautions readers to avoid being like the "doty juryman" and instead to see beneath the surface of gendered performances.

"The Country in the Woman" and "She Rock" also explore the impact migration has on identity and marriage, as well as the tensions between rural and urban life. The plot of both stories revolves around Caroline, a married woman who uses her ax to end the affairs of her philandering husband. This pattern appears four times across the body of Hurston's work. Rural versions of the tales set in Hurston's hometown of Eatonville, Florida, appear in "The Eatonville Anthology" (collected here) and in her autobiography. In "The Country in the Woman" and in "She Rock," Hurston relocates the plot to Harlem to critique urban constructions of female identity.

"The Country in the Woman" (1927) focuses narrowly on Caroline and her wayward husband in Harlem. In exchanges between Caroline and her husband, Mitchell, readers see Caroline perform for her audiences. The story opens on a Harlem street as Caroline confronts Mitchell and his "side gal." Rural African American vernacular permeates Caroline's speech, as she threatens the other woman: "I'll kick her clothes up round her neck like a horse collar. She'll think lightnin' struck her all right, now." A "dark brown lump of country contrariness," this wife has publicly and humorously vanquished previous rivals when the couple lived in the South, but Mitchell mistakenly believes that in urban Harlem he can carry on an affair without her knowledge. Mitchell has adopted "Seventh Avenue corners and a man about town air" and a new, store-bought wardrobe. Caroline, however, continues to sleep in "yellow homespun." Because homespun cloth and the clothing it became were made in the home, that nightgown symbolizes the independence necessary for the survival of rural women like Caroline. Her idioms and her "'way-down-in-Dixie' look" also foreshadow the rural weapon Caroline will use to end Mitchell's liaison. Readers laugh at the humorous conflict between husband and wife and between rural and urban norms as Caroline emerges the victor by rejecting conventional, urban, middle-class norms of femininity.[42]

The final and latest of the recovered stories is "She Rock." In 2004, Hugh Davis noted his discovery in *The Zora Neale Hurston Forum*.[43] He serendipitously found it while browsing the *Courier* for the writings of another Harlem Renaissance scribe, George Schuyler.[44] Written in 1933, "She Rock" explores the same central plot as "The Country in the Woman," but in this version traditional narration gives way to the numbered mock biblical chapters and verses that Hurston had employed in "The

Book of Harlem" and "Monkey Junk." In "She Rock" Hurston allows readers to migrate with Caroline and her husband when Oscar's brother recruits him to work for the "Kings and Princes in Great Babylon" to earn "many sheckels." Once in the city, Oscar is advised to "shake that thing," and he does, as Hurston riffs on the Ethel Waters hit by the same name: "Yea, shook the fat with the lean, the rich with the poor; the aged with the young, verily was there not a shaking like unto this before nor after it." More explicitly than in "The Country in the Woman," Hurston critiques the relationship between Oscar and his girlfriend. The portraits are funny but unflattering. He is arrogant, and she is a gold-digging manipulator. The result of Hurston's revisions is a less playful tale, one more critical of New Negro gender constructions that would keep Caroline passively at home while her husband roams the streets with another woman.[45]

EXPLORING THE POLITICS OF RACE AND CLASS

Hurston's fiction interrogating race receives less attention than it should, particularly given that her more direct treatments of race and power appear in stories in which she blends folklore and fiction. African American folklore, particularly in song and story, serves important functions within the black community. It also has a long history as a weapon in the fight against slavery and racism. While Zora's treatment of race differs considerably from the angry, confrontational work of her contemporary Richard Wright, her fiction nevertheless explores what it means to be black in America. Her decision to write about black communities with white characters appearing only on the fringes—if at all—is a political choice, one that marginalizes whites and puts African Americans at the center and affirms that black folk are worthy of stories. As we have seen, using her "crooked stick" Hurston strikes at the intraracial politics of complexion, called colorism or shadeism, which exists in dialogue with whiteness and the belief that lighter is somehow better. Likewise, her fiction resists New Negro attempts to rehabilitate the image of blacks in the eyes of the whites by shunning folk culture as backward, ignorant, or undesirable. These are intentional treatments of race that Wright and his contemporaries overlooked.[46] But Hurston also wrote stories that address race more directly. She turned to folklore to do so.

The neglected story "Black Death" apparently never appeared in print in Hurston's lifetime. She submitted it to the 1925 *Opportunity* literary contest, where it won honorable mention.[47] All evidence suggests the story waited until the appearance of *The Collected Stories* (1995) to finally find an audience, perhaps because it explores conjure's role in a southern black community. Like "Spunk," the story illustrates the ways in which the weak take their vengeance on the strong. Fiction and folklore blend in "Black Death," blurring the lines between genres. The frame for the plot of "Black Death" reads like an essay and emphasizes different ways of knowing, illustrating that blacks know and understand things about the world that whites do not. At the heart of the story is a lothario who comes to town, seduces a girl he works with, and abandons her when she becomes pregnant. The girl's mother, distraught and helpless in this world, turns to Old Man Morgan, the local conjure man, for justice. Hemenway tells us that both the lothario's name, Beau Diddely, and the plot itself are "traditional," and they exist elsewhere in Hurston's anthropological publications.[48] Clearly, then, the story is not entirely fiction, but Hurston transforms the folktale, frames it, and, like Charles W. Chesnutt did before her in his conjure tales, reveals the ways in which power works—in the material world and beyond. While some middle-class readers might have been put off by or embarrassed by a conjure story, Hurston's pride in her culture prevented any such discomfort for her. Further, the frame of the story suggests that whites are inferior because they live only in a material world and thus fail to understand the additional dimensions of the spirit world.

In "'Possum or Pig" (1926), Hurston takes a similar approach by blending genres. Julius Lester, the African American storyteller, explains that folklore is like water in that as it passes from one pitcher to another "its essential properties are not harmed or changed . . . . A folktale assumes the shape of its teller."[49] Hurston's oral performances at parties were legendary, and here she may well have transferred to paper part of her repertoire for the magazine *Forum*, where editors included commentary praising the value of African American folklore and supporting the New Negro movement. Set in the days before emancipation, the story features a plot that hinges on John, the classic African American trickster figure, who has stolen and butchered one of Master's pigs. When Master comes to John's cabin, the pig is steaming in a pot above the fire. Unable to deter Master from entering his humble cabin without enduring a whipping, John claims to be cooking a "dirty lil' possum": "Ah put dis heah critter in heah a possum,—if it comes out a pig, 'tain't mah fault." The open-ended tale emphasizes John's willingness to match wits with his master, and readers pull for the less powerful character. Lurking beneath the surface, however, are also the larger dynamics of American slavery. John steals pigs to feed himself because he is not provided enough to eat. His cabin is not his own. The man defined by law as his "owner" can do what he wills to John without fear of retribution. John must use his wits to survive. The seriousness of this history embedded within a funny, traditional tale reveals Hurston "hitting a straight lick with a crooked stick" to address the politics of race, which had evolved painfully little in the years between emancipation and the Harlem Renaissance, especially for those sharecropping in the South.

Near the end of the period, Hurston published one of her finest stories, "The Gilded Six-Bits" (1933), which offers one of her most direct critiques of the politics of race. Her critique is embedded in an interesting reversal of other migration stories (in that one of the characters migrates south) and provides a subtle interrogation of masculinity. In its conclusion, however, Hurston turns the reader's attention to the politics of race. When "The Gilded Six-Bits" appeared in *Story* magazine, it caught the attention of editors at J. B. Lippincott and ultimately led to the publication of Hurston's first novel, *Jonah's Gourd Vine*. Again, the complexities of marriage take center stage in a love triangle, but this time a northerner participates in reverse migration when he moves from Chicago to Eatonville to open an ice cream parlor. There he meets Joe and Missie May, a young married couple. Joe puts the urbanite on a pedestal, talking repeatedly about this urban interloper with "de finest clothes . . . ever seen on a colored man's back" and a five-dollar gold coin for a lapel pin. Missie, on the other hand, seems decidedly unimpressed. Readers then are almost as shocked as Joe is to find Missie and the northerner in bed together. When Joe discovers the affair, he also finds that the gold pin he had admired is nothing more than a gilded coin. It and the urbanite are both fakes. Things are not always as they seem. In the final lines, Hurston turns this story about love and marriage to illuminate yet another way in which appearance and reality collide, this time in the politics of race. She confronts readers with racism in the one scene in which a white character appears. When Joe finally spends the northerner's gilded coin in a local shop, the white store clerk articulates the stereotype he has imposed on Joe: "Wisht I could be like those darkies. Laughin' all the time. Nothin' worries 'em." The ironic claim rings hollow for readers who know just how painful the acquisition of that gilded coin was for Joe. The clerk's use of the term "darky" reveals that he sees Joe as a minstrel figure untroubled by the woes of the modern world. Through dramatic irony, Hurston points out that Joe's life is far more complicated than the racist clerk can imagine. The line contrasts what readers, white and black, know about Joe's life with what the clerk *thinks* he knows. In this way, Hurston undermines the stereotype, revealing its distortion of a man's complex humanity.

THE END OF THE ERA

In the late 1920s and early 1930s, Hurston took a break from writing short fiction as she traveled the South collecting African American folklore. During this period she drafted the material that would eventually become three distinct books: *Mules and Men* (1935), *Every Tongue Got to Confess: Negro Folk-tales from the Gulf States* (2001), and *Barracoon: The Story of the Last "Black Cargo"* (2018). She and Langston Hughes fell out over their failed collaboration on *Mule Bone* in 1929, which did not appear in print until 1991. And she worked to bring authentic folk performances to the stage to great critical acclaim but with little financial success.[50] Zora's fiction was changing, too. The last story from Hurston's Harlem Renaissance years, "The Fire and the Cloud" (1934), marks a significant departure from her earlier stories in terms of themes, characters, and settings. There is no love triangle, no Eatonville or Harlem settings, no vernacular speech. Instead, "The Fire and the Cloud" focuses on the Old Testament figure of Moses. Hurston's attention has shifted from identity politics to the complexities of leadership. "The Fire and the Cloud" appeared five years before her novel *Moses, Man of the Mountain* (1939), in which she develops Moses as a magical figure—a masterful hoodoo practitioner, one not only dependent on God but powerful in his own right. Building on a long tradition of the Exodus story serving as an inspiration in African American culture, Hurston shifts the focus from the plight of the people being led out of bondage to the struggles of the leader. In the short story, readers see Hurston exploring for the first time the isolation and burdens of leadership. Set in the days after Moses has led the people to the Promised Land, the story opens on a mountain where the great liberator sits overlooking his people. Although seemingly without companionship, Moses strikes up a series of conversations with a lizard, in which he reveals he is alone after forty years of leadership. He is unconvinced that the people he served will remember or appreciate his sacrifices. After all, he points out, "The heart of man is an ever empty abyss into which the whole world shall fall and be swallowed up." At the end of thirty days on the mountain, Moses symbolically inters his role as leader and walks away, leaving his powerful staff leaning on the pile of stone. He passes the role of leader to Joshua, who will find the staff and assume that Moses has passed away. The story's conclusion literally and symbolically severs the role of leader from the human being who assumes the mantle, suggesting it is a performative role. While followers might naively put their leaders on a pedestal and idealize them, leaders take on the role their followers need them to assume, sometimes at great personal cost.

In the years between "The Fire and the Cloud" and *Their Eyes*

Were Watching God (1937), Hurston traveled to Haiti and Jamaica on two prestigious Guggenheim fellowships. She wrote the novel on her first trip as she tried to "smother [her] feelings" after leaving her longtime love affair behind in the United States. "The plot was far from the circumstances, but I tried to embalm all the tenderness of my passion for him in 'Their Eyes Were Watching God,'" she writes in her autobiography.[51] While Hurston's black contemporaries were critical of the book when it appeared because it did not explicitly confront class issues, it has been largely responsible for her ascending to the canons of American literature.[52] When the author returned to the United States after her fellowships in 1938, she would focus on producing books and essays. The peak of her productivity as a short story writer was behind her.

Almost a century later, Hurston's contributions to American literary culture continue to inform the ways we talk about the Harlem Renaissance, Modernism, women's literature, folk literature and folklore, ethnography, migration fiction, and Southern literature. Her groundbreaking stories and bodacious personality have made her one of the most-storied and most-studied Harlem Renaissance writers. Hurston's finest stories have made her a hypercanonical figure, a giant of the twentieth century, an icon. This collection of Hurston's Harlem Renaissance short fiction, particularly the addition of once-lost stories to her canon, requires readers to rethink her legacy. In these recovered stories, we see her explore the urban experience and the educated New Negro, two elements of Harlem Renaissance culture that seemed to have been lacking in her oeuvre. We see her use her "crooked stick" to critique the politics of gender, class, and race. Situated within the better-known body of Hurston's work, as they are in this volume, these recovered stories reveal the broader scope of her writings, both in terms of theme and form. Hurston's keen ear for vernacular speech, her devotion to depicting proudly and completely the folk she knew, and her persistent attention to the intersections of race, class, and gender have left us a beautiful, complicated, and unsurpassed legacy of Harlem Renaissance short stories.

Genevieve West

October 22, 2019

Hitting a Straight Lick with a Crooked Stick

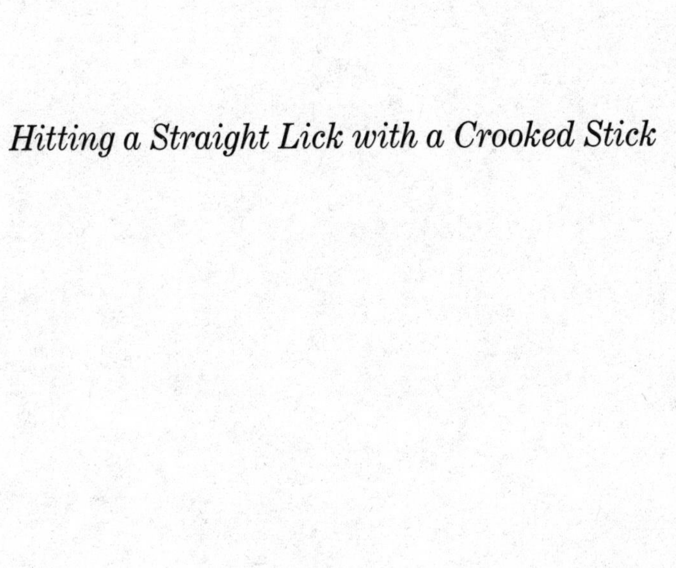

John Redding Goes to Sea

The Villagers said that John Redding was a queer child. His mother thought he was too. She would shake her head sadly, and observe to John's father, "Alf, it's too bad our boy's got a spell on him." The father always met this lament with indifference, if not impatience.

"Aw, woman, stop dat talk 'bout conjure. 'Tain't so nohow. Ah doan want Jawn tuh git dat foolishness in him."

"Case you allus tries tuh know mo' than me, but Ah aint so ign'rant. Ah knows a heap mahself. Many and manys the people been drove outa their senses by conjuration, or rid tuh deat' by witches."

"Ah, keep on telling yur, woman, 'taint so. B'lieve it all you wants tuh, but dontcher tell mah son none of it."

Perhaps ten-year-old John was puzzling to the simple folk there in the Florida woods, for he was an imaginative child and fond of daydreams. The St. John River flowed a scarce three hundred feet from his back door. On its banks at this point grew numerous palms, luxuriant magnolias and bay trees with a dense undergrowth of ferns, cat-tails and rope-grass. On the bosom of the stream float millions of delicately colored hyacinths. The little brown boy loved to wander down to the water's edge and cast in dry twigs, and watch them sail away down stream to Jacksonville, the sea, and the wide world and John Redding wanted to follow them.

Sometimes in his dreams he was a prince, riding away in a gorgeous carriage. Often he was a knight bestride a fiery charger prancing down the white shellroad that led to distant lands. At other times he was a steamboat Captain piloting his craft down the St. John River to where the sky seemed to touch the water. No matter what he dreamed or whom he fancied himself to be, he always ended by riding away to the horizon, for in his childish ignorance he thought this to be the farthest land.

But these twigs, which John called his ships, did not always sail away. Sometimes they would be swept in among the weeds growing in the shallow water, and be held there. One day his father came upon him scolding the weeds for stopping his seagoing vessels.

"Let go mah ships! you old mean weeds, you!" John screamed and stamped impotently, "They wants tuh go 'way, you let 'em go on."

Alfred laid his hand on his son's head lovingly. "What's mattah, son?"

"Mah ships, Pa," the child answered weeping. "Ah throwed 'em in to go way off an them ole weeds won't let 'em."

"Well, well, doan cry. Ah thought youse uh grown up man. Men doan cry lak babies. You mustnt take it too hard bout yo ships. You gotter git uster things gitten tied up. They's lotsa folks that 'ud go 'on off too ef somethin didn' ketch 'em and hol' 'em!"

Alfred Redding's brown face grew wistful for a moment, and

the child noticing it asked quickly, "Do weeds tangle up folks too, Pa?"

"Now, now chile, doan be takin' too much stock of what ah say. Ah talks in parables sometimes. Come on, le's go on tuh supper."

Alf took his son's hand, and started slowly toward the house. Soon John broke the silence.

"Pa, when ah gets as big as you ah'm goin' farther than them ships. Ah'm going to where the sky touches the ground."

"Well, son, when ah waz a boy, ah said ah waz going too, but heah ah am. Ah hopes you have better luck than I had."

"Pa, ah betcher ah seen somethin in th' wood that you ain't seen."

"What?"

"See dat tallest pine tree ovah dere how it looks like a skull wid a crown on!"

"Yes, indeed," said the father looking toward the tree designated, "it do look lak a skull since you call mah 'tention to it. You 'magine lotser things nobody evah did, son."

"Sometimes, Pa, dat ole tree waves to me just after th' sun goes down, an' makes me sad an' skeered too."

"Ah specks youse skeered of de dahk, thas all, sonny. When you gits biggah you wont think of sich."

Hand in hand these two trudged across the plowed land and up to the house—the child dreaming of the days when he should wander to far countries, and the man of the days when he might have—and thus they entered the kitchen.

Matty Redding, John's mother, was setting the table for supper. She was a small wiry woman with large eyes that might have been beautiful when she was young, but too much weeping had left them watery and weak.

"Matty," Alf began as he took his place at the table, "dontcher know our boy is different from any othah chile roun' heah. He 'lows he's goin to sea when he gits grown, an' ah reckon ah'll let 'im."

The woman turned from the stove, skillet in hand. "Alf, you aint gone crazy is you? John kaint help wantin tuh stray off, cause he's got a spell on 'im, but you oughter be shamed to be encouragin' 'im."

"Aint ah done tol you forty times not tuh tawk dat low-life mess in front of mah boy?"

"Well, if taint no conjure in de world, how come Mitch Potts been layin' on his back six mont's an' de doctah kaint do 'im no good? Answer me dat. The very night John wuz bawn, Granny seed ole witch Judy Davis creepin outer dis yahd. You knows she had swore tuh fix me fuh marryin' you 'way from her darter Edna. She put travel dust down fuh mah chile, dats what she done, to make him walk 'way fum me. An' evah sence he's been able tuh crawl, he's been tryin tuh go."

"Matty, a man doan need no travel dust tuh make 'im wanter hit de road. It jes comes natcheral fuh er man tuh travel. Dey all wants tuh go at some time or other but they kaint all git away. Ah wants mah John tuh go an' see, cause ah wanted to go mahself. When he comes back ah kin see them furrin places wid his eyes. He kaint help wantin tuh go cause he's a man chile."

Mrs. Redding promptly went off into a fit of weeping but the man and boy ate supper unmoved. Twelve years of married life had taught Alfred that, far from being miserable when she wept, his wife was enjoying a bit of self-pity.

Thus John Redding grew to manhood, playing, studying and dreaming. He attended the village school as did most of the youth about him, but he also went to high school at the county seat where none of the villagers went. His father shared his dreams and ambitions, but his mother could not understand why he should wish to go to strange places where neither she nor his father had been. No one of their community had been farther away than Jacksonville. Few, indeed, had ever been there. Their own gardens, general store, and occasional trips to the County seat—seven miles away—sufficed for all their needs. Life was simple indeed with these folk.

John was the subject of much discussion among the country folk. Why didn't he teach school instead of thinking about strange places and people? Did he think himself better than any of the belles thereabout that he would not go a courting any of them? He must be "fixed" as his mother claimed, else where did his queer notions come from? Well, he was always queer, and one could not expect the man to be different from the child. They never failed to stop work at the approach of Alfred in order to be at the fence to inquire after John's health and ask when he expected to leave.

"Oh," Alfred would answer, "yes, as soon as his ma gets reconciled to th' notion. He's a mighty dutiful boy mah John is. He doan wanna hurt her feelings."

The boy had on several occasions attempted to reconcile his mother to the notion, but found it a difficult task. Matty always took refuge in self-pity and tears. Her son's desires were incomprehensible to her, that was all. She did not want to hurt him. It was love, mother love, that made her cling so desperately to John.

"Lawd knows," she would sigh, "Ah nevah wuz happy an' I nevah specks tuh be."

"An from yo actions," put in Alfred hotly, "you's determined not to be."

"Thas right, Alfred, go on an' 'buse me. You allus does. Ah know Ah'm ig'nrant an' all dat, but dis is mah son. Ah bred an' born 'im. He kaint help from wantin' to go rovin' cuz travel dust been put down fuh him. But mabbe we kin cure 'im by discouragin' the idea."

"Well ah wants mah son tuh go, an' he wants tuh go too. He's a man now, Matty, an' we mus let John hoe his own row. If it's travellin', 'twont be for long. He'll come back tuh us bettah than when he went off. Anyhow he'll learn dat folks is human all ovah de world. Dats worth a lot to know, an' it's worth going a long way tuh fin out. What do you say, son?"

"Mama," John began slowly, "it hurts me to see you so troubled over me going away, but I feel that I must go. I'm stagnating here. This indolent atmosphere will stifle every bit of ambition that's in me. Let me go, Mama, please. What is there here for me? Give me two or three years to look around and I'll be back here with you and Papa, and I'll never leave you again. Mama, please let me go."

"Now, John, it's bettah for you to stay heah and take over the school. Why won't you marry and settle down?"

"I'm sorry Mama that you won't consent. I am going, nevertheless."

"John, John, mah baby! You wouldn't kill yo' po' ole mama, would you? Come kiss me, Son."

The boy flung his arms about his mother and held her closely while she sobbed on his breast. To all of her pleas, however, he answered that he must go.

"I'll stay at home this year, Mama, then I'll go for a while, but it won't be long. I'll come back and make you and Papa oh so very happy. Do you agree, Mama dear?"

"Ah reckon t'ain't nothin' 'tall fuh me to do else."

Things went on very well around the Reddings home for some time. During the day John helped his father about the farm and read a great deal at night.

Then the unexpected happened. John married Stella Kanty, a neighbor's daughter. The courtship was brief but ardent—on John's part at least. He danced with Stella at a candy-pulling, walked with her home and in three weeks declared himself. Mrs. Redding declared she was happier than she had ever been in her life. She therefore indulged in a whole afternoon of weeping. John's change was occasioned possibly by the fact that Stella was really beautiful, he was young and red-blooded, and the time was spring.

Spring time in Florida is not a matter of peeping violets or bursting buds merely. It is a riot of color, in nature—glistening green leaves, pink, blue, purple, yellow blossoms that fairly stagger the visitor from the north. The miles of hyacinths are like an undulating carpet on the surface of the river and divide reluctantly when the slow-moving alligators push their way log-like across. The nights are white nights as the moon shines with dazzling splendor, or in the absence of that goddess, the soft darkness creeps down laden with innumerable scents. The heavy fragrance of magnolias mingled with the delicate sweetness of jasmine and wild roses.

If time and propinquity conquered John, what then? These forces have overcome older men.

The raptures of the first few weeks over, John began to saunter out to the gate to gaze wistfully down the white dusty road, or to wander again to the river as he had done in childhood. To be sure he did not send forth twig-ships any longer, but his thoughts would in spite of himself, stray down river to Jacksonville, the sea, the wide world—and poor home-tied John Redding wanted to follow them.

He grew silent and pensive. Matty accounted for this by her ever-ready explanation of conjuration. Alfred said nothing, but smoked and puttered about the barn more than ever. Stella accused her husband of indifference and pouting. At last John decided to bring matters to a head and broached the subject to his wife.

"Stella, dear, I want to go roving about the world for a spell, would you stop here with Papa and Mama and wait for me to come back?"

"John, is you crazy sho 'nuff? If you don't want me, say so, an' I kin go home to mah folks."

"Stella, darling, I do want you, but I want to go away too. I can have both if you'll let me. We'll be so happy when I return."

"Now, John, you cain't push me off one side like that. You didn't hafta marry me. There's a plenty others that would hev been glad enhuff tuh get me. You know ah want educated befo han'."

"Don't make me too conscious of my weakness, Stella. I know I should have never married you with my inclinations, but its done now. No use to talk about what is past. I love you and I want to keep you, but I can't stifle that longing for the open road, rolling seas, for peoples and countries I have never seen. I'm suffering too, Stella, I'm paying for my rashness in marrying before I was ready. I'm not trying to shirk my duty—you'll be well taken care of in the meanwhile."

"John, folks allus said you was queer and tol me not to marry yuh, but ah jes loved yuh so ah couldn't help it, an now to think you wants tuh sneak off an' leave me."

"But I'm coming back, darling. Listen, Stella—" But the girl would not. Matty came in and Stella fell into her arms weeping. John's mother immediately took up arms against him. The two women carried on such an effective war against him for the next few days that finally Alfred was forced to take his son's part.

"Matty, let dat boy alone ah tell yuh! Ef he wuz uh home-boddy he'd be drove 'way by you-all's racket."

"Well, Alf, dats all we po' wommen kin do. We wants our husbands an' our sons. John's got a wife now, an' he ain't got no business to be talkin' bout goin' nowhere. I 'lowed dat marryin' Stella would settle him."

"Yas, das all you wimmen study 'bout—settlin' some man. You takes all de get-up, out of 'em. Jes let uh fellah mak a motion lak gettin' somewhere an' some 'oman'll begin tuh hollah 'Stop theah! wheres you goin'? don't fuhgit you b'long tuh me!'"

"My Gawd! Alf! What you reckon Stella's gwine do? Let John walk off an leave huh?"

"Naw. Git outer huh foolishness an' go 'long wid him. He'd take huh."

"Stella ain't got no call tuh go crazy 'cause John is. She ain't no woman tuh be floppin' roun' from place tuh place lak some uh dese reps follerin' uh section gang."

The man turned abruptly from his wife and stood in the kitchen door. A blue haze hung over the river and Alfred's attention seemed fixed upon this. In reality his thoughts were turned inward. He was thinking of the numerous occasions upon which he and his son had sat on the fallen log at the edge of the water and talked of John's proposed travels. He had encouraged his son, given him every advantage his poor circumstances would permit. And now John was home-tied.

The young man suddenly turned the corner of the house and approached his father.

"Hello, Papa."

"'Lo, Son."

"Where's Mama and Stella?"

The older man merely jerked his thumb toward the interior of the house and once more gazed pensively toward the river. John entered the kitchen and kissed his mother fondly.

"Great news, Mama."

"What now."

"Got a chance to join the Navy, Mama, and go all around the world. Ain't that grand!"

"John, you shorely ain't gointer leave me and Stella, is yuh?"

"Yes, I think I am, I know how both of you feel, but I know how I feel also. You preach to me the gospel of self-sacrifice for the happiness of others, but you are unwilling to practice any of it youself. Stella can stay here—I am going to support her and spend all the time I can with her. I am going; that's settled, but I want to go with your blessing. I want to do something worthy of a strong man. I have done nothing so far but look to you and Papa for everything. Let me learn to strive and think—in short, be a man."

"Naw, John, Ah'll nevah give mah consent. I know you's hard headed jus lak you Paw, but if you leave dis place ovah mah head, ah nevah wants you tuh come back heah no mo. Ef I wuz laid on de coolin' board, ah doan' want yun standin' ovah me, young man. Doan never come neah mah grave, you ongrateful wretch!"

Mrs. Redding arose and flung out of the room. For once, she was too incensed to cry. John stood in his tracks, his eyes dilated with terror at his mother's pronouncement. Alfred, too, was moved. Mrs. Redding banged the bed-room door violently and startled John slightly. Alfred took his son's arm saying softly, "Come, son, let's go down to the river."

At the water's edge they halted for a short space before seating themselves on the log. The sun was setting in a purple cloud.

Hundreds of mosquito hawks darted here and there, catching gnats and being themselves caught by the lightening-swift bull-bats. John abstractedly snapped in two the stalk of a slender young bamboo. Taking no note of what he was doing, he broke it into short lengths and tossed them singly into the stream. The old man watched him silently for a while, but finally he said, "Oh, yes, my boy, some ships get tangled in the weeds."

"Yes, Papa, they certainly do; I guess I'm beaten—might as well surrender."

"Nevah say die. Yuh nevah kin tell what will happen."

"What can happen? I have courage enough to make things happen, but what can I do against Mama! What man wants to go on a long journey with his mother's curses ringing in his ears? She doesn't understand. I'll wait another year, but I am going because I must."

Alfred threw an arm about his son's neck and drew him nearer but he quickly removed it. Both men instantly drew apart, ashamed for having been so demonstrative. The father looked off to the wood-lot and asked with a reminiscent smile, "Son, do you remember showing me the tree dat looked lak a skeleton head?"

"Yes I do. It's still there. I look at it sometimes when things have become too painful for me at the house, and I run down here to cool off and think."

"You wuz always imaginin' things, John, things that nobody else evah thought on."

"Oh, yes, I'm a dreamer. I have such wonderfully complete dreams, Papa. They never come true. But even as my dreams fade, I have others."

The men arose without more conversation. Possibly they feared to trust themselves to speech. As they walked leisurely toward the house Alfred remarked the freshness of the breeze.

"It's about time the rains set in," added his son. "The year is wearin' on."

After a gloomy supper, John strolled out into the spacious front yard and seated himself beneath a China-berry tree. The breeze had grown a trifle stronger since sunset and continued down from the southwest. Matty and Stella sat on the deep front porch, but Alfred joined John under the tree. The family was divided into two armed camps and the hostilities had reached that stage where no quarter could be asked or given.

About nine o'clock an automobile came flying down the dusty white road and halted at the gate. A white man slammed the gate and hurried up the walk towards the house, but stopped abruptly before the men under the China-berry tree. It was Mr. Hill, the builder of the new bridge that spanned the river.

"Howdy John, howdy Alf, I'm mighty glad I found you; I am in trouble."

"Well, now, Mist. Hill," answered Alfred slowly but pleasantly, "we'se glad you foun' us too. What trouble could you be having now?"

"It's the bridge. The weather bureau says that the rains will be upon us in forty-eight hours. If it catches the bridge as it is now, I'm afraid all my work of the past five months will be swept away, to say nothing of half a million of dollars' worth of labor and material. I've got all my men at work now and I thought to get as many extra hands as I could to help out tonight and tomorrow. We can make her weather tight in that time if I can get about twenty more."

"I'll go Mister Hill," said John with a great deal of energy. "I don't want Papa out on that bridge—too dangerous."

"Good for you, John!" cried the white man. "Now if I had a few more men of your brawn, I could build an entirely new bridge in forty-eight hours. Come on and jump into the car. I am taking the men down as I find them."

"Wait a minute. I must put on my blue jeans. I won't be long." John arose and strode to the house. He knew his mother and wife had overheard everything, but he paused for a moment to speak to them.

"Mama, I am going to work all night on the bridge."

There was no answer. He turned to his wife.

"Stella, don't be lonesome, I'll be home at daybreak."

His wife was as silent as his mother. John stood for a moment on the steps, then resolutely strode past the women and into the house. A few minutes later he emerged clad in his blue jeans and brogans. This time he said nothing to the silent figures rocking back and forth on the porch. But when he was a few feet from the steps he called back, "Bye Mama, bye Stella," and hurried down the walk to where his father sat.

"So long, Papa. I'll be home around seven."

Alfred roused himself and stood. Placing both hands upon his son's broad shoulders he said softly, "Be keerful, son don't fall or nothin'."

"I will, Papa. Don't you get into a quarrel on my account."

John hurried on to the waiting car and was whirled away.

Alfred sat for a long time beneath the tree where his son had left him and smoked on. The women soon went in doors. On the night breeze were borne the mingled scents of jasmine, of roses, of damp earth, of the river, of the pine forest near by. A solitary whip-poor-will sent forth his plaintive call from the nearby shrubbery. A giant owl hooted and screeched from the wood lot. The calf confined in the barn bleated and was answered by his mother's sympathetic "Moo" from his pen.

Around ten o'clock the breeze freshened, growing stiffer until midnight when it became a gale. Alfred fastened the doors and bolted the wooden shutters at the windows. The three persons sat about a round table in the kitchen upon which stood a bulky kerosene lamp, flickering and sputtering in the wind that came through the numerous cracks in the walls. The wind rushed down the chimney blowing puffs of ashes about the room. It banged the cooking utensils on the walls. The drinking gourd hanging outside the door played a weird tattoo, hallow and unearthly, against the thin wooden wall.

The man and the women sat silently. Even if there had been no storm they would not have talked. They could not go to bed because the women were afraid to retire during a storm and the man wished to stay awake and think of his son. Thus they sat: the women hot with resentment toward the man and terrified by the storm, the man hardly mindful of the tempest, but eating his heart out in pity for his boy. Time wore heavily on.

And now a new element of terror was added. A screech-owl alighted on the roof and shivered forth his doleful cry. Possibly he had been blown out of his nest by the wind. Matty started up at the sound but fell back in her chair pale as death. "My Gawd!" She gasped, "dats a sho' sign of death."

Stella hurriedly thrust her hand in the salt jar and threw some into the chimney of the lamp. The color of the flame changed from yellow to blue-green, but this burning of the salt did not have the desired effect—to drive away the bird from the roof. Matty slipped out of her blue calico wrapper and turned it wrong side out before replacing it. Even Alfred turned one sock.

"Alf," said Matty, "what do you reckon's gonna happen from this?"

"How do ah know, Matty?"

"Ah wisht John hadner went way from heah tuh night."

"Huh."

Outside the tempest raged. The palms rattled dryly, and the giant pines groaned and sighed in the grip of the wind. Flying leaves and pine-mast filled the air. Now and then a brilliant flash of lightning disclosed a bird being blown here and there with the wind. The prodigious roar of the thunder seemed to rock the earth. Black clouds hung so low that the tops of the pines among them moaned slowly before the wind and made the darkness awful. The screech-owl continued his tremulous cry.

The wind ceased and the rain commenced. Huge drops clattered down upon the shingle roof like buckshot and ran from the eaves in torrents. It entered the house through the cracks in the walls and under the doors. It was a deluge in volume and force, but subsided before morning. The sun came up brightly on the havoc of the wind and rain, calling forth millions of feathered creatures. The white sand everywhere was full of tiny cups dug out by the force of the falling rain drops. The rims of the little depressions crunched noisily underfoot.

At daybreak Mr. Redding set out for the bridge. He was uneasy. On arriving he found that the river had risen twelve feet during the cloudburst and was still rising. The slow St. John was swollen far beyond its banks and rushing on to the sea like a mountain stream, sweeping away houses, great blocks of earth, cattle, trees, in short, anything that came within its grasp. Even the steel framework of the new bridge was gone.

The siren of the fibre factory was tied down for half an hour, announcing the disaster to the country side. When Alfred arrived therefore he found nearly all the men of the district there.

The river, red and swollen, was full of floating debris. Huge trees were swept along as relentlessly as chicken coops and fence rails. Some steel piles were all that was left of the bridge.

Alfred went down to a group of men who were fishing members of the ill-fated construction gang out of the water. Many were able to swim ashore unassisted. Wagons backed up and were hurriedly driven away loaded with wet, shivering men. Two men had been killed outright; others seriously wounded. Three men had been drowned. At last all had been accounted for except John Redding. His father ran here and there, asking for him or calling him. No one knew where he was. No one remembered seeing him since daybreak.

Dozens of women had arrived at the scene of the disaster by this time. Matty and Stella, wrapped in woolen shawls, were among them. They rushed to Alfred in alarm and asking where was John.

"Ah doan' know," answered Afred impatiently, "that's what ah'm tryin' to fin' out now."

"Do you reckon he's run away?" asked Stella thoughtlessly.

Matty bristled instantly.

"Naw," she answered sternly, "he ain't no sneak."

The father turned to Fred Mimms, one of the survivors, and asked him where John was and how had the bridge been destroyed.

"You see," said Mimms, "when dat terrible win' come up we wuz out 'bout de middle of the river. Some of us wuz on de bridge, some on de derrick. De win' blowed so hahd we could skeercely stan'; and Mist. Hill tol' us tuh set down fuh a speel. He's afraid some of us mought go overboard. Den all of a sudden de lights went out—guess de wires wuz blowed down. We wuz all skeered tuh move for slippin' overboard. Den dat rain commenced—and ah nevah seed such a downpour since the flood. We set dere an' someone begins tuh pray. Lawd, how we did pray tuh be spared! Den somebody raised a song and we sung, you hear me. We sung from the bottom of our hearts till daybreak. When the first light come we couldn't see nothin' but fog everywhere. You couldn't tell which wuz water an' which wuz lan'. But when de sun come up de fog began to lift, and we could see da water. Dat fog was so thick an' so heavy dat it was huggin' dat river lak a windin' sheet. And when it rose we saw dat de river had rose way up durin' the rain. My Gawd, Alf, it was running high—so high it nearly teched de bridge an red as blood, so much clay, you know, from lan' she done overflowed. Coming down stream, as fast as 'press train, was three big pine trees. De fust one wasn't forty feet from us and there wasn't no chance to do nothin' but pray. De fust one struck us and shock de whole works, an' befo it could stop shakin' the other two hit us an' down we went. Ah thought ah'd never see home again."

"But Mimms, where's John?"

"Ah ain't seen him, Alf, since de logs struck us. Mebee he's swum ashore, mebbe dey picked him up. What's dat floatin' way out dere in de water?"

Alfred shaded his eyes with his guarded brown hand, and gazed out into the stream. Sure enough there was a man floating on a piece of timber. He lay prone upon his back. His arms were outstretched and the water washed over his brogans, but his feet were lifted out of the water whenever the timber was buoyed up by the stream. His blue overalls were nearly torn from his body. A heavy piece of steel or timber had struck him in falling, for his left side was laid open by the thrust. A great jagged hole, wherein the double fists of a man might be thrust, could plainly be seen from the shore. The man was John Redding.

Everyone seemed to see him at once. Stella fell to the wet earth in a faint. Matty clung to her husband's arm weeping hysterically. Alfred stood very erect with his wife clinging tearfully to him, but he said nothing. A single tear hung on his lashes for a time, then trickled slowly down his wrinkled brown cheek.

"Alf! Alf!" screamed Matty, "dere's our son. Ah knowed when ah heard dat owl las' night."

"Ah see 'im Matty," returned her husband softly.

"Why is yuh standin' heah? Go git mah boy."

The men were manning a boat to rescue the remains of John Redding when Alfred spoke again.

"Mah po boy, his dreams never come true."

"Alf," complained Matty, "why doan't-cher hurry an' git mah boy. Doan't-cher see he's floatin' on off?"

Her husband paid her no attention, but addressed himself to the rescue party.

"You all stop. Leave my boy go on. Doan stop 'im. He wants tuh go. Ah'm happy 'cause dis mawnin' mah boy is going tuh sea, he's goin' tuh sea."

Out on the bosom of the river, bobbing up and down as if waving good-bye, John Redding floated away to Jacksonville, the sea, the wide world—at last.

The Conversion of Sam

Jim's restaurant is a dingy little place on Poplar Street. Now, Poplar Street, be it known, lies in a down-at-the-heel locality such as is found in all American cities, where the derelicts of all nations drag out their aimless existences.

Drab, tottering old houses with grimy doors and broken windows squat along the narrow thoroughfare; heavy wagons lumber over the uneven cobble-stones, and all manner of filth and trash litter the side-walk and gutter. Indeed, the whole width of the street appears to be a gutter.

The unwashed of both sexes and all races stroll up and down and hover in front of the slatternly business places, "The Bucket of Blood," a notorious saloon, receiving the most attention.

Jim was fat, black, and indolent; and his eating house reflected the character of its owner. In his fly-specked shop-window were displayed fish, pigs' feet and ears, and chitterlings that one more than half suspected had had the same attention from the flies as the window itself.

While his wife slaved in the hot kitchen, Jim lounged in one of the greasy chairs talking loudly on the solution of the race problem with two of his cronies, the Reverend Zephaniah Solomon Meggs and Professor Cicero Omega Butts. They argued loud, they argued long, but all finally agreed that the salvation of the Negro lay in leisure. Too much work was sapping the vitality of the race—Booker T. Washington was all wrong.

There is no telling how many problems these three worthies might have solved had not a slim octoroon stepped into the shop.

She was young, fresh-looking and clean, which marked her a stranger in these parts. Jim jumped up as quickly as his immense body would permit, grinning from ear to ear.

"Mornin' miss, whut'll yer have?"

The girl shifted from one foot to the other and looked shyly about her. "I come ter see ef yer er—er high me fer er waittruss."

Now Jim had never considered hiring help in his small place. His wife did the cooking and he, himself, waited on his patrons except when he got drunk, which was frequent; then his wife did both cooking and waiting. But his mind was made up immediately; in fact, the girl could have gotten most anything that Jim had to give.

"Why, yas, miss er—er—ah wuz jes lookin' fer er nice gal ter wait on de place—is yer ready ter staht now? an' er—whut's yer name?"

"Mah name's Stella, an' ah come from Virginia yestiddy, an' ah 'lowed ter git er job right er way."

"Wa-al, Miss Stella, youse hiahed at five dollahs er week, fur es long es yer wants ter stay—walk right bak en tek off yer things."

Stella started toward the rear, and the eyes of the men followed her. Seeing this, Jim began to tire of all problem discussions; yea grew weary of the fellowship of the Reverend and Professor and wished them far from Poplar Street. As they made no motion to leave, Jim mumbled something about "looking after things" and followed Stella.

It was a very easy matter to convince Mrs. Jim that she needed a waitress—the eyes of her husband told her it would be unhealthy for her to object; so Stella became a part of Poplar Street.

The news of the coming of Stella spread like wild-fire. The crowd of "lillies" who usually sunned themselves in front of the barber-shop across the way, promptly moved over to Jim's corner. Business picked up one-hundred per cent; the place was always crowded. Moreover, Stella washed the window and scoured the floor and the cleanliness was an added attraction.

The Reverend and Professor became rivals for the favors of this country girl who was unconscious of her power to attract, and even Jim began to talk of "getting out papers agin Mrs. Jim en gittin' mah'ied ergin."

For days Stella showed no preference for any of her admirers. She blushed and giggled, giggled and blushed, and continued to look clean and fresh and made everything about her look the same.

Then one evening a tall figure, shabbily clad, entered the eating-house. The genial, brown-skinned face was cracked in a broad grin, a black water spaniel followed closely with a pipe between its teeth. A titter ran over the room, then the assembly laughed outright. People usually laughed when Sam and his dog made their appearance.

Sam Simpson was shiftless. He never did any work unless exhibiting his trained dog could be called work. Good-natured and witty, he was liked by both colored and white folks alike.

On seeing Stella, Sam made a grotesque bow and exclaimed, "Saint Peter sho mus' be sleep on his job, en lettin' angels fly 'way fum Heben."

The recipient of this crude compliment giggled and looked confused, and haltingly asked Sam what he would have to eat.

Sam bestowed his most winning smile on Stella for a full minute, then answered, "Well, since *you* goin' to wait on me, ah *will* eat sumpin'; guess ah'll tek er grave-yard stew."

"Whut's dat?"

"Doll-baby, aint yo' never hearn tell of er grave-yard stew? Where yo come fum?"

"Ah come fum Virginia."

"Oh, Ah see. Well, er grave-yard stew is milk toas'. Folks eat dat when they's 'bout ter croak."

"Is you 'bout ter croak?"

"Ah wuz, but since Ah seen *you*, Ah reckon Ah kin hol' out er little longer."

The loungers were listening and laughing at Sam's chaff. To them, he was Hitchcock, Bert Williams, Jolson, Lauder, Clifton Crawford, and all other first class comedians in one.

Stella went into the kitchen. The Professor C. Omega Butts turned on Sam. The green-eyed monster was at his vitals. He was determined that Sam should not win more by sugary smiles and airy persiflage in a few minutes than he had in many days by assiduous attention and lengthy, weighty words. What added to his fury, he noticed that Stella thought Sam clever. He, therefore, felt it time to squelch this Sam person once [and] for all. He cleared his throat, thrust forward his chest and began.

"Sam, do you know this young lady's entrimmings?"

"Naw, Ah don't, an' Ah aint worryin' 'bout what kin of trimmin' she wears."

"That aint whut Ah means, do you know her intitlems?"

"Ah dunno whut she's entitled ter nuther, en Ah aint worryin' 'bout dat."

The room rang with boisterous laughter, and the Professor found it difficult to make himself heard.

"Ah'm axin you ef you knows de lady's name, but youse too ignant ter perceive de logic of mah discussion," Professor Butts replied witheringly.

Sam jumped to his feet and shook his fist under the nose of the other and shouted, "Looker hyaer, shad-mouf nigger! Ah doan' perceive non er yo' logic, en' Ah doan wanter, but Ah *does* perceive dat yo' trousers need haff-solin, en Ah'm gwine ter wreck 'em fuder, ef yo' doan' shet up wid me. Goin' 'roun' tryin ter get respect'ble by wearin' whiskers, ef er man is hones' he doan need whiskers ter hide behind."

It was now the Professor's turn to rise. He did so slowly, haughtily.

"Ah perceives dat—"

"Aw, Ah'm tiahed er yo perceivin', whut meks yer call yerseff er perfesser? Whut is yo' perfesser of?"

More tittering.

"Wal, Ah'm perfesser ob ebery t'ing, not er no one thing, Ah'm er all-roun' perfesser."

Sam turned to his dog and gave him a playful kick. "Stan' up Perfesser Vicious en shake han's wid Perfesser Butts."

The dog arose and offered his front paw to the irate man, who strode to the door pompously, trying to look pityingly on the assembly. As he stepped to the sidewalk, Sam yelled after him, "Say Butts, de street-cleaning Depahtment wants er nice 'fesser lak yo 'ter lif' garbage-cans offen de side-walk."

The Professor fled.

Stella was beaming on Sam—whom she considered, in spite of his shabby clothes, the wittiest, most charming being on earth. Sam saw this and acted up to her. He told his funniest stories, put the dog through all his tricks, and told her in detail of the Mummers' Parade, in which he and his dog always figured.

"Yaas, Miss Stella, Ah'd be mekin' money eve'y day ef Ah had er girl lak you."

Stella smiled and wriggled in her confusion.

"Aw, Mr. Sam, youse jokin' now, Ah 'clare ef yo' aint de funniest, de teasinest man Ah ever seed."

"Deed, ah hope er shad may shoot me, ef ah doan lak you."

No shad appeared with deadly weapons so Sam continued, "Co'se, Ah knows Ah ain't got no call ter be sayin' dis, but ef any er dese 'Lillies' en sea-buzzards whut hang 'roun' hyar gits too fresh fer yer, jes yo' lemme know, en Ah'll tek keer uf 'em."

Sam looked hungrily into Stella's eyes for some sort of encouragement, but the girl only hung her head and traced a pattern on the floor with the toe of her shoe. She was a country girl, and knew not the ways of city folk, of whose perfidy she had heard so often. Except for his clothes, Sam was her idea of a swell fellow—saying snappy things, and defying all other aspirants to her hand. He was tall too—a comforting thought. But how could she know that Sam really liked her? She had been told how city fellows made fools of country girls, and what would Sam Simpson do with a stupid thing like Stella? And besides, this was the first time that she had ever seen him, and her aunt had cautioned her against taking strange men seriously. So it was more than self-consciousness that kept the girl silent.

Being neither accepted or refused as Lord Protector of Stella's person, Sam was hopeful and made up his mind to win her somehow. He took stock of his personal appearance that night in the mirror in the barber-shop and decided that a new suit, a shave and a hair-cut might help some. But how was he to get all this money? His dog brought in no such sums. He must get a job. He felt that he was tired of loafing anyway.

Stella did not see Sam for two weeks. Then he surprised all by walking into Jim's, dressed in a snuff-colored suit. Tho the suit was not new, it was clean and well-pressed. He wore patent-leather shoes with grey tops, and a snuff-colored felt hat set rakishly over one eye. He strolled leisurely to a vacant chair, drinking in the admiration he was receiving from the assembly.

Stella's heart jumped up and down so violently that she dropped a glass of water she was carrying. Sam was at her side instantly, helping her to collect the fragments. For a minute neither spoke, then the man found his tongue.

"Miss Stella, how you been makin' it sence Ah seen you las'?"

"Yes indeed,—Mr. Sam,—putty good,—Ah mean al'right. Whut yo' gonner eat?"

"Bring me er reg'lar twenty-five cent dinnah, please, miss, an' yer needn't hurry 'tall."

While Stella was in the kitchen, Sam struck up a general conversation with three or four men who were sitting about for the pleasure of seeing Stella smile. He broke the news to these worthies that he was a working man now; had a job at Wescott's lumber yard at fifteen dollars per week, subject to a raise and was thinking of settling down.

When Stella returned, Sam asked her if she had been to a "movie" since she had been in town.

"No, but ah'd jes lufter go."

"Git yer bunnet an' we'll jes run eround dere dis ehenin."

"Ah dunno if mistah Jim 'll lemme go."

"Doan you worry 'bout dat, chile. Ah'll speak ter him."

And so he did, or rather spoke to Mrs. Jim when she poked her head into the dining room to see how things were going.

Now, Mrs. Jim did not like Sam. She suspected him of making her person the butt of many of his witticisms. His clothes surprised her, but did not allay her dislike for him. So when he spoke, she was ready to refuse as soon as he finished his request.

"Now, Sam, you ain't nobuddy fer Stella ter be goin 'round wid."

"Why?"

Mrs. Jim flung her head up and closed her eyes in an attempt to look imposing.

"Cause you ain't nothin' 'tall but trash."

"Ah'm jes es good es you er Jim either. An you'se glad enuff ter git *him*."

"W'en Ah wuz Stella's age, Ah's very purtickler who I 'cepted fer mah escorts, Ah kin tell yer."

"Well, yer didn't pick much. But Ah doan reckon yer had much chance."

"Who, *me*? Ev'ey buddy said Ah'se putty as a pink when—"

"Yas, Ah reckon you'se bout whut you is now—er kitchen bokay. An Ah reckon Jim married yer w'en he's drunk."

"Git outer mah place, Sam!"

"Oh, Ah ain't hurryin'. But ef you chunk one er dem baked insults at me dat *you* calls biscuits, Ah'll wish Ah had er went. You call dis joint er rest'rant? Why, dis ain't nothin' 'tall but a munition fact'ry."

Stella entered from the rear with hat and coat on, and Mrs. Jim, glad to escape from Sam's ridicule, turned on her.

"Stella, ef you leaves yo wuk ter go out wid dis scalawag, you needn't come back hyar no mo'."

The girl wilted and turned to go to the rear, with a sorrowful expression, but Sam detained her.

"Stella, come on. She ain't got nuthin' 'tall ter do wid you. She's jes er darned ole anteek dat's jealous er yer looks. Ef she kin mek out widout *you,* you kin more'n mek out widout *her.* You kin git er job mos' any place, an besides, I'se got a job."

Stella hesitated. She wanted her job and she wanted to go with Sam. At this juncture, Jim came waddling in, reeling under his load of "bottled in bond." He did not know what was going on, but he could see that his wife was angry and that Stella, his goldmine, his prosperity, had on her hat and coat, and that she was almost in tears. Even in his befuddled state, he could see that his prosperity would go with Stella. And if his wife was driving her out, she'd suffer for it. He rushed forward and fairly bellowed.

"Whut's gwine on? Mattie, whut yo doin out er de kitchen? Meddlin in mah affairs ah reckon, jes es usual."

Mattie fairly quaked, and Sam seeing her confusion completed the rout he had begun.

"Jim, I axed Miss Stella to 'comp'ny me ter de movies an yo' wife say ef she go she cain't come back hyar to work no mo'. Now Ah cain't see why. Ain't she a good waitress 'en ev'eything?"

Jim glared fiercely at Mattie, as she shuffled toward the kitchen.

"I knowed it! Ah knowed it!" he triumphantly exclaimed. "The minute Ah come in dat do', Ah could see dat Mattie hed been up mo' devilment. An' dog-damn her, ef she doan' git back in dat kitchen and stay dere Ah'm gwine knock ev'ey one er dem naps offen her haid one by one. Co'se Stella kin go ter de show wid her gen'leman frens', when she gits ready." Sam gathered the blushing Stella upon his arm and proudly fared forth.

Whereupon Jim flopped into a chair and held forth at great length on the necessity of keeping wives in their places; to wit: speechless and expressionless in the presence of their lords and masters and cited several instances where men had met their downfall and utter ruin by ill advisedly permitting their wives to air their ignorance by talking. His audience, composed entirely of males, agreed with him. Wife-beaters are numberous in Poplar Street.

Sam went to work next morning a happy man. Stella had accepted him as her "fellow." How he did work! Mr. Bronner, the boss, remarked the fact to some of the men. He was due for a raise and at the beginning of the next month he got it.

Sam strode proudly into the restaurant the night following the afternoon upon which he had been informed of his good fortune. Stella accompanied him to a "movie" as usual where he broke the news to her.

"Co'se we kin git mah'ied now," he fumbled with his hat awhile, "ef you'll have me."

Stella looked down at her feet, played with her fingers a bit, but said nothing.

"Will yer?" Sam urged. "Ah kin tek keer un yer lak yer oughter be took keer un, en Ah'll wuk mah toe-nails off fer yer. Den atter dat, Ah'll go git a reglar job ef yer say de word. Does yer love me jes' a little, Stella?"

Stella was thrilled to the heart by this passionate appeal. She loved Sam surely, and she wanted to be his wife, but she couldn't find a word of acceptance that didn't sound bold and brazen to her. But every woman, whether she be college-bred and city reared, the daughter of wealth and fashion; or just a country girl like Stella has felt that same lack of words under the same circumstance. After a while Stella nodded her head in the affirmative. Sam grabbed her hand and pressed his suit with zeal.

"Yer gonna ma'y me, Stella?"

Stella nodded her head again in the affirmative. Sam squeezed her hand more tightly. Both lost sight of the screen story, and sat there silently, their hearts beating audibly. It was a holy moment.

Poplar Street was dumbfounded. No one thought a pretty girl like Stella would marry Sam. When the news went its rounds, the other aspirants to the hand of Stella rushed upon her, hoping and expecting a denial of the report, but no denial forthcoming, they shuffled away chagrined. Sam ostentatiously displayed his "catch." The nuptials were to be celebrated in September, three months later. Stella had insisted on this interval so that she might have time to get ready.

Sam's employer was very fond of him, because, besides being a good worker, Sam radiated good humor wherever he happened to be, and his witticisms kept the men about him in a cheerful mood and made good workers out of them too. So when he gleefully told Mr. Bronner of his approaching marriage, Sam's employer mentally resolved to do the handsome thing by him. A week before the date set for the nuptials, the Negro was agreeably surprised by Mr. Bronner's calling him into the office and asking him where he was going to live.

"Well, boss, Ah 'lowed ter git some rooms dere in Poplar Street."

"Sam, it would be better for you and better for your wife if you lived in a more respectable neighborhood."

"Yessah, Ah guess hit would."

"Well, I'm going to call up Mr. Hill, a friend of mine. He has some houses and flats to rent to colored people. I'll see if he hasn't something up-town where the better class of Negroes live. How about it?"

"Dat ud be jis fine, boss. Yer know, Stella, mah Stella, is ez putty ez a pitcher, boss, an' Ah reckon some er dem low-down shad-mouf niggers in Poplar Street gwine gimme truble ef Ah keeps her dere. Tryter put her 'gin me, yer know."

"That's just it, Sam. Get away from the riff-raff. You don't want your wife to associate with those women and listen to the kind of conversation that's common down there."

"Ah see do dat, boss. 'Fo' Gawd Ah will. Call up de man."

There was such a note of sincerity in Sam's voice that the white man stared at him for a moment. Respect for the black man was born in him, but he answered in an offhand manner.

"All right, Sam. Now, another thing. Don't go buying a lot of furniture on the installment plan. You may go now. I'll let you know when you can see the house. And Sam, comb your hair once or twice before you get married."

Sam, with his hand on the door, turned and looked at Bronner and grinned.

"Yer reckon she notice things lak dat?"

"Sure she does, Sam. Do as I tell you now; get the habit."

Sam went back to his work happy but thoughtful. He was going to live up-town with the "dickties," those members of his race who were professional or well off businessmen! Well, Stella deserved it. There was no woman among them possessed of more physical charms, and Stella was a lady, too. She never talked dirt nor mingled with the toughs. But it was hard to comb his hair, even for the sake of a goddess. Nevertheless, he went to a barbershop that evening and had his hair combed, trimmed, greased and slicked down. My, how sore his head was after the operation! But he would gladly have gone through it every hour to win such admiring glances from Stella as she bestowed upon him that evening. He resolved to comb his hair every day after that.

Two days before his wedding, Sam was summoned to inspect the house that Mr. Bronner had selected for him. Sam went up the stone steps proudly. There was a tiny, tiled vestibule, a brass door-bell, and a door with the upper-half beveled glass.

But when he stepped inside, he received the surprise of his life. The house was furnished! To be sure, the furniture was not new, but it was in good condition. The bewildered Sam turned to Mr. Bronner.

"Boss, de folks whut lef' ain't moved yit?"

"Yes, Sam."

"Well, how did dis all git hyar?"

"My wife wanted new furniture at home and we didn't have any place to put this. Then I thought you and Stella might have use for it, and so here you are. Take good care of it, Sam. It's the stuff my wife and I started out with. I was an ordinary laborer then." Mr. Bronner paused and dropped upon the davenport. "You won't need any more furniture except for the kitchen until you've accumulated five thousand dollars. We didn't have any old furniture for that."

Sam's eyes were rolling around in his head from surprise and joy. Wouldn't Stella be a queen though? He seized the hand of his benefactor and wrung it (not a natural act for a character like Sam).

"Deed, boss, Ah dunno whut ter say, Ah'm dat glad en happy."

"Don't say anything, Sam, just live an honest life and stick with me down at the works and above all, respect and honor the woman you are marrying. Keep her clean. Here's your key. Mr. Hill says your rent is $20.00 per month. Pay promptly. Now come on and get into the car and I'll drop you at your present address."

So Samuel Simpson or Sam Shambles, as he was called, married Stella Potts and moved up town into the red brick house with the white marble steps.

Stella worked some wonderful changes in Sam; for instance, she combed his hair so often that it was almost bereft of its ancestral kinks, and persuaded him that a person might bathe between Saturdays without unsettling the universe; and that it was expected of a "dickty" to clean his fingernails at least once a day.

Things went on very well for five or six months. Sam was becoming more proud and self assured every day. He could see the neighbors casting admiring glances at his wife as they went forth arm in arm. He never went near Poplar Street anymore, for he had a bank account and was thinking of buying a piano. No "dickties" lived in Poplar Street.

But one day he met "Blue-front," one of his old cronies, upon Poplar Street. "Blue-front" noted Sam's neatness, his air of importance, and hated him. He wondered if Sam would speak. Sam was polite but reserved.

"'Lo, Blue!"

"'Lo, Sam, Ah doan see yer no mo'."

"Naw, Ise busy wid mah fambly."

"Ah hyar yer er 'dickty' dese days—"

Sam stiffened. Here was jealousy sticking out all over "Blue."

"Reckon das' 'bout it."

"No hard feelins, come on hab a drink."

"Nope, doan drink no mo'."

"Well, a seegar den."

"Nope, got a whole box at home."

"Blue-front's" anger was kindled at Sam's rebuffs. Sam, who had been the rattiest of rats! He could barely suppress a snort of anger and scorn. Never mind, he'd pull him off his pinnacle and bring him back to his before-meeting-Stella state, sooner or later. So he must hide his chagrin.

"Mister Simpson, yer doan ject ter mah walkin' up town wid yer 'en seein' yo house do yer?"

Sam's first impulse was to refuse, but his pride in his home led him to grudgingly consent.

"Blue-front" was taken off his feet. He never thought to find Sam living so well. Stella was a gracious hostess, and while her husband proudly showed the envious "Blue-front" around, put supper on the table, and invited him to stay. She had veal-cutlet and fried sweet potato, tea and hot biscuit.

"Blue-front" fairly guzzled. But his envy mounted till he could almost have murdered Sam for having a pretty wife and a comfortable home. And, too, after supper that box of cigars came out and while he grabbed two and thrust them into his pocket, he was plotting how to pull his host off his perch.

At last, he rose to go.

"Gawd, Sam, youse in sof'. An' Miss Simpson, ya supper sho wuz good."

Sam's chest protruded.

"Yap mah lil' girl kin really cook. Them wuz *biskits,* not baked insults, and dat wuz *tea,* instid er dat Red Seal Lye Jim sells down in Poplar Street, ter say nothin' tall 'bout de gravy." Sam beamed on Stella, and she flushed with happiness.

"So long, Sam, see yer latah," said the departing guest, as the host closed the door after him.

"Now, Honey, he's gwine down in Poplar Street an' tell all de niggers 'bout'n us. Dey'll all turn green from jealousy. Come on, Honey, an gimme er kiss. You sholy mekin' er man outer me."

Stella kissed him more than dutifully and sitting on his lap they planned many things to be bought in the near future.

Tho "Blue-front" did not come home with Sam again, he frequently accosted him on the way and walked a few blocks, flattering and praising him. Sam, being only human, warmed toward "Blue" and was persuaded one afternoon to go through Poplar Street.

His old cronies gathered about admiring and flattering.

"Come on, Sam, an' drink sumpin' on me. Das er han'some suit yer got on—yer lookin' sharp as er tack."

Sam patronized and held a bit aloof, but he was pleased by the homage he was receiving.

"Sorry, gen'l'men, but Ah ain't indulging no mo'. Hi dere 'High-pocket'!"

"Sam, come on, shoot er game er bones."

"Kaint do it, 'Fen-cloes,' mah supper is waitin'."

"Huh, Ah reckon mah'ed life done strap yer up so yer ain't got no change ter spare."

Sam grinned, thrust his hand into his pocket, and brought forth a roll of one-dollar bills generously sprinkled with fives and tens.

"Guess Ah got de price all right."

"Ah, Sam, come on; jes one game."

"Naw." Sam was weakening, but he managed to tear himself away and go home. He had never been late before, and Stella was worried. He resolved never to go down there again. But the next afternoon when he stepped into the street from the lumberyard "Blue-front" and "High-pocket" were waiting for him. This time he yielded. Into Poplar Street he went and when once in Poplar Street, his old self seemed to take possession of him and he gambled as in days gone by. Fortune favored him and he went home six dollars richer in this world's goods, but much poorer in spirit than since he first saw Stella. Though Stella said nothing, Sam felt the hurt shining out of her eyes, striking through him. He told her he had been detained at work.

That was the beginning. Night after night he visited Poplar Street; night after night he lost money, sleep, and self-respect. Each day he resolved to stay away, but his past years told on him now. He lacked moral strength. He was twenty-five years old and for fifteen of those twenty-five years he had lived in the streets and alleys blacking boots, selling papers, and winning stakes at petty gamblin.

He would creep home to Stella, cringing and evasive of manner. She never questioned or scolded, though she knew that he could not be at work at twelve or one o'clock in the morning.

Sam gradually lost all of his savings and one first of the month found himself unable to pay his rent. Mr. Hill waited two weeks, then went to Mr. Bronner. That gentleman was surprised but, when he recalled to mind having seen, at various times, disreputable looking men hanging around waiting for Sam, light dawned upon him. He called Sam in, not the laughing Sam of yore, but a slinking, servile, Sam, whose dog even seemed to feel his master's disgrace, and slunk too.

Sam was questioned closely, advised and dismissed. He was utterly lost now. No job, no money, soon no home, for how could he get another job with Mr. Bronner's unfavorable recommendation? That night he did not go home; he simply could not face Stella with tidings so unwelcome. He knew she would not reprove him and that made it harder, for Sam loved his wife.

He did not go home that night, nor the next. A dozen times he started up-town, half-crazed by his longing to see and reassure his young wife, but each time his courage failed him. He attempted again and again to borrow enough money to pay his rent, but failed. A few days before, he could have borrowed five times that sum at a moment's notice, but to the world now he was no longer Samuel Simpson, but merely "Sam," jobless and penniless. He was in appearance no longer "sharp as a tack."

In the meanwhile, Stella—poor, trusting Stella—was weeping and looking out of the window at irregular intervals, expecting to see the body of her lord brought to the door at any moment.

She could not believe that Sam could be alive and remain away from her for two whole days.

At last, she dried her tears and went down to Mr. Bronner's office to inquire for Sam. She was surprised to hear that he was no longer employed by the lumberman.

The kind-hearted man felt sorry for the unsophisticated negress because he thought that Sam had tired of her and had gone back to his shiftless ways and left her to her own devices. After he discovered that she did not know her rent was unpaid, he telephoned his wife and influenced her to hire her as a chambermaid, and advised the stricken girl to give up the house and take a room.

Stella agreed to begin working for Mrs. Bronner on the following morning. She went home more unhappy than ever, believing that Sam had cast her off, and that city-folk were just as wicked as provincials thought them to be.

Sam wandered about Poplar Street his dog at his heels from pool-room to barber-shop and from barber-shop to bar, disconsolate and weary. His late admirers stood, like Pharisees, afar off. Sam no longer interested them. He was, in the language of the curb, "on the bricks" or "burnt up."

Early that night, he heard that there was to be a crap-game in "Sweetie's" flat, the home of a disreputable woman in Poplar Street. He felt in his pockets and found he still possessed eighty-five cents. In desperation he resolved to sit in that game and try to win enough money to purchase his self-respect with his wife. If he lost the eighty-five cents, he would not be much worse off than he was at present; if he won,—he clapped his hands over his eyes to shut out the vision of Stella which was too much for him just now. So he went to "Sweetie's" and sat in the game.

About nine o'clock that night, Stella felt that she could bear

Sam's absence no longer. She would seek him the world over and ask him why he did not love her still. Perhaps he might come home again and she could win his love once more. Anyway, if she could only see him once again, she felt she would be justified in a month's journey afoot.

She went from room to room looking at and touching things dear by association. The morris chair, the smoking stand, the pillows in the window seat, where she always watched for Sam's coming in the evenings, and where he found and invariably kissed her; the "kewpie" that hung by a ribbon about its waist from the bed-post. They had always taken the doll to bed and pretended it was their first-born. Sam would ask about the baby as soon as he reached home, and Stella would run and fetch it, pretending at times that it had been fretful and cried for its dad. She decided that she could never disturb things, that if she could not find her husband, or if he refused to return to her, then perhaps God would, in his great love and kindness, let her go to sleep. She knew she would be very weary if she returned without Sam.

So Stella put on her prettiest dress and went out to seek her lord.

She went first to Poplar Street—no sign of Sam. People spoke to her; she answered timidly and glided away, peeping first into one den, then another, as she walked down the line. At last she asked "Squeegee," "Sweetie's" pal, if she had seen him, and "Squeegee" glibly told her where he was.

Stella turned and walked briskly in the direction pointed out by the woman. As she left the curb in her anxiety she did not notice a swiftly approaching automobile. Stepping straight in front of it, she was felled to the ground. "Squeegee" saw the accident and ran forward. The occupants of the car, two men, quickly picked up the girl and placed her in the car. A policeman came up and, after going thru the usual preliminaries, permitted the men to take her to the hospital. "Squeegee" gave the officer Stella's address.

In a few minutes she burst into the room where Sam was gambling. There was no hesitation in proclaiming to all the news. In an instant Sam was in the street hatless and breathless, on his way to the hospital. When he burst through the swinging doors, he was told that no visitors were allowed at that hour, but he might telephone later and find out her condition.

Sam flung out of the place a madman. His conscience smote him piteously. His fears seemed to possess voices and to shriek themselves into his ears.

He found himself in Poplar Street once more and in "Jim's Place." Everyone down there was talking of the accident.

Sam slunk into a chair. Mrs. Jim was jubilant. Sam's suffering gave her pleasure; for she remembered the jokes he had coined at her expense, his proud days, and his arrogance. She stood akimbo in front of the unhappy man and sneered.

"Sam, Ah reckon yo' satisfied now, ya done kilt Stella."

Sam was on his feet in a moment. The spectators thought he would strike his tormenter.

"Youse a nappy-headed liah! Ah ain't kilt mah' Stella. Youse oughter been dead er hunded yeahs ergo." Sam's voice sank to a whisper. "Gawd knows Ah didn't kill mah Stella, deed Ah didn't." He hurried to the nearest telephone booth and called the Hospital.

He was told over the phone that Stella had sustained a broken rib and several minor scratches and bruises, and that he might call on her at two o'clock the next day. This was eleven o'clock at night.

At eleven forty, Mr. Bronner was awakened by a violent ringing of his door-bell. Hastily slipping into his bath-robe, he hurried down to find Sam on the door-step.

"Come in, Sam. What do you want at this hour of the night?"

"Boss, Ah wants mah job back. Ah jes' gotta have it. Stella, mah Stella, done got hit by a car while she wuz huntin' fer me, boss. Gawd bless her, I believe she loves me yet. Jis' try me one mo' time."

"But, Sam, you know how you behaved last time. I don't hire gamblers, nor drunkards, nor even those who associate with such. I treated you white, but you didn't appreciate it. Your wife is a fine woman. My wife thinks so, too, but—"

Sam grabbed the lapels of Mr. Bronner's bath-robe, and his voice shook with the intensity of his emotion.

"Boss, gimme one mo' trial. Das all Ah ast. Ah hope a shad may shoot me ef Ah doan mek good dis time. Ah gotta git mah Stella back. Ah kaint go down ter de hospital termorrer en say Ah ain't got no job." His voice broke to a sob and he hastily drew the back of his hand across his eyes.

"Stella will think Ah aint no good, en she's de bes' 'oman on yearth; deed she is! Das reason Ah ain't been home. My Gawd, boss, yer cain't turn me down!"

"Sam, are you going down to your wife a sensible, steady man tomorrow and will you try, God helping you, to never, never give her cause to doubt your manliness again? Are you going to keep her clean and trusting and womanly? If so, you are hired again."

Sam's right hand shot up into the air above his head and his eyes were elevated as he answered reverently, "Befoah Gawd, I will, boss."

And Sam kept his word.

—FINIS—

A Bit of Our Harlem

He came into the shop with a pitifully small amount of cheap candy to sell. The men gruffly refused to buy or to even look at his wares, and he shuffled toward the door with such a forlorn air that the young lady called him back. She was smiling partly because she liked to smile, and did so whenever fate gave her a chance, and partly to put the tattered little hunch-back at his ease.

The boy approached the table where the girl sat with the air of a homeless dog who hopes that he has found a friend.

"Let me see your candy, little boy." She toyed with the paper-wrapped packages for a while. She knew that she would buy one even though she had but fifteen cents in her pocket-book and a very vague notion as to where her next week's rent would come from. The hunched-back boy looked too dejected to turn away, however. She handed him a nickel.

"Thank yuh ma'am," said the boy. "You certainly is a nice lady. You aint mean lak some folks."

"Thank you," rejoined the girl, "and where do you live?"

"I lives down in Fifty-Third Street. My mama, she dead when I wuz a baby an' my fadder, too, he dead."

"Who takes care of you?"

"My grand'ma, an' she teached me th' Lawd's prayer an' I goes tuh Sunday school when I got shoes. See this coat? Aint it nice? A lady gave it to me."

"It is a pretty coat," agreed the young woman, "and do you belong to the church yet?"

"Naw, not yet, but I guess I will some day. A lady that used to live wid us she got religion, but after a while her sins come back on her. Do you know my teacher?"

"No, I don't. What does she teach you?"

"She, she teach me how to read and count a hundred, but I forgot what comes after ninety-seven. Do you know? Let's see, ninety-five, ninety-six, ninety-seven—gee. I can't learn that."

"Of course," laughed the girl, "ninety-eight, ninety-nine, one hundred. What else does she teach you?"

"She say when I go to Heben I be white as snow an' the angels goin' to take this lump out of my back an' make me tall. I guess maybe they roll something over my back like dat machine, what dey rolls out the street wid."

The girl felt very much like laughing at this original idea, but seeing his serious face she resisted and asked him very kindly how old he was.

"Let's see," answered the boy. "Grand'ma she say I'm fifteen, teacher she say I'm sixteen. I guess I'm sixteen cause once, long time ago, I wuz fifteen before."

The young lady exhibited signs of flagging interest and asked no more questions but the boy showed no inclination to go. His eyes never left her face, and at last he asked, "Where is yo' mama and papa?"

"Both dead."

"Who takes keer of you, then?"

"Why, I do, myself."

"Nobody buys you nothin' to eat, neither?"

"No."

The hunch-back looked pitying at the girl, at himself, at the floor, and at last said in a voice full of pity, "I guess maybe I can put on some long pants an' marry you an' then I'll buy you something to eat."

The girl would have laughed but the world of sympathy, understanding, and fellowship that showed in the boy's face and choked his voice restrained her. How often had she sought that same understanding fellowship within her own class, but how seldom had she found it!

"Well, lady, I'm goin' now cause I got to make a fire in the stove for Grand'ma. But I come back again some time cause youse a nice lady. Maybe I bring you some Easter candy if I have some nickels—that's the day the Jews nailed Jesus in a box an' put rocks on it, but he got out—ask the Bible, he knows."

Drenched in Light

"You Isie Watts! Git 'own offen dat gate post an' rake up dis yahd!"

The little brown figure perched upon the gate post looked yearningly at the gleaming shell road that lead to Orlando, and down the road that led to Sanford and shrugged her thin shoulders. This heaped kindling on Grandma Potts' already burning ire.

"Lawd a-mussy!" she screamed, enraged—"Heah Joel, gimme dat wash stick. Ah'll show dat limb of Satan she kain't shake huhseff at *me*. If she ain't down by de time Ah gets dere, Ah'll break huh down in de lines" (loins).

"Aw Gran'ma, Ah see Mist' George and Jim Robinson comin' and Ah wanted to wave at 'em," the child said petulantly.

"You jes wave dat rake at dis heah yahd, madame, else Ah'll take you down a button hole lower. You'se too 'oomanish jumpin' up in everybody's face dat pass."

This struck the child in a very sore spot for nothing pleased her so much as to sit atop of the gate post and hail the passing vehicles on their way south to Orlando, or north to Sanford. That white shell road was her great attraction. She raced up and down the stretch of it that lay before her gate like a round eyed puppy hailing gleefully all travelers. Everybody in the country, white and colored, knew little Isis Watts, the joyful. The Robinson brothers, white cattlemen, were particularly fond of her and always extended a stirrup for her to climb up behind one of them for a short ride, or let her try to crack the long bull whips and yee whoo at the cows.

Grandma Potts went inside and Isis literally waved the rake at the "chaws" of ribbon cane that lay so bountifully about the yard in company with the knots and peelings, with a thick sprinkling of peanut hulls.

The herd of cattle in their envelope of gray dust came alongside and Isis dashed out to the nearest stirrup and was lifted up.

"Hello theah Snidlits, I was wonderin' wheah you was," said Jim Robinson as she snuggled down behind in the saddle. They were almost out of the danger zone when Grandma emerged.

"You Isie-s!" she bawled.

The child slid down on the opposite side from the house and executed a flank movement through the corn patch that brought her into the yard from behind the privy.

"You lil' hasion you! Wheah you been?"

"Out in de back yahd," Isis lied and did a cart wheel and a few fancy steps on her way to the front again.

"If you doan git tuh dat yahd, Ah make a mommuk of you!" Isis observed that Grandma was cutting a fancy assortment of switches from peach, guana and cherry trees.

She finished the yard by raking everything under the edge of the porch and began a romp with the dogs, those lean, floppy eared 'coon hounds that all country folks keep. But Grandma vetoed this also.

"Isie, you set 'own on dat porch! Uh great big 'lebon yeah old gal racin' an' rompin' lak dat—set 'own!"

Isis impatiently flung herself upon the steps.

"Git up offa dem steps, you aggavatin' limb, 'fore Ah git dem hick'ries tuh you, an' set yo' seff on a cheah."

Isis petulantly arose and sat down as violently as possible in a chair, but slid down until she all but sat upon her shoulder blades.

"Now look atcher," Grandma screamed, "Put yo' knees together, an' git up offen yo' backbone! Lawd, you know dis hellion is gwine make me stomp huh insides out."

Isis sat bolt upright as if she wore a ramrod down her back and began to whistle. Now there are certain things that Grandma Potts felt no one of this female persuasion should do—one was to sit with the knees separated, "settin' brazen" she called it; another was whistling, another playing with boys, neither must a lady cross her legs.

Up she jumped from her seat to get the switches.

"So youse whistlin' in mah face, huh!" She glared till her eyes were beady and Isis bolted for safety. But the noon hour brought John Watts, the widowed father, and this excused the child from sitting for criticism.

Being the only girl in the family, of course she must wash the dishes, which she did in intervals between frolics with the dogs. She even gave Jake, the puppy, a swim in the dishpan by holding him suspended above the water that reeked of "pot likker"—just high enough so that his feet would be immersed. The deluded puppy swam and swam without ever crossing the pan, much to his annoyance. Hearing Grandma she hurriedly dropped him on the floor, which he tracked up with feet wet with dishwater.

Grandma took her patching and settled down in the front room to sew. She did this every afternoon and invariably slept in the big red rocker with her head lolled back over the back, the sewing falling from her hand.

Isis had crawled under the center table with its red plush cover with little round balls for fringe. She was lying on her back imagining herself various personages. She wore trailing robes, golden slippers with blue bottoms. She rode white horses with flaring pink nostrils to the horizon, for she still believed that to be land's end. She was picturing herself gazing over the edge of the world into the abyss when the spool of cotton fell from Grandma's lap and rolled away under the whatnot. Isis drew back from her contemplation of the nothingness at the horizon and glanced up at the sleeping woman. Her head had fallen back. She breathed with a regular "snark" intake and soft "poosah" exhaust. But Isis was a visual minded child. She heard the snores only subconsciously but she saw straggling beard on Grandma's chin, trembling a little with every "snark" and "poosah." They were long gray hairs curled here and there against the dark brown skin. Isis was moved with pity for her mother's mother.

"Poah Gran'ma needs a shave," she murmured, and set about it. Just then, Joel, next older than Isis, entered with a can of bait.

"Come on, Isie, les' we all go fishin'. The perch is bitin' fine in Blue Sink."

"Sh-h—" cautioned his sister, "Ah got to shave Gran'ma."

"Who say so?" Joel asked, surprised.

"Nobody doan hafta tell me. Look at her chin. No ladies don't weah no whiskers if they kin help it. But Gran'ma gittin' ole an' she doan know how to shave like me."

The conference adjourned to the back porch lest Grandma wake.

"Aw, Isie, you doan know nothin' 'bout shavin' a-tall—but a *man* lak *me*—"

"Ah do so know."

"You don't not. Ah'm goin' shave her mahseff."

"Naw, you won't neither, Smarty. Ah saw her first an' thought it all up first," Isis declared, and ran to the calico covered box on the wall above the wash basin and seized her father's razor. Joel was quick and seized the mug and brush.

"Now!" Isis cried defiantly, "Ah got the razor."

"Goody, goody, goody, pussy cat, Ah got th' brush an' you can't shave 'thout lather—see! Ah know mo' than you," Joel retorted.

"Aw, who don't know dat?" Isis pretended to scorn. But seeing her progress blocked for lack of lather she compromised.

"Ah know! Les' we all shave her. You lather an' Ah shave."

This was agreeable to Joel. He made mountains of lather and anointed his own chin, and the chin of Isis and the dogs, splashed the walls and at last was persuaded to lather Grandma's chin. Not that he was loath but he wanted his new plaything to last as long as possible.

Isis stood on one side of the chair with the razor clutched cleaver fashion. The niceties of razor-handling had passed over her head. The thing with her was to *hold* the razor—sufficient in itself.

Joel splashed on the lather in great gobs and Grandma awoke.

For one bewildered moment she stared at the grinning boy with the brush and mug but sensing another presence, she turned to behold the business face of Isis and the razor-clutching hand. Her jaw dropped and Grandma, forgetting years and rheumatism, bolted from the chair and fled from the house, screaming.

"She's gone to tell papa, Isie. You didn't have no business wid his razor and he's gonna lick yo hide," Joel cried, running to replace mug and brush.

"You too, chuckle-head, you, too," retorted Isis. "You was playin' wid his brush and put it all over the dogs—Ah seen you put it on Ned an' Beulah." Isis shaved some slivers from the door jamb with the razor and replaced it in the box. Joel took his bait and pole and hurried to Blue Sink. Isis crawled under the house to brood over the whipping she knew would come. She had meant well.

But sounding brass and tinkling cymbal drew her forth. The local lodge of the Grand United Order of Odd Fellows, led by a braying, thudding band, was marching in full regalia down the road. She had forgotten the barbecue and log-rolling to be held today for the benefit of the new hall.

Music to Isis meant motion. In a minute, razor and whipping forgotten, she was doing a fair imitation of the Spanish dancer she had seen in a medicine show some time before. Isis' feet were gifted—she could dance most anything she saw.

Up, up went her spirits, her brown little feet doing all sorts of intricate things and her body in rhythm, hand curving above her head. But the music was growing faint. Grandma nowhere in sight. She stole out of the gate, running and dancing after the band.

Then she stopped. She couldn't dance at the carnival. Her dress was torn and dirty. She picked a long stemmed daisy and thrust it behind her ear. But the dress, no better. Oh, an idea! In the battered round topped trunk in the bedroom!

She raced back to the house, then, happier, raced down the white dusty road to the picnic grove, gorgeously clad. People laughed good naturedly at her, the band played and Isis danced because she couldn't help it. A crowd of children gather[ed] admiringly about her as she wheeled lightly about, hand on hip, flower between her teeth with the red and white fringe of the tablecloth—Grandma's new red tablecloth that she wore in lieu of a Spanish shawl—trailing in the dust. It was too ample for her meager form, but she wore it like a gypsy. Her brown feet twinkled in and out of the fringe. Some grown people joined the children about her. The Grand Exalted Ruler rose to speak; the band was hushed, but Isis danced on, the crowd clapping their hands for her. No one listened to the Exalted one, for little by little the multitude had surrounded the brown dancer.

An automobile drove up to the Crown and halted. Two white men and a lady got out and pushed into the crowd, suppressing mirth discreetly behind gloved hands. Isis looked up and waved them a magnificent hail and went on dancing until—

Grandma had returned to the house and missed Isis and straightway sought her at the festivities expecting to find her in her soiled dress, shoeless, gaping at the crowd, but what she saw drove her frantic. Here was her granddaughter dancing before a gaping crowd in her brand new red tablecloth, and reeking of lemon extract, for Isis had added the final touch to her costume. She *must* have perfume.

Isis saw Grandma and bolted. She heard her cry: "Mah Gawd, mah brand new tablecloth Ah jus' bought f'um O'landah!" as she fled through the crowd and on into the woods.

II

She followed the little creek until she came to the ford in a rutty wagon road that led to Apopka and laid down on the cool grass at the roadside. The April sun was quite hot.

Misery, misery and woe settled down upon her and the child wept. She knew another whipping was in store for her.

"Oh, Ah wish Ah could die, then Gran'ma an' papa would be sorry they beat me so much. Ah b'leeve Ah'll run away an' never go home no mo'. Ah'm goin' drown mahseff in th' creek!" Her woe grew attractive.

Isis got up and waded into the water. She routed out a tiny 'gator and a huge bull frog. She splashed and sang, enjoying herself immensely. The purr of a motor struck her ear and she saw a large, powerful car jolting along the rutty road toward her. It stopped at the water's edge.

"Well, I declare, it's our little gypsy," exclaimed the man at the wheel, "What are you doing here, now?"

"Ah'm killin' mahseff," Isis declared dramatically, "cause Gran'ma beats me too much."

There was a hearty burst of laughter from the machine.

"You'll last sometime the way you are going about it. Is this the way to Maitland? We want to go to the Park Hotel."

Isis saw no longer any reason to die. She came up out of the water, holding up the dripping fringe of the tablecloth.

"Naw, indeedy. You go to Maitland by the shell road—it goes by mah house—an' turn off at Lake Sebelia to the clay road that takes you right to the do'."

"Well," went on the driver, smiling furtively, "could you quit dying long enough to go with us?"

"Yessuh," she said thoughtfully, "Ah wanta go wid you."

The door of the car swung open. She was invited to a seat beside the driver. She had often dreamed of riding in one of these heavenly chariots but never thought she would, actually.

"Jump in then, Madame Tragedy, and show us. We lost ourselves after we left your barbecue."

During the drive Isis explained to the kind lady who smelt faintly of violets and to the indifferent men that she was really a princess. She told them about her trips to the horizon, about the trailing gowns, the gold shoes with blue bottoms—she insisted on the blue bottoms—the white charger, the time when she was Hercules and had slain numerous dragons and sundry giants. At last the car approached her gate over which stood the umbrella China-berry tree. The car was abreast of the gate and had all but passed when Grandma spied her glorious tablecloth lying back against the upholstery of the Packard.

"You Isie-e!" she bawled, "You lil' wretch you! come heah *dis instunt!*"

"That's me," the child confessed, mortified, to the lady on the rear seat.

"Oh, Sewell, stop the car. This is where the child lives. I hate to give her up though."

"Do you wanta keep me?" Isis brightened.

"Oh, I wish I could, you shining little morsel. Wait, I'll try to save you a whipping this time."

She dismounted with the gaudy lemon flavored culprit and advanced to the gate where Grandma stood glowering, switches in hand.

"You're gointuh ketchit f'um yo' haid to yo' heels m'lady. Jes' come in heah."

"Why, good afternoon," she accosted the furious grandparent. "You're not going to whip this poor little thing, are you?" the lady asked in conciliatory tones.

"Yes, Ma'am. She's de wustest lil' limb dat ever drawed bref. Jes' look at mah new tablecloth dat ain't never been washed. She done traipsed all over de woods, uh dancin' an' uh prancin' in it. She done took a razor to me t'day an' Lawd knows whut mo'."

Isis clung to the white hand fearfully.

"Ah wuzn't gointer hurt Gran'ma, miss—Ah wuz jus' gointer shave her whiskers fuh huh 'cause she's old an' can't."

The white hand closed tightly over the little brown one that was quite soiled. She could understand a voluntary act of love even though it miscarried.

"Now, Mrs. er—er—I didn't get the name—how much did your tablecloth cost?"

"One whole big silvah dollar down at O'landah—ain't had it a week yit."

"Now here's five dollars to get another one. The little thing loves laughter. I want her to go on to the hotel and dance in that tablecloth for me. I can stand a little light today—"

"Oh, yessum, yessum," Grandma cut in, "Everything's alright, sho' she kin go, yessum."

The lady went on: "I want brightness and this Isis is joy itself, why she's drenched in light!"

Isis, for the first time in her life, felt appreciated and danced up and down in an ecstasy of joy for a minute.

"Now, behave yo'seff, Isie, ovah at de hotel wid de white folks," Grandma cautioned, pride in her voice, though she strove to hide it. "Lawd, ma'am, dat gal keeps me so frackshus, Ah doan know mah haid f'um mah feet. Ah orter comb huh haid, too, befo' she go wid you all."

"No, no, don't bother. I like her as she is. I don't think she'd like it either, being combed and scrubbed. Come on, Isis."

Feeling that Grandma had been somewhat squelched did not detract from Isis' spirit at all. She pranced over to the waiting motor and this time seated herself on the rear seat between the sweet, smiling lady and the rather aloof man in gray.

"Ah'm gointer stay wid you all," she said with a great deal of warmth, and snuggled up to her benefactress. "Want me tuh sing a song fuh you?"

"There, Helen, you've been adopted," said the man with a short, harsh laugh.

"Oh, I hope so, Harry." She put an arm about the red draped figure at her side and drew it close until she felt the warm puffs of the child's breath against her side. She looked hungrily ahead of her and spoke into space rather than to anyone in the car. "I want a little of her sunshine to soak into my soul. I need it."

Spunk

I

A giant of a brown-skinned man sauntered up the one street of the Village and out into the palmetto thickets with a small pretty woman clinging lovingly to his arm.

"Looka theah, folkses!" cried Elijah Mosely, slapping his leg gleefully. "Theah they go, big as life an' brassy as tacks."

All the loungers in the store tried to walk to the door with an air of nonchalance but with small success.

"Now pee-eople!" Walter Thomas gasped. "Will you look at 'em!"

"But that's one thing Ah likes about Spunk Banks—he ain't skeered of nothin' on God's green footstool—*nothin'!* He rides that log down at saw-mill jus' like he struts 'round wid another man's wife—jus' don't give a kitty. When Tes' Miller got cut to giblets on that circle-saw, Spunk steps right up and starts ridin'. The rest of us was skeered to go near it."

A round-shouldered figure in overalls much too large, came nervously in the door and the talking ceased. The men looked at each other and winked.

"Gimme some soda-water. Sass'prilla Ah reckon," the new-comer ordered, and stood far down the counter near the open pickled pig-feet tub to drink it.

Elijah nudged Walter and turned with mock gravity to the new-comer.

"Say, Joe, how's everything up yo' way? How's yo' wife?"

Joe started and all but dropped the bottle he held in his hands. He swallowed several times painfully and his lips trembled.

"Aw 'Lige, you oughtn't to do nothin' like that," Walter grumbled. Elijah ignored him.

"She jus' passed heah a few minutes ago goin' thata way," with a wave of his hand in the direction of the woods.

Now Joe knew his wife had passed that way. He knew that the men lounging in the general store had seen her, moreover, he knew that the men knew *he* knew. He stood there silent for a long moment staring blankly, with his Adam's apple twitching nervously up and down his throat. One could actually *see* the pain he was suffering, his eyes, his face, his hands and even the dejected slump of his shoulders. He set the bottle down upon the counter. He didn't bang it, just eased it out of his hand silently and fiddled with his suspender buckle.

"Well, Ah'm goin' after her to-day. Ah'm goin' an' fetch her back. Spunk's done gone too fur."

He reached deep down in his trouser pocket and drew out a hollow ground razor, large and shiny, and passed his moistened thumb back and forth over the edge.

"Talkin' like a man, Joe. Course that's *yo'* fambly affairs, but Ah like to see grit in anybody."

Joe Kanty laid down a nickel and stumbled out into the street.

Dusk crept in from the woods. Ike Clarke lit the swinging oil lamp that was almost immediately surrounded by candle-flies.

The men laughed boisterously behind Joe's back as they watched him shamble woodward.

"You oughtn't to said whut you did to him, 'Lige—look how it worked him up," Walter chided.

"And Ah hope it did work him up. 'Tain't even decent for a man to take and take like he do."

"Spunk will sho' kill him."

"Aw, Ah don't know. You never kin tell. He might turn him up an' spank him fur gettin' in the way, but Spunk wouldn't shoot no unarmed man. Dat razor he carried outa heah ain't gonna run Spunk down an' cut him, an' Joe ain't got the nerve to go up to Spunk with it knowing he totes that Army .45. He makes that break outa heah to bluff us. He's gonna hide that razor behind the first likely palmetto root an' sneak back home to bed. Don't tell me nothin' 'bout that rabbit-foot colored man. Didn't he meet Spunk an' Lena face to face one day las' week an' mumble sumthin' to Spunk 'bout lettin' his wife alone?"

"What did Spunk say?" Walter broke in—"Ah like him fine but tain't right the way he carries on wid Lena Kanty, jus' cause Joe's timid 'bout fightin'."

"You wrong theah, Walter. 'Tain't cause Joe's timid at all, it's cause Spunk wants Lena. If Joe was a passle of wile cats Spunk would tackle the job just the same. He'd go after *anything* he wanted the same way. As Ah wuz sayin' a minute ago, he tole Joe right to his face that Lena was his. 'Call her,' he says to Joe. 'Call her and see if she'll come. A woman knows her boss an' she answers when he calls.' 'Lena, ain't I yo' husband?' Joe sorter whines out. Lena looked at him real disgusted but she don't answer and she don't move outa her tracks. Then Spunk reaches out an' takes hold of her arm an' says: 'Lena, youse mine. From now on Ah works for you an' fights for you an' Ah never wants you to look to nobody for a crumb of bread, a stitch of close or a shingle to go over yo' head, but *me* long as Ah live. Ah'll git the lumber foh owah house to-morrow. Go home an' git yo' things together!' 'Thass mah house,' Lena speaks up. 'Papa gimme that.' 'Well,' says Spunk, 'doan give up whut's yours, but when youse inside don't forgit youse mine, an' let no other man git outa his place wid you!' Lena looked up at him with her eyes so full of love that they wuz runnin' over an' Spunk seen it an' Joe seen it too, and his lip started to tremblin' and his Adam's apple was galloping up and down his neck like a race horse. Ah bet he's wore out half a dozen Adam's apples since Spunk's been on the job with Lena. That's all he'll do. He'll be back heah after while swallowin' an' workin' his lips like he wants to say somethin' an' can't."

"But didn't he do *nothin'* to stop 'em?"

"Nope, not a frazzlin' thing—jus' stood there. Spunk took Lena's arm and walked off jus like nothin' ain't happened and he stood there gazin' after them till they was outa sight. Now you know a woman don't want no man like that. I'm jus' waitin' to see whut he's goin' to say when he gits back."

II

But Joe Kanty never came back, never. The men in the store heard the sharp report of a pistol somewhere distant in the palmetto thicket and soon Spunk came walking leisurely, with his big black Stetson set at the same rakish angle and Lena clinging to his arm, came walking right into the general store. Lena wept in a frightened manner.

"Well," Spunk announced calmly, "Joe come out there wid a meatax an' made me kill him."

He sent Lena home and led the men back to Joe—Joe crumpled and limp with his right hand still clutching his razor.

"See mah back? Mah cloes cut clear through. He sneaked up an' tried to kill me from the back, but Ah got him, an' got him good, first shot," Spunk said.

The men glared at Elijah, accusingly.

"Take him up an' plant him in 'Stoney lonesome,'" Spunk said in a careless voice. "Ah didn't wanna shoot him but he made me do it. He's a dirty coward, jumpin' on a man from behind."

Spunk turned on his heel and sauntered away to where he knew his love wept in fear for him and no man stopped him. At the general store later on, they all talked of locking him up until the sheriff could come from Orlando, but no one did anything but talk.

A clear case of self-defense, the trial was a short one, and Spunk walked out of the court house to freedom again. He could work again, ride the dangerous log-carriage that fed the singing, snarling, biting, circle-saw; he could stroll the soft dark lanes with his guitar. He was free to roam the woods again; he was free to return to Lena. He did all of these things.

III

"Whut you reckon, Walt?" Elijah asked one night later. "Spunk's gittin' ready to marry Lena!"

"Naw! Why Joe ain't had time to git cold yit. Nohow Ah didn't figger Spunk was the marryin' kind."

"Well, he is," rejoined Elijah. "He done moved most of Lena's things—and her along wid 'em—over to the Bradley house. He's buying it. Jus' like Ah told yo' all right in heah the night Joe wuz kilt. Spunk's crazy 'bout Lena. He don't want folks to keep on talkin' 'bout her—thass reason he's rushin' so. Funny thing 'bout that bob-cat, wan't it?"

"What bob-cat, 'Lige? Ah ain't heered 'bout none."

"Ain't cher? Well, night befo' las' was the fust night Spunk an' Lena moved together an' jus' as they was goin' to bed, a big black bob-cat, black all over, you hear me, *black*, walked round and round that house and howled like forty, an' when Spunk got his gun an' went to the winder to shoot it, he says it stood right still an' looked him in the eye, an' howled right at him. The thing got Spunk so nervoused up he couldn't shoot. But Spunk says twan't no bob-cat nohow. He says it was Joe done sneaked back from Hell!"

"Humph!" sniffed Walter, "he oughter be nervous after what he done. Ah reckon Joe come back to dare him to marry Lena, or to come out an' fight. Ah bet he'll be back time and again, too. Know what Ah think? Joe wuz a braver man than Spunk."

There was a general shout of derision from the group.

"Thass a fact," went on Walter. "Lookit whut he done; took a razor an' went out to fight a man he knowed toted a gun and wuz a crack shot, too; 'nother thing, Joe wuz skeered of Spunk, skeered plumb stiff! But he went jes' the same. It took him a long time to get his nerve up. 'Tain't nothin' for Spunk to fight when he ain't skeered of nothin'. Now Joe's done come back to have it out wid the man that's got all he ever had. Y'll know Joe ain't never had nothin' nor wanted nothin' besides Lena. It musta been a h'ant cause ain' nobody never seen no black bob-cat."

"'Nother thing," cut in one of the men, "Spunk wuz cussin' a blue streak today 'cause he 'lowed dat saw wuz wobblin'—almos' got 'im once. The machinist come, looked it over an' said it wuz alright. Spunk musta been leanin' t'wards it some. Den he claimed somebody pushed 'im but 'twant nobody close to 'im. Ah wuz glad when knockin' off time come. I'm skeered of dat man when he gits hot. He'd beat you full of button holes as quick as he's look atcher."

IV

The men gathered the next morning in a different mood, no laughter. No badinage this time.

"Look, 'Lige, you goin' to set up wid Spunk?"

"Naw, Ah reckon not, Walter. Tell yuh the truth, Ah'm a lil bit skittish. Spunk died too wicket—died cussin' he did. You know he thought he wuz done outa life."

"Good Lawd, who'd he think done it?"

"Joe."

"Joe Kanty? How come?"

"Walter, Ah b'leeve Ah will walk up thata way an' set. Lena would like it Ah reckon."

"But whut did he say, 'Lige?"

Elijah did not answer until they had left the lighted store and were strolling down the dark street.

"Ah wuz loadin' a wagon wid scantlin' right near the saw when Spunk fell on the carriage but 'fore Ah could git to him the saw got him in the body—awful sight. Me an' Skint Miller got him off but it was too late. Anybody could see that. The fust thing he said wuz: 'He pushed me, 'Lige—the dirty hound pushed me in the back!'—He was spittin' blood at ev'ry breath. We laid him on the sawdust pile with his face to the East so's he could die easy. He helt mah han' till the last, Walter, and said: 'It was Joe, 'Lige—the dirty sneak shoved me . . . he didn't dare come to mah face . . . but Ah'll git the son-of-a-wood louse soon's Ah git there an' make hell too hot for him . . . Ah felt him shove me . . . !' Thass how he died."

"If spirits kin fight, there's a powerful tussle goin' on somewhere ovah Jordan 'cause Ah b'leeve Joe's ready for Spunk an' ain't skeered any more—yas, Ah b'leeve Joe pushed 'im mahself."

They had arrived at the house. Lena's lamentations were deep and loud. She had filled the room with magnolia blossoms that gave off a heavy sweet odor. The keepers of the wake tipped about whispering in frightened tones. Everyone in the village was there, even old Jeff Kanty, Joe's father, who a few hours before would have been afraid to come within ten feet of him, stood leering triumphantly down upon the fallen giant, as if his fingers had been the teeth of steel that laid him low.

The cooling board consisted of three sixteen-inch boards on saw horses, a dingy sheet was his shroud.

The women ate heartily of the funeral baked meats and wondered who would be Lena's next. The men whispered coarse conjectures between guzzles of whiskey.

Magnolia Flower

The brook laughed and sang. When it encountered hard places in its bed, it hurled its water in sparkling dance figures up into the moonlight.

It sang louder, louder; danced faster, faster, with a coquettish splash! at the vegetation on its banks.

At last it danced boisterously into the bosom of the St. John's, upsetting the whispering hyacinths who shivered and blushed, drunk with the delight of moon kisses.

The Mighty One turned peevishly in his bed and washed the feet of the Palmetto palms so violently that they awoke and began again the gossip they had left off when the Wind went to bed. A palm cannot speak without wind. The river had startled it also, for the winds sleep on the bosom of waters.

The palms murmured noisily of seasons and centuries, mating and birth and the transplanting of life. Nature knows nothing of death.

The river spoke to the brook.

"Why, O Young Water, do you hurry and hurl yourself so riotously about with your chatter and song? You disturb my sleep."

"Because, O Venerable One," replied the brook, "I am young. The flowers bloom, the trees and wind say beautiful things to me; there are lovers beneath the orange trees on my banks,—but most of all because the moon shines upon me with a full face."

"That is not sufficient reason for you to disturb my sleep," the river retorted. "I have cut down mountains and moved whole valleys into the sea, and I am not so noisy as you are."

The river slapped its banks angrily.

"But," added the brook diffidently, "I passed numbers of lovers as I came on. There was also a sweet-voiced night-bird."

"No matter, no matter!" scolded the river. I have seen millions of lovers, child. I have borne them up and down, listened to those things that uttered more with the breath than the lips, gathered infinite tears, and some lovers have even flung themselves upon the soft couch I keep in my bosom and slept."

"Tell me about some of them!" eagerly begged the brook.

"Oh, well," the river muttered, "I am wide awake now, and I suppose brooks must be humored."

THE RIVER'S STORY

"Long ago, as men count years, men who were pale of skin held a dark race of men in a bondage. The dark ones cried out in sorrow and travail,—not here in my country, but farther north. Many rivers carried their tears to the sea and the tide would bring some of them to me. The Wind brought cries without end.

"But there were some among the slaves who did not weep, but fled in the night to safety,—some to the far north, some to the far south, for here the red man, the panther, and the bear alone were to be feared. One of them from the banks of the Savannah came here. He was large and black and strong. His heart was strong and thudded with an iron sound in his breast. The forest made way for him, the beasts were afraid of him, and he built a house. He gathered stones and bits of metal, yellow and white—such as men love and for which they die—and grew wealthy. How? I do not know. Rivers take no notice of such things. We sweep men, stones, metal—all, **ALL** to the sea. All are as grass; all must to the sea in the end.

"He married Swift Deer, a Cherokee Maiden, and five years—as men love to clip Time into bits—passed.

"They had now a daughter, Magnolia Flower they called her, for she came at the time of them opening.

"When they had been married five years, she was four years old.

"Then the tide brought trouble rumors to me of hate, strife and destruction—war, war, war.

"The blood of those born in the North flowed to sea, mingled with that of the southern-born. Bitter Waters, Troubled Winds. Rains that washed the dust from Heaven but could not beat back the wails of anguish, the thirst for blood and glory; the prayers for that which God gives not into the hands of man,—Vengeance,—fires of hate to sear and scorch the ground; wells of acid tears to blight the leaf.

"Then all men walked free in the land, and Wind and Water again grew sweet.

"The man-made time notches flew by, and Magnolia Flower was in full-bloom. Her large eyes burned so brightly in her dark-brown face that the Negroes trembled when she looked angrily upon them. 'She curses with her eyes,' they said. 'Some evil surely will follow.'

"Black men came and went now as they pleased and the father had many to serve him, for now he had built a house such as white men owned when he was in bondage.

"His heart, of the ex-slave Bentley, was iron to all but Magnolia Flower. Swift Deer was no longer swift. Too many kicks and blows, too many grim chokings had slowed her feet and heart.

"He had done violence to workmen. There was little law in this jungle, and that was his,—'Do as I bid you or suffer my punishment.'

"He was hated, but feared more.

"He hated anything that bore the slightest resemblance to his former oppressors. His servants must be black, very black or Cherokee.

"The flower was seventeen and beautiful. Bentley thought often of a mate for her now, but one that would not offend him either in spirit or flesh. He must be full of humility, and black.

"One day, as the sun gave me a good-night kiss and the stars began their revels, I bore a young Negro yet not a Negro, for his skin was the color of freshly barked cypress, golden with the curly black hair of the white man.

"There were many Negroes in Bentley's Village and he wished to build a school that would teach them useful things.

"Bentley hated him at once; but ordered a school-house to be built, for he wished Magnolia to read and write.

"But before two weeks had passed, the teacher had taught the Flower to read strange marvels with her dark eyes, and she had taught the teacher to sing with his eyes, his hands, his whole body in her presence or whenever he thought of her,—not in her father's house, but beneath that clump of palms, those three that bathe their toes eternally and talk.

"They busied themselves with dreams of creation, while Bentley swore the foundation of the school-room into place.

"'Nothing remains for me to do, now that I have your consent, but to ask your father for your sweet self. I know I am poor, but I have a great Vision, a high purpose, and he shall not be ashamed of me!'

"She clung fearfully to him.

"'No, don't, John, don't. He'll say "Naw!" and cuss. He—he don't like you at all. Youse too white.'

"'I'll get him out of that, just trust me, precious. Then I can just own you—just let me talk to him!'

"She wept and pleaded with him—told him of Bentley's terrible anger and violence, begged him to take her away and send her father word; but he refused to hear her, and walked up to her house and seated himself upon the broad verandah to wait for the father of Magnolia Flower.

"She flew to Swift Deer and begged her to persuade her lover not to brave Bentley's anger. The older woman crept out and tearfully implored him to go. He stayed.

"At dusk Bentley came swearing in. It had been a hot day; the men had cut several poor pieces of timber and seemed all bent on driving him to the crazy-house, he complained.

"Swift Deer slunk into the house at his approach, dragging her daughter after her.

"What followed was too violent for words to tell,—strength against strength, steel against steel. Threats bellowed from Bentley's bull throat seemed no more than little puffs of air to the lover. Of course, he would leave Bentley's house; but he would stay in the vicinity until he was told to leave by the Flower,—his Flower of sweetness and purity—and he would marry her unless hell froze over.

"'Better eat up dem words an' git out whilst ah letcher,' the old man growled.

"Bentley drew up his lips in a great roll glare.

"'No!' John shouted, giving him glare for his rage boiling and tumbling out from behind these ramparts, as it were. His eye reddened, a vessel in the center of his forehead stood out, gorged with blood, and his great hands twitched. For good or evil, Bentley was a strong man, mind and body.

"Swift Deer could no longer restrain her daughter. Magnolia Flower burst triumphantly upon the verandah.

"'Well, papa, you don't say that I haven't picked a man. No one else in forty miles round would stand up to you like John!'

"'Ham! Jim! Israel!' Bentley howled, on the verge of apoplexy. The men appeared. 'Take dis here yaller skunk an' lock him in dat back-room. I'm a gonna hang 'im high as Hamon come sun up, law uh no law.'

"A short struggle, and John was tied hand and foot.

"'Stop!' cried Magnolia Flower, fighting, clawing, biting, kicking like a brown fiend for her lover. One brawny worker held her until John was helplessly bound.

"But when she looked at all three of the men with her eye of fire, they shook in superstitious fear.

"'Oh, Mah Gawd!' breathed Ham, terrified. 'She's cussing us, she's cussing us all wid her eyes. Sump'm sho gwine happen.'

"Her eye was indeed something to affright the timid and even give the strong heart pause. A woman robbed of her love is more terrible than an army with banners.

"'Oh, I wish I could!' she uttered in a voice flat with intensity. 'You'd all drop dead on the spot.'

"Swift Deer had crept out and stood beside the child. She screamed and clasped her hands over her daughter's lips.

"'Say not such words, Magnolia,' she pleaded. 'Take them back into your bosom unsaid.'

"'Leave her be,' Bentley laughed acidly. 'Ah got a dose uh mah medicine ready for her too. Befo' ah hangs dis yaller pole-cat ahm gwinter marry her to Crazy Joe, an' John kin look on; den ah'll hang him, and she kin look on. Magnolia and Joe oughter have fine black chillen. Ha! Ha!'

"The girl never uttered a sound. She smiled with her lips but her eyes burned every bit of courage to cinders in those who saw her.

"John was locked in the stout back-room. The windows were guarded and Ham sat with a loaded gun at the door.

"Magnolia was locked in the parlor where she ran up and down, tearing her heavy black hair. She beat helplessly upon the doors, she hammered the windows, making little mewing noises in her throat like a cat deprived of her litter.

"The house grew grimly still. Bentley had forced his wife to accompany him to their bedroom. She lay fearfully awake but he slept peacefully, if noisily.

"'Magnolia Flower!' Ham called softly as he turned the key stealthily in the lock of her prison. 'Come on out. Ah caint stan' dis here weekedness uh yo pappy!'

"'No thank you, Ham. I'll stay right here and make him kill me long with John, if you don't let him out too.'

"'Lawd a mussy knows ah wisht ah could, but de ole man's got de key in his britches.'

"'I'm going and get it, Ham,' she announced as she stepped over the threshold to freedom.

"'Lawd! He'll kill me sho's you born.'

"Her feet were already on the stairs.

"'I'll have that key or die. Ham, you put some victuals in that rowboat.'

"Half for love, half for fear, Ham obeyed.

"No one but Magnolia Flower would have entered Bentley's bed-room as she did under the circumstances but to her the circumstances were her reasons for going. The big horse pistol under his pillow, the rack of guns in the hall, and her father's giant hands—none of these stopped her. She knew three lives,—her own, her lover's, and Ham's—hung on her success; but she went and returned with that key.

"One minute more and they flew down the path to the three leaning palms into the boat away northward.

"The morning came. Bentley ate hugely. The new rope hung ominously from the arm of the giant oak in the yard. Preacher Ike had eaten his breakfast with Bentley and the idiot, Crazy Joe, had forced himself into a pair of clean hickory pants.

"Bentley turned the key and flung open the door, stood still a minute in a grey rage and stalked to the back-room door, feeling for the key meanwhile.

"When he had fully convinced himself that the key was gone, he did not bother to open the door.

"'Ham, it 'pears dat Magnolia an' dat yaller dog aint heah dis mawnin', so you an' Swift Deer will hafta do, being ez y'all let 'em git away.' He said this calmly and stalked toward the gun rack; but his anger was too large to be contained in one human heart. His arteries corded his face, his eyes popped, and he fell senseless as he stretched his hand for the gun. Rage had burst his heart at being outwitted by a girl.

"This all happened more than forty years ago, as men reckon time. Soon Swift Deer died, and the house built by strong Bentley fell to decay. White men came and built a town and Magnolia Flower and her eyes passed from the hearts of people who had known her."

* * *

THE BROOK HAD LISTENED, tensely thrilled to its very bottom at times. The river flowed calmly on, shimmering under the moon as it moved ceaselessly to the sea.

An old couple picked their way down to the water's edge. He had once been tall—he still bore himself well. The little old woman clung lovingly to his arm.

"It's been forty-seven years, John," she said sweetly, her voice full of fear. "Do you think we can find the place?"

"Why yes, Magnolia, my Flower, unless they have cut down our trees; but if they are standing, we'll know 'em—couldn't help it."

"Yes, sweetheart, there they are. Hurry and let's sit on the roots like we used to and trail our fingers in the water. Love is wonderful, isn't it, dear?"

They hugged the trunks of the three clustering palms lovingly; then hugged each other and sat down shyly upon the heaped up roots.

"You never have regretted, Magnolia?"

"Of course not! But John, listen, did you ever hear a river make such a sound? Why it seems almost as if it were talking—that murmuring noise, you know."

"Maybe, it's welcoming us back. I always felt that it loved you and me, somehow."

Black Death

We Negroes in Eatonville know a number of things that the hustling, bustling white man never dreams of. He is a materialist with little care for overtones.

For instance, if a white person were halted on the streets of Orlando and told that Old Man Morgan, the excessively black Negro hoodoo man, can kill any person indicated and paid for, without ever leaving his house or even seeing his victim, he'd laugh in your face and walk away, wondering how long the Negro would wallow in ignorance and superstition. But no black person in a radius of twenty miles will smile, not much. They *know*.

His achievements are far too numerous to mention singly. Besides many of his cures or "conjures" are kept secret. But everybody knows that he put the loveless curse on Della Lewis. She has been married seven times but none of her husbands have ever remained with her longer than twenty-eight days that Morgan had prescribed as the limit.

Hiram Lester's left track was brought to him with five dollars and when the new moon came again, Lester was stricken with paralysis while working in his orange grove.

There was the bloody-flux that he put on Lucy Potte; he caused Emma Taylor's teeth to drop out; he put the shed skin of a black snake in Horace Brown's shoes and made him as the Wandering Jew; he put a sprig of Lena Merchant's hair in a bottle, corked it and threw it into a running stream with the neck pointing upstream, and she went crazy; he buried Lillie Wilcox's finger-nails with lizard's feet and dried up her blood.

All of these things and more can easily be proved by the testimony of the villagers. They ought to know.

He lives alone in a two-room hut down by Lake Blue Sink, the bottomless. His eyes are reddish and the large gold hoop ear-rings jan[gl]ing on either side of his shrunken black face make the children shrink in terror whenever they meet him on the street or in the woods where he goes to dig roots for his medicines.

But the doctor can not spend his time merely making folks ill. He has sold himself to the devil over the powerful black cat's bone that alone will float upstream, and many do what he wills. Life and death are in his hands—he sometimes kills.

He sent Old Lady Crooms to her death in the lake. She was a rival hoodoo doctor and laid claims to equal power. She came to her death one night. That very morning Morgan had told several that he was tired of her pretences—he would put an end to it and prove his powers.

That very afternoon near sundown, she went down to the lake to fish, telling her daughter, however, that she did not wish to go, but something seemed to be forcing her. About dusk someone heard her scream and rushed to the lake. She had fallen in and drowned. The white coroner from Orlando said she met her death by falling into the water during an epileptic fit. But the villagers *knew*. White folks are very stupid about some things. They can think mightily but cannot *feel*.

But the undoing of Beau Diddely is his masterpiece. He had come to Eatonville from up North somewhere. He was a waiter at the Park House Hotel over in Maitland where Docia Boger was a chamber-maid. She had a very pretty brown body and face, sang alto in the Methodist Choir and played the blues on her guitar. Soon Beau Diddely was with her every moment he could spare from his work. He was stuck on her all right, for a time.

They would linger in the shrubbery about Park Lake or go for long walks in the woods on Sunday afternoon to pick violets. They are abundant in the Florida woods in winter.

The Park House always closed in April and Beau was planning to go North with the white tourists. It was then Docia's mother discovered that Beau should have married her daughter weeks before.

"Mist' Diddely," said Mrs. Boger, "Ah'm a widder 'oman an' Doshy's all Ah got, an' Ah know youse gointer do what you orter." She hesitated a moment and studied his face. "'Thout no trouble. [Illegible] Ah doan wanta make no talk 'round town."

In a split second the vivacious, smiling Beau had vanished. A very hard vitriolic stranger occupied his chair.

"Looka heah, Mis' Boger. I'm a man that's travelled a lot—been most everywhere. Don't try to come that stuff over me—what I got to marry Docia for?"

"'Cause—'cause"—the surprise of his answer threw the old woman into a panic. "Youse the cause of her condition, aintcher?"

Docia, embarrassed, mortified, began to cry.

"Oh, I see the little plot now!" He glanced maliciously toward the girl and back again to her mother. "But I'm none of your down-South-country-suckers. Go try that on some of these clod-hoppers. Don't try to lie on *me*—I got money to fight."

"Beau," Docia sobbed, "you ain't callin' *me* a liah, is you?" And in her misery she started toward the man who through four months' constant association and assurance she had learned to love and trust.

"Yes! You're lying—you sneaking little—oh you're not even good sawdust! Me marry you! Why I could pick up a better woman out of the gutter than you! I'm a married man anyway, so you might as well forget your little scheme!"

Docia fell back stunned.

"But, but Beau, you said you wasn't," Docia wailed.

"Oh," Beau replied with a gesture of dismissal of the whole affair. "What difference does it make? A man will say anything at times. There are certain kinds of women that men always lie to."

In her mind's eye Docia saw things for the first time without her tinted glasses and real terror seized her. She fell upon her knees and clenched the nattily clad legs of her seducer.

"Oh Beau," she wept, struggling to hold him, as he, fearing for the creases in his trousers, struggled to free himself—"You said—you—you promised"— — —

"Oh, well, you ought not to have believed me—you ought to have known I didn't mean it. Anyway I'm not going to marry you, so what're you going to do? Do whatever you feel big enough to try—my shoulders are broad."

He left the house hating the two women bitterly, as only we hate those we have injured.

At the hotel, omitting mention of his shows of affection, his pleas, his solemn promises to Docia, he told the other waiters how that piece of the earth's refuse had tried to inveigle, to force him into a marriage. He enlarged upon his theme and told them all, in strict confidence, how she had been pursuing him all winter; how she had waited in ambush time and again and dragged him down by the lake, and well, he was only human. It couldn't have happened with the *right* kind of a girl, and he thought too much of himself to marry any other than the country's best.

So the next day Eatonville knew; and the scourge of tongues was added to Docia's woes.

Mrs. Boger and her daughter kept strictly indoors, suffering, weeping, growing bitter.

"Mommer, if he jus' hadn't tried to make me out a bad girl, I could look over the rest in time, Mommer, but—but he tried to make out—ah— —"

She broke down weeping again.

Drip, drip, drip went her daughter's tears on the old woman's heart, each drop calcifying a little the fibers till at the end of four days the petrifying process was complete. Where once had been warm, pulsing flesh was now a cold heavy stone, that pulled down pressing out normal life and bowing the head of her. The woman died, and in that heavy cold stone a tiger, a female tiger—was born.

She was ready to answer the questions Beau had flung so scornfully at her old head: "Well, what are you going to do?"

Docia slept, huddled on the bed. A hot salt tear rose to Mrs. Boger's eyes and rolled heavily down the quivering nose. Must Docia awake always to that awful desolation? Robbed of *everything,* even faith. She knew then that the world's greatest crime is not murder—its most terrible punishment is meted to her of too much faith—too great a love.

She turned down the light and stepped into the street.

It was near midnight and the village slept. But she knew of one house where there would be a light; one pair of eyes still awake.

As she approached Blue Sink she all but turned back. It was a dark night but the lake shimmered and glowed like phosphorous near the shore. It seemed that figures moved about on the quiet surface. She remembered that folks said Blue Sink, the bottomless, was Morgan's graveyard and all Africa awoke in her blood.

A cold prickly feeling stole over her and stood her hair on end. Her feet grew heavy and her tongue dry and stiff.

In the swamp at the head of the lake, she saw a Jack-O-Lantern darting here and there and three hundred years of America passed like the mist of morning. Africa reached out its dark hand and claimed its own. Drums, tom, tom, tom, tom, tom, beat in her ears. Strange demons seized her. Witch doctors danced before her, laid hands upon her alternately freezing and burning her flesh, until she found herself within the house of Morgan.

She was not permitted to tell her story. She opened her mouth but the old man chewed a camphor leaf or two, spat into a small pail of sand and asked:

"How do yuh wanta kill 'im? By water, by sharp edge, or a bullet?"

The old woman almost fell off of the chair in amazement that he knew her mind. He merely chuckled a bit and handed her a drinking gourd.

"Dip up a teeny bit of water an' po' hit on de flo',—by dat time you'll know."

She dipped the water out of a wooden pail and poured it upon the rough floor.

"Ah wanta shoot him, but how kin ah 'thout . . ."—

"Looka heah," Morgan directed and pointed to a huge mirror scarred and dusty. He dusted its face carefully. "Look in dis glass 'thout turnin' yo' head an' when he comes, you shoot tuh kill. Take good aim!"

Both faced about and gazed hard into the mirror that reached from floor to ceiling. Morgan turned once to spit into the pail of sand. The mirror grew misty, darker, near the center, then Mrs. Boger saw Beau walk to the center of the mirror and stand looking at her, glaring and sneering. She all but fainted in superstitious terror.

Morgan thrust the gun into her hand. She saw the expression on Beau Diddely's face change from scorn to fear and she laughed.

"Take good aim," Morgan cautioned. "You cain't shoot but once."

She leveled the gun at the heart of the apparition in the glass and fired. It collapsed; the mirror grew misty again, then cleared.

In horror she flung her money at the old man who seized it greedily, and fled into the darkness, dreading nothing, thinking only of putting distance between her and the house of Morgan.

* * *

The next day Eatonville was treated to another thrill.

It seemed that Beau Diddely, the darling of the ladies, was in the hotel yard making love to another chamber-maid. In order that she might fully appreciate what a great victory was hers, he was reciting the Conquest of Docia, how she loved him, pursued him, knelt down and kissed his feet, begging him to marry her,—when suddenly he stood up very straight, clasped his hand over his heart, grew rigid and fell dead.

The coroner's verdict was death from natural causes—heart failure. But they were mystified by what looked like a powder burn directly over the heart.

But the Negroes knew instantly when they saw that mark, but everyone agreed that he got justice. Mrs. Boger and Docia moved to Jacksonville where she married well.

And the white folks never knew and would have laughed had anyone told them,—so why mention it?

The Bone of Contention

Eatonville, Florida is a colored town and has its colored interests. It has not now, nor ever has had anything to rank Brazzle's yellow mule. His Yaller Highness was always mentioned before the weather, the misery of the back or leg, or the hard times.

The mule was old, rawbony and mean. He was so rawbony that he creaked as he ambled about the village street with his meanness shining out through every chink and cranny in his rattling anatomy. He worked little, ate heartily, fought every inch of the way before the plow and even disputed with Brazzle when he approached to feed him. Sale, exchange or barter was out of the question, for everybody in the county knew him.

But one day he died. Everybody was glad, including Brazzle. His death was one of those pleasant surprises that people hope for, but never expect to happen.

The city had no refuse plant so H.Y.H. went the way of all other domestic beasts who died among us. Brazzle borrowed Watson's two grey plugs and dragged the remains out to the edge of the cypress swamp, three miles beyond city limits and abandoned them to the natural scavengers. The town attended the dragging out to a man. The fallen gladiator was borne from the arena on his sharp back, his feet stiffly raised as if a parting gesture of defiance. We left him on the edge of the cypress swamp and returned to the village satisfied that the only piece of unadulterated meanness that the Lord had ever made was gone from among us forever.

Three years passed and his bones were clean and white. They were scattered along the swamp edge. The children still found them sufficiently interesting to tramp out to gaze upon them on Sunday afternoons. The elders neglected his bones, but the mule remained with them in song and story as a simile, as a metaphor, to point a moral or adorn a tale. But as the mean old trouble-making cuss, they considered him gone for good.

II

It was early night in the village. Joe Clarke's store porch was full of chewing men. Some chewed tobacco, some chewed cane, some chewed straws, for the villager is a ruminant in his leisure. They sat thus every evening ostensibly waiting for the mail from Number 38, the south-bound express. It was seldom that any of them got any but it gave them a good excuse to gather. They all talked a great deal, and every man jack of them talked about himself. Heroes all, they were, of one thing or another.

Ike Pearson had killed a six-foot rattler in a mighty battle that grew mightier every time Ike told about it; Walter Thomas had chinned the bar twenty times without stopping; Elijah Moseley had licked a "cracker"; Brazzle had captured a live catamount; Hiram Lester had killed a bear; Sykes Jones had won the soda-cracker eating contest; AND JOE CLARKE HAD STARTED THE TOWN!

Reverend Simms, the Methodist preacher, a resident of less than a year, had done nothing to boast of, but it was generally known that he aspired to the seat of Joe Clarke. He wanted to be the mayor. He had observed to some of his members that it wasnt no sense in one man staying in office all the time.

"Looka heah," Clarke cut across whoever it was that [was] talking at the time, "when Ah started dis town, Ah walked right up to de white folks an' laid down TWO HUN'DED DOLLARS WID DIS RIGHT HAND YOU SEE BEFO' YOU AN' GOT MAH PAPERS AN' PUT DIS TOWN ON DE MAP! It takes uh powerful lot uh sense an' grit tuh start uh town, yessirree!"

"Whut map did you put it on, Joe?" Lindsay disrespectfully asked. "Ah aint seed it on no map."

Seeing Clarke gored [him] to his liver. Rev. Simms let out a gloating snicker and tossed a cane knot to Tippy, the Lewis' dejected dog frame hovering about the group hoping for something more tempting to a dog's palate than cane chews and peanut shells might drop. He tossed the knot and waited for Clarke to answer. His Honor ignored the thrust as being too low for him to stoop and talked on. Was he not mayor, postmaster, storekeeper and Pooh Bah general? Insults must come to him from at least the county seat.

"Nother thing," Clarke continued, giving Simms a meaning look, "there's a heap goin' on 'round heah under the cover dat Ahm gointer put a stop to. Jim Weston done proaged through mah hen house enough. Last Sat'day Ah missed three uh mah bes' layin' hens, an' Ah been tol' he buried feathers in his backyard the very next day. Cose Ah caint prove nothin', but de minute he crooks his little finger, he goes 'way from mah town. He aint de onliest one Ah got mah eye on neither."

Simms accepted the challenge thrown at him.

"Fact is, the town aint run lak it might be. We oughta stop dat foolishness of runnin' folks outa town. We oughta jail 'em. They's got jails in all de other towns, an' we oughta bring ours up to date!"

"Ah'll be henfired! Simms, you tries to know mo' 'bout runnin' de town than me! Dont you reckon a man thats got sense enough to start uh town, knows how tuh run it. Dont you reckon if de place had uh needed uh jailhouse Ah would have got one built 'long befo' you come heah?"

"We do so need a jail," Lindsay contended. "Jus' cause you stahted the town, dat dont mean yo' mouf no prayer book nor neither yo' lips no Bible. They dont flap lak none tuh *me*."

Lindsay was a little shriveled up man with gray hair and bow-legs. He was the smallest man in the village, who nevertheless did the most talk of fighting. That was because the others felt he was too small for them to hit. He was harmless, but known to be the nastiest threatener in the county.

Clarke merely snorted contemptuously at his sally and remarked dryly that the road was right there for all those who were not satisfied with the way he was running the town.

"Meaning to insult me?" Lindsay asked belligerently.

"Ah dont keer HOW yuh take it. Jus' take yo' rawbony cow an' gwan tuh de woods, fuh all I keer," Clarke answered.

Lindsay leaped from the porch and struck his fighting pose. "Jus' hit de ground an' Ah'll strow yuh all over Orange County! Aw, come on! Come on! Youse a big seegar, but Ah kin smoke yuh!"

Clarke looked at the little man, old, and less than half his size, and laughed. Walter Thomas and 'Lige Mosely rushed to Lindsay and pretended to restrain him.

"That's right," Lindsay panted, "you better hold me offen him. Cause if I lay de weight uh dis right hand on him, he wont forget it long as he live."

"Aw, shet up, Lin'say, an' set down. If you could fight as good as you kin threaten, you'd be world's champeen 'stead uh Jack Dempsey. Some uh dese days when youse hollerin' tuh be let loose, somebody's gointer take you at yo' word, then it will be jus' too bad about yuh," Lester admonished.

"Who?—"

The war was about to begin all over on another front when Dave Carter, the local Nimrod, walked, almost ran up the steps of [the] porch. He was bareheaded, excited and even in the poor light that seeped to the porch from the oil lamps within, it was seen that he was bruised and otherwise unusually mussed up.

"Mist' Clarke, Ah wants tuh see yuh," he said. "Come on inside."

"Sholy, Dave, sholy." The mayor responded and followed the young man into the store and the corner reserved for City Administration. The crowd from the porch followed to a man.

Dave wiped a bruise spot on his head. "Mist' Clarke, Ah wants uh warrant took out fuh Jim Weston. Ahm gointer law him outa dis town. He caint lam me over mah head wid no mule bone and steal mah turkey and go braggin' about it!"

Under the encouraging quiz of the mayor, Dave told his story. He was a hunter and fisherman, as everybody knew. He had discovered a drove of wild turkeys roosting in the trees along the edge of the cypress swamp near the spot where Brazzle's old mule had been left. He had watched them for weeks, had seen the huge gobbler that headed the flock and resolved to get him.

"Yes," agreed Clarke, "you said something to me about it yesterday when you bought some shells."

"Yes, and thats how Jim knowed Ah was goin' turkey huntin'. He was settin' on de store porch and heard me talkin' to you. Today when Ah started out, jes 'bout sundown—dats de bes' time tuh get turkeys, when they goes tuh roost—he ups and says he's goin' long. Ah didnt keer 'bout dat, but when them birds goes tuh roost, he aint even loaded, so Ah had shot dat gobbler befo' he took aim. When he see dat great big gobbler fallin' he fires off his gun and tries tuh grab him. But Ah helt on. We got tuh pushin' and shovin' and tusslin' 'till we got to fightin'. Jim's a bully, but Ah wuz beatin' his socks offa him 'till he retched down and picked up de hock-bone of Brazzle's ol' mule and lammed me ovah mah head wid it and knocked me out. When Ah come to, he had done took mah turkey and gone. Ah wants uh warrant, Mist' Clarke. Ahm gointer law him outa dis town."

"An' you sho gointer get [him], Dave. He oughter be run out. Comes from bad stock. Every last one of his brothers been run out as fast as they grow up. Daddy hung for murder."

Clarke busied himself with the papers. The crowd looking on and commenting.

"See whut you Meth'dis' niggahs will do?" asked Brazzle, a true Baptist. "Goin' round lammin' folks ovah the head an' stealin they turkeys."

"Cose everybody knows dem Westons is a set uh bullies, but you Baptists aint such a much," Elijah Moseley retorted.

"Yas, but Ah know yuh know," put in Lindsay. "No Baptis' aint never done nothin' bad as dat. Joe Clarke is right. Jail is too good fuh 'em. The last one uh these half-washed Christians oughta be run 'way from heah."

"When it comes tuh dat, theres jus' as many no count Baptists as anybody else. Jus' aint caught 'em," Thomas said, joining the fray.

"Yas," Lindsay retorted, "but we done kotched yo' Meth'dis' niggah. Kotched him knockin' people ovah de head wid mule bones an' stealin' they turkeys, an' wese gointer run him slap outa town sure as gun's iron. The dirty onion!"

"We dont know whether you will or no, Joe Lindsay. You Baptists aint runnin' this town exactly."

"Trial set for three o'clock tomorrow at de Baptis' church, that being the largest meetin' place in the town," Clarke announced with a satisfied smile and persuaded the men to go back to the porch to argue.

Clarke, himself was a Methodist, but in this case, his interests lay with the other side. If he could get Jim to taste the air of another town, chicken mortality, of the sudden and unexplained variety, would drop considerably, he was certain. He was equally certain that the ambitious Simms would champion Jim's cause and losing the fight, lose prestige. Besides, Jim was a troublesome character. A constant disturber of the village peace.

III

It was evident to the simplest person in the village long before three o'clock that this was to be a religious and political fight. The assault and the gobbler were unimportant. Dave was a Baptist, Jim a Methodist, only two churches in the town and the respective congregations had lined up solidly.

At three the house was full. The defendant had been led in and seated in the amen corner to the left of the pulpit. Rev. Simms had taken his place beside the prisoner in the role of defense counsel. The plaintiff, with Elder Long, shepherd of the Baptist flock in the capacity of prosecution, was seated at the right. The respective congregations were lined up behind their leaders.

Mutual glances of despisement and gloating are exchanged across the aisle. Not a few verbal sorties were made during this waiting period as if they were getting up steam for the real struggle.

Wize Anderson (Meth.) Look at ole Dave tryin' to make out Jim hurt his head! Yuh couldnt hurt a Baptist head wid a hammer—they're that hard.

Brother Poke (Bapt.) Well, anyhow we dont lie an' steal an' git run outa town lak de softhead Meth'dis niggahs.

Some Baptist wag looked over at Jim and crowed like a rooster, the others took it up immediately and the place was full of hen-cackling and barnyard sounds. The implication was obvious. Jim stood up and said, "If I had dat mule bone heah, Ahd teach a few mo' uh you mud-turtles something." Enter His Honor at this moment. Lum Boger pompously conducted him to his place, the pulpit, which was doing duty as the bench for the occasion. The assembly unconsciously moderated its tone. But from the outside could still be heard the voices of the children engaged in fisticuffy trials of the case.

The mayor began rapping for order at once. "Cote is set. Cote is set! Looka heah, DIS COTE IS DONE SET! Ah wants you folks tuh dry up."

The courtroom grew perfectly still. The mayor prepared to read the charge to the prisoner, when Brother Stringer (Meth.) entered, hot and perspiring with coat over his arm. He found a seat near the middle of the house against the wall. To reach it, he must climb over the knees of a bench length of people. Before seating himself, he hung his coat upon an empty lamp bracket above his head.

Sister Lewis, of the Baptist persuasion, arose at once, her hands akimbo, her eyes flashing.

"Brothah Stringah, you take yo' lousy coat down off dese sacred walls! Aint you Methdis got no gumption in the house uh washup?"

Stringer did not answer her, but he cast over a glance that said as plain as day 'Just try and make me do it!'

Della Lewis snorted, but Stringer took his seat complacently. He took his seat, but rose up again as if he had sat on a hot needle point. The reason for this was that Brother Hambo on the Baptist side, a nasty scrapper, rose and rolled his eyes to the fighting angle, looking at Stringer. Stringer caught the look, and hurriedly pawed that coat down off that wall.

Sister Taylor (M) took up the gauntlet dropped like a hot potato by Stringer. "Some folks," she said with a meaning look, "is a whole lot moh puhticalar bout a louse in they church than they is in they house." A very personal look at Sister Lewis.

"Well," said that lady, "mah house mought not be exactly clean but nobody caint say *dat*"—indicating an infinitesimal amount on the end of her finger—"about my chaRACter! They didnt hafta git de sheriff to make Ike marry ME!"

Mrs. Taylor leaped to her feet and struggled to cross the aisle to her traducer but was restrained by three or four men. "Yas, they did git de sheriff tuh make Sam marry me!" She shouted as she panted and struggled. "And Gawd knows you sho oughter git him agin and make *some* of these men marry yo' Ada!"

Mrs. Lewis now had to be restrained. She gave voice and hard, bone-breaking words flew back and forth across the aisle. Each was aided and abetted by her side of the house. His Honor was all the time beating the pulpit with his gavel and shouting for order. At last he threatened to descend in person upon the belligerents.

"Heah! You moufy wimmen! Shet up. Aint Ah done said cote was set? Lum Boger, do yo' duty. Make them wimmen dry up or put 'em outa heah."

Marshall Boger who wore his star for the occasion was full of the importance of his office for nineteen is a prideful age; he hurried over to Mrs. Taylor. She rose to meet him. "You better gwan 'way from me, Lum Boger. Ah jes' wish you would lay de weight of yo' han' on me! Ahd kick yo' close up round yo' neck lak a horse-collar. You impident limb you."

Lum retreated before the awful prospect of wearing his suit about his neck like a horse-collar. He crossed the aisle to the fiery Della and frowned upon her. She was already standing and ready to commence hostilities. One look was enough. He said nothing, but her threats followed him down the aisle as he retreated to the vestibule to shoo the noisy children away. The women subsided and the Mayor began.

"We come heah on very important business," he said. "Stan' up dere, Jim Weston. You is charged wid 'ssaultin' Dave Carter here wid a mule bone, and robbin' him uh his wild turkey. Is you guilty or not guilty."

Jim arose, looked insolently around the room and answered the charge. "Yes, Ah hit him and took de turkey cause it wuz mine. Ah hit him and Ahll hit him again, but it wasnt no crime this time."

His Honor's jaw dropped. There was surprise on the faces of all the Baptist section, surprise and perplexity. Gloating and laughter from the Methodists. Simms pulled Jim's coattail.

"Set down Jim," he cooed, "youse one of mah lambs! Setdown. Yo' shepard will show them that walks in de darkness wid sinners and republicans de light."

Jim sat down and the pastor got to his feet.

"Lookah heah, Jim, this aint for no foolishness. Do you realize dat if youse found guilty, youse gonna be run outa town?"

"Yeah," Jim answered without rising. "But Ah aint gonna be found no guilty. You caint find me." There was a pleasurable stir on his side of the house. The Baptists were still in the coma which Jim's first statement had brought on.

"Ah say too, he aint guilty," began Rev. Simms with great unction in his tones. "Ah done been to de cot-house at Orlando an' set under de voice of dem lawyers an' heard 'em law from mornin' tell night. They says yuh got tuh have a weepon befo' you kin commit uh 'ssault. Ah done read dis heah Bible fum lid tuh lid (he made a gesture to indicate the thoroughness of his search) and it aint in no Bible dat no mule bone is a weepon, an' it aint in no white folks law neither. Therefo' Brother Mayor, Ah ast you tuh let Jim go. You gotta turn 'im loose, cause nobody kin run 'im outa town when he aint done no crime."

A deep purple gloom settled down upon the Mayor and his follows. Over against this the wild joy of the Methodists. Simms already felt the reins of power in his hands. Over the protest of the Mayor he raised a song and he and his followers sang it with great gusto.

"Oh Mary dont you weep, dont you mourn
Oh Mary, dont you weep dont you mourn
Pharaoh's army got drownded
O-O-oh Mary, dont you weep"

The troubled expression on the face of the Baptist leader, Rev. Long, suddenly lifted. He arose while yet the triumphant defense is singing its hallelujah. Mayor Clarke quieted the tumult with difficulty. Simms saw him rise but far from being worried, he sank back upon the seat, his eyes half closed, hands folded fatly across his fat stomach. He smirked. Let them rave! He had built his arguments on solid rock, and the gates of Baptist logic could not prevail against it!

When at last he got the attention of the assembly, he commanded Dave to stand.

"Ah jus want you all tuh take a look at his head. Anybody kin see dat big knot dat Jim put on dere." Jim, the Rev. Simms, and all his communicants laughed loudly at this, but Long went on calmly. "Ah been tuh de cot-house tuh Orlando an' heard de white folks law as much as any body heah. And dey dont ast whether de thing dat a person gits hurt wid is uh weepon or not. All dey wants tuh fin' out is, 'did it hurt?' Now you all kin see dat mule bone did hurt Dave's head. So it must be a weepon cause it hurt 'im.—"

Rev. Simms had his eyes wide open now. He jumped to his feet.

"Never mind bout dem white folks laws at O'landa, Brother Long. Dis is a colored town. Nohow we oughter run by de laws uh de Bible. Dem white folks laws dont go befo' whuts in dis sacred book."

"Jes' hold yo' hot potater, Brother Simms, Ahm comin' tuh dat part right now. Jes lemme take yo' Bible a minute."

"Naw, indeed. You oughter brought one of yo' own if you got one. Furthemo' Brother Mayor, we got work to do. Wese workin' people. Dont keep us in heah too long. Dis case is through wid."

"Oh, naw it aint," the Mayor disagreed, "you done talked yo' side, now you got tuh let Brother Long talk his. So fur as de work is concerned, it kin wait. One thing at a time. Come on up heah in yo' pulpit an' read yo' own Bible, Brother Long. Dont mind me being up heah."

Long ascended the pulpit and began to turn the leaves of the large Bible. The entire assembly slid forward to the edges of the seat.

"Ah done proved by de white folks law dat Jim oughter be run outa town an' now Ahm gointer show by de Bible—"

Simms was on his feet again. "But Brother Mayor—"

"Set down Simms" was all the answer he got. "Youse *entirely* outa order."

"It says heah in Judges 15:16 dat Samson slewed a thousand Philistines wid de jaw-bone of a ass," Long drawled.

"Yas, but this wasnt no ass, this was a mule," Simms objected.

"And now dat bring us to de main claw uh dis subjick. It sho want no ass, but everybody knows dat a donkey is de father of every mule what ever wuz born. Even little chillen knows dat. Everybody knows dat dat little as a donkey is, dat if he is dangerous, his great big mule son is mo' so. Everybody knows dat de further back on a mule you goes, de mo' dangerous he gits. Now if de jawbone is as dangerous as it says heah in de Bible, by de time you gits clear back tuh his hocks hes rank pizen."

"AMEN!! Specially Brazzle's ol' mule," put in Hambo.

"An' dat makes it double 'ssault an' batt'ry," Long continued. "Therefo' Brother Mayor, Ah ast dat Jim be run outa town fuh 'ssaultin Dave wid a deadly weepon an' stealin' his turkey while de boy wuz unconscious."

It was now the turn of the Baptists to go wild. The faint protests of Simms were drowned in the general uproar.

"I'll be henfired if he aint right!" the Mayor exclaimed when he could make himself heard. "This case is just as plain as day."

Simms tried once more. "But Brother Mayor—"

"Aw be quiet, Simms. You done talked yo'self all outa joint already." His Honor cut him short. "Jim Weston, you git right outa *mah* town befo sundown an' dont lemme ketch you back heah under two yeahs, neither. You folks dats so rearin' tuh fight, gwan outside an' fight all you wants tuh. But dont use no guns, no razors nor no mule-bones. Cote's dismissed."

A general murmur of approval swept over the house. Clarke went on, unofficially, as it were. "By ziggity, dat ol' mule been dead three years an' still kickin'! An' he done kicked more'n one person outa whack today." And he gave Simms one of his most personal looks.

Muttsy

The piano in Ma Turner's back parlor stuttered and wailed. The pianist kept time with his heel and informed an imaginary deserter that "she might leave and go to Halimufack, but his slow-drag would bring her back," mournfully with a memory of tom-toms running rhythm through the plaint.

Fewclothes burst through the portieres, a brown chrysalis from a dingy red cocoon, and touched the player on the shoulder.

"Say Muttsy," he stage whispered, "Ma's got a new lil' biddy in there—just come. And say—her foot would make all of dese Harlem babies a Sunday face."

"Whut she look like?" Muttsy drawled, trying to maintain his characteristic pose of indifference to the female.

"Brown skin, patent leather grass on her knob, kinder tallish. She's a lil' skinny," he added apologetically, "but ah'm willing to buy corn for that lil' chicken."

Muttsy lifted his six feet from the piano bench as slowly as his curiosity would let him and sauntered to the portieres for a peep.

The sight was as pleasing as Fewclothes had stated—only

more so. He went on in the room which Ma always kept empty. It was her receiving room—her "front."

From Ma's manner it was evident that she was very glad to see the girl. She could see that the girl was not overjoyed in her presence, but attributed that to southern greenness.

"Who you say sentcher heah, dearie?" Ma asked, her face trying to beam, but looking harder and more forbidding.

"Uh-a-a man down at the boat landing where I got off—North River. I jus' come in on the boat."

Ma's husband from his corner spoke up.

"Musta been Bluefront."

"Yeah, musta been him," Muttsy agreed.

"Oh, it's all right, honey, we New Yorkers likes to know who we'se takin' in, dearie. We has to be keerful. Whut did you say yo' name was?"

"Pinkie, yes mam, Pinkie Jones."

Ma stared hard at the little old battered reticule the girl carried for luggage—not many clothes if that was all—she reflected. But Pinkie had everything she needed in her face—many, many trunks full. Several of them for Ma. She noticed the cold-reddened knuckles of her bare hands too.

"Come on upstairs to yo' room—thass all right 'bout the price—we'll come to some 'greement tomorrow. Jes' go up and take off yo' things."

Pinkie put back the little rusty leather purse of another generation and followed Ma. She didn't like Ma—her smile resembled the smile of the Wolf in Red Riding Hood. Anyway back in Eatonville, Florida, "ladies," especially old ones, didn't put powder and paint on the face.

"Forty-dollars-Kate sure landed a pippin' dis time," said Muttsy sotto voce, to Fewclothes back at the piano. "If she ain't, then there ain't a hound dawk in Georgy. Ah'm goin' home an' dress."

No one else in the crowded back parlor let alone the house knew of Pinkie's coming. They danced on, played on, sang their "blues," and lived on hotly their intense lives. The two men who had seen her—no one counted ole man Turner—went on playing too, but kept an ear cocked for her coming.

She followed Ma downstairs and seated herself in the parlor with the old man. He sat in a big rocker before a copper-lined gas stove, indolence in every gesture.

"Ah'm Ma's husband," he announced by way of making conversation.

"Now you jus' shut up!" Ma commanded severely. "You gointer git yo' teeth knocked down yo' thoat yit for runnin' yo' tongue. Lemme talk to dis gal—dis is *mah* house. You sets on the stool un do nothin' too much tuh have anything to talk over!"

"Oh, Lawd," groaned the old man feeling a knee that always pained him at the mention of work. "Oh, Lawd, will you sen' yo' fiery chariot an' take me 'way from heah?"

"Aw shet up!" the woman spit out. "Lawd don't wantcher—devil wouldn't have yuh." She peered into the girl's face and leaned back satisfied.

"Well, girlie, you kin be a lotta help tuh me 'round dis house if you takes un intrus' in things—oh Lawd!" She leaped up from her seat. "That's mah bread ah smell burnin! . . ."

No sooner had Ma's feet cleared the room than the old man came to life again. He peered furtively after the broad back of his wife.

"Know who she is," he asked Pinkie in an awed whisper. She shook her head. "You don't? Dat's Forty-dollars-Kate!"

"Forty-dollars-Kate?" Pinkie repeated open eyed. "Naw, I don't know nothin' 'bout her."

"Sh-h," cautioned the old man. "Course you don't. I fuhgits

you ain't nothin' tall but a young 'un. Twenty-five years ago they all called her dat 'cause she *wuz* 'Forty-dollars-Kate.' She sho' wuz some p'utty 'oman—great big robus' lookin' gal. Men wuz glad 'nough to spend forty dollars on her if dey had it. She didn't lose no time wid dem dat didn't have it."

He grinned ingratiatingly at Pinkie and leaned nearer.

"But you'se better lookin' than she ever wuz, you might—taint no tellin' what you might do ef you git some sense. I'm a gointer teach you, here?"

"Yessuh," the girl managed to answer with an almost paralyzed tongue.

"Thass a good girl. You jus' lissen to me an' you'll pull thew alright."

He glanced at the girl sitting timidly upon the edge of the chair and scolded.

"Don't set dataway," he ejaculated. "Yo' back bone ain't no ram rod. Kinda scooch down on the for'ard edge uh da chear lak dis." (He demonstrated by "scooching" forward so far that he was almost sitting on his shoulder-blades.) The girl slumped a trifle.

"Is you got a job yit?"

"Nawsuh," she answered slowly, "but I reckon I'll have one soon. Ain't been in town a day yet."

"You looks kinda young—kinda little biddy. Is you been to school much?"

"Yessuh, went thew eight reader. I'm goin' again when I get a chance."

"Dat so? Well ah reckon ah kin talk some Latin tuh yuh den." He cleared his throat loudly, "Whut's you entitlum?"

"I don't know," said the girl in confusion.

"Well den, whut's yo' entrimmins," he queried with a bit of braggadocio in his voice.

"I don't know," from the girl, after a long awkward pause.

"You chillun don't learn nothin' in school dese days. Is you got to 'goes into' yit?"

"You mean long division?"

"Ain't askin' 'bout de longness of it, dat don't make no difference," he retorted.

"Sence you goin' stay heah ah'll edgecate yuh—do yuh know how to eat a fish—uh nice brown fried fish?"

"Yessuh," she answered quickly, looking about for the fish.

"How?"

"Why, you jus' eat it with corn bread," she said, a bit disappointed at the non-appearance of the fish.

"Well, ah'll tell yuh," he patronized. "You starts at de tail and liffs de meat off de bones sorter gentle and eats him clear tuh de head on dat side; den you turn 'im ovah an' commence at de tail agin and eat right up tuh de head; den you push *dem* bones way tuh one side an' takes another fish an' so on 'till de end—well, 'till der ain't no mo'!"

He mentally digested the fish and went on. "See," he pointed accusingly at her feet, "you don't even know how tuh warm yoself! You settin' dere wid yo' feet ev'y which a way. Dat ain't de way tuh git wahm. Now look at *mah* feet. Dass right put bofe big toes right togethah—now shove 'em close up tuh de fiah; now lean back so! Dass de way. Ah knows uh heap uh things tuh teach yuh sense you gointer live heah—ah learns all of 'em while de ole lady is paddlin' roun' out dere in de yard."

Ma appeared at the door and the old man withdrew so far into his rags that he all but disappeared. They went to supper where there was fried fish but forgot all rules for eating it and just ate heartily. She helped with the dishes and returned to the parlor. A little later some more men and women knocked and were admitted after the same furtive peering out through the merest crack of the door. Ma carried them all back to the kitchen and Pinkie heard the clink of glasses and much loud laughter.

Women came in by ones and twos, some in shabby coats turned up about the ears, and with various cheap but showy hats crushed down over unkempt hair. More men, more women, more trips to the kitchen with loud laughter.

Pinkie grew uneasy. Both men and women stared at her. She kept strictly to her place. Ma came in and tried to make her join the others.

"Come on in, honey, a lil' toddy ain't gointer hurt nobody. Evebody knows *me*, ah wouldn't touch a hair on yo' head. Come on in, dearie, all th' men wants tuh meetcher."

Pinkie smelt the liquor on Ma's breath and felt contaminated at her touch. She wished herself back home again even with the ill treatment and squalor. She thought of the three dollars she had secreted in her shoe—she had been warned against pickpockets—and flight but where? Nowhere. For there was no home to which *she* could return, nor any place she knew of. But when she got a job, she'd scrape herself clear of people who took toddies.

A very black man sat on the piano stool playing as only a Negro can with hands, stamping with his feet and the rest of his body keeping time.

"Ahm gointer make me a graveyard of mah own
Ahm gointer make me a graveyard of mah own
Carried me down on de smoky Road"—

Pinkie, weary of Ma's maudlin coaxing, caught these lines as she was being pulled and coaxed into the kitchen. Everyone in there was shaking shimmies to music, rolling eyes heavenward as they picked imaginary grapes out of the air, or drinking. "Folkes," shouted Ma. "Look a heah! Shut up dis racket! Ah wantcher tuh meet Pinkie Jones. She's de bes' frien' ah got." Ma flopped into a chair and began to cry into her whiskey glass.

"Mah comperments!" The men almost shouted. The women were less, much less enthusiastic.

"Dass de las' run uh shad," laughed a woman called Ada, pointing to Pinkie's slenderness.

"Jes' lak a bar uh soap aftah uh hard week's wash," Bertha chimed in and laughed uproariously. The men didn't help.

"Oh, Miss Pinkie," said Bluefront, removing his Stetson for the first time. "Ma'am, also Ma'am, ef you wuz tuh see me settin' straddle of uh Mud-cat leadin' a minner whut ud you think?"

"I-er, oh I don't know suh. I didn't know you—or anybody could ride uh fish."

"Stick uh roun' me, baby, an you'll wear diamon's." Bluefront swaggered. "Look heah lil' Pigmeat, youse *some* sharp! If you didn't had but one eye ah'd think you wuz a needle—thass how sharp you looks to me. Say, mah right foot is itchin'. Do dat mean ah'm goingter walk on some strange ground wid you?"

"Naw, indeedy," cut in Fewclothes. "It jes' means you feet needs to walk in some strange water—wid a lil' Red Seal Lye thowed in."

But he was not to have a monopoly. Fewclothes and Shorty joined the chase and poor Pinkie found it impossible to retreat to her place beside the old man. She hung her head, embarrassed that she did not understand their mode of speech; she felt the unfriendly eyes of the women, and she loathed the smell of liquor that filled the house now. The piano still rumbled and wailed that same song—

"Carried me down on de Smoky Road
Brought me back on de coolin' board
Ahm gointer make me a graveyard of mah own."

A surge of cold, fresh air from the outside stirred the smoke and liquor fumes and Pinkie knew that the front door was open. She turned her eyes that way and thought of flight to the clean outside. The door stood wide open and a tall figure in an overcoat with a fur collar stood there.

"Good Gawd, Muttsy! Shet 'at do'," cried Shorty. "Dass a pure razor blowing out dere tonight. Ah didn't know you wuz outa here nohow."

"Carried me down on de Smoky Road
Brought me back on de coolin' board
Ahm gointer make me a graveyard of mah own,"

sang Muttsy, looking as if he sought someone and banged the door shut on the last words. He strode on in without removing hat or coat.

Pinkie saw in this short space that all the men deferred to him, that all the women sought his notice. She tried timidly to squeeze between two of the men and return to the quiet place beside old man Turner, thinking that Muttsy would hold the attention of her captors until she had escaped. But Muttsy spied her through the men about her and joined them. By this time her exasperation and embarrassment had her on the point of tears.

"Well, whadda yuh know about dis!" he exclaimed. "A real lil' pullet."

"Look out dere, Muttsy," drawled Dramsleg with objection, catching Pinkie by the arm and trying to draw her toward him. "Lemme tell dis lil' Pink Mama how crazy ah is 'bout her mahself. Ah ain't got no lady atall an'—"

"Aw, shut up, Drams," Muttsy said sternly, "put yo' pocketbook where yo' mouf is, an' somebody will lissen. Ah'm a heavy-sugar papa. Ah eats fried chicken when the rest of you niggars is drinking rain water."

He thrust some of the others aside and stood squarely before her. With her downcast eyes, she saw his well polished shoes, creased trousers, gloved hands and at last timidly raised her eyes to his face.

"Look a heah!" he frowned, "you roughnecks done got dis baby ready tuh cry."

He put his forefinger under her chin and made her look at him. And for some reason he removed his hat.

"Come on in the sittin' room an' le's talk. Come on befo' some uh dese niggers sprinkle some salt on yuh and eat yuh clean up lak a radish." Dramsleg looked after Muttsy and the girl as they swam through the smoke into the front room. He beckoned to Bluefront.

"Hey, Bluefront! Ain't you mah fren'?"

"Yep," answered Bluefront.

"Well, then why cain't you help me? Muttsy done done me dirt wid the lil' pig-meat—throw a louse on 'im."

Pinkie's hair was slipping down. She felt it, but her self-consciousness prevented her catching it and down it fell in a heavy roll that spread out and covered her nearly to the waist. She followed Muttsy into the front room and again sat shrinking in the corner. She did not wish to talk to Muttsy nor anyone else in that house, but there were fewer people in this room.

"Phew!" cried Bluefront, "dat baby sho got some righteous moss on her keg—dass reg'lar 'nearow mah Gawd tuh thee' stuff." He made a lengthy gesture with his arms as if combing out long, silky hair.

"Shux," sneered Ada in a moist, alcoholic voice. "Dat ain't nothin' mah haih uster be so's ah could set on it."

There was general laughter from the men.

"Yas, ah know it's de truth!" shouted Shorty. "It's jes' ez close tuh yo' head *now* as ninety-nine is tuh uh hund'ed."

"Ah'll call Muttsy tuh you," Ada threatened.

"Oh, 'oman, Muttsy ain't got you tuh study 'bout no 'mo cause he's parkin' his heart wid dat lil' chicken wid white-folks' haih. Why, dat lil' chicken's foot would make you a Sunday face."

General laughter again. Ada dashed the whiskey glass upon the floor with the determined stalk of an angry tiger and arose and started forward.

"Muttsy Owens, uh nobody else ain't gointer make no fool outer *me*. Dat lil' kack girl ain't gointer put *me* on de bricks—not much."

Perhaps Muttsy heard her, perhaps he saw her out of the corner of his eye and read her mood. But knowing the woman as he did he might have known what she would do under such circumstances. At any rate he got to his feet as she entered the room where he sat with Pinkie.

"Ah know you ain't lost yo' head sho 'nuff 'oman. 'Deed, Gawd knows you bettah go 'way 'fum me." He said this in a low, steady voice. The music stopped, the talking stopped and even the drinkers paused. Nothing happened, for Ada looked straight into Muttsy's eyes and went on outside.

"Miss Pinkie, Ah votes you g'wan tuh bed," Muttsy said suddenly to the girl.

"Yes-suh."

"An' don't you worry 'bout no job. Ah knows where you kin git a good one. Ah'll go see em first an tell yuh tomorrow night."

She went off to bed upstairs. The rich baritone of the piano player came up to her as did laughter and shouting. But she was tired and slept soundly.

Ma shuffled in after eight the next morning. "Darlin', ain't you got 'nuff sleep yit?"

Pinkie opened her eyes a trifle. "Ain't you the puttiest lil' trick! An Muttsy done gone crazy 'bout yuh! Chile, he's lousy wid money an' diamon's an' everything—Yuh better grab him quick. Some folks has all de luck. Heah ah is—got uh man dat hates work lak de devil hates holy water. Ah gotta make dis house pay!"

Pinkie's eyes opened wide. "What does Mr. Muttsy do?"

"Mah Gawd, chile! He's de bes' gambler in three states, cards, craps un hawses. He could be a boss stevedore if he so wanted. The big boss down on de dock would give him a fat job—just begs him to take it cause he can manage the men. He's the biggest hero they got since Harry Wills left the waterfront. But he won't take it cause he makes so much wid the games."

"He's awful good-lookin," Pinkie agreed, "an' he been mighty nice tuh me—but I like men to work. I wish he would. Gamblin' ain't nice."

"Yeah, 'tis, ef yuh makes money lak Muttsy. Maybe yo ain't noticed dat diamon' set in his tooth. He picks women up when he wants tuh an' puts 'em down when he choose."

Pinkie turned her face to the wall and shuddered. Ma paid no attention.

"You doan hafta git up till you git good an' ready, Muttsy says. Ah mean you kin stay roun' the house 'till you come to, sorter."

Another day passed. Its darkness woke up the land east of Lenox—all that land between the railroad tracks and the river. It was very ugly by day, and night kindly hid some of its sordid homeliness. Yes, nighttime gave it life.

The same women, or others just like them, came to Ma Turner's. The same men, or men just like them, came also and treated them to liquor or mistreated them with fists or cruel jibes. Ma got half drunk as usual and cried over everyone who would let her.

Muttsy came alone and went straight to Pinkie where she sat trying to shrink into the wall. She had feared that he would not come.

"Howdy do, Miss Pinkie."

"How'do Mistah Owens," she actually achieved a smile. "Did you see bout m' job?"

"Well, yeah—but the lady says she won't needya fuh uh week yet. Doan worry. Ma ain't gointer push yuh foh room rent. Mah wrist ain't got no cramps."

Pinkie half sobbed: "Ah wantsa job now!"

"Didn't ah say dass alright? Well, Muttsy doan lie. Shux! Ah might jes' es well tell yuh—ahm crazy 'bout yuh—money no objeck."

It was the girl herself who first mentioned "bed" this night. He suffered her to go without protest.

The next night she did not come into the sitting room. She went to bed as soon as the dinner things had been cleared. Ma begged and cried, but Pinkie pretended illness and kept to her bed. This she repeated the next night and the next. Every night Muttsy came and every night he added to his sartorial splendor; but each night he went away, disappointed, more evidently crestfallen than before.

But the insistence for escape from her strange surroundings grew on the girl. When Ma was busy elsewhere, she would take out the three one dollar bills from her shoe and reconsider her limitations. If that job would only come on! She felt shut in, imprisoned, walled in with these women who talked of nothing but men and numbers and drink, and men who talked of nothing but the numbers and drink and women. And desperation took her.

One night she was still waiting for the job—Ma's alcoholic tears prevailed. Pinkie took a drink. She drank the stuff mixed with sugar and water and crept to bed even as the dizziness came on. She would not wake tonight. Tomorrow, maybe, the job would come and freedom.

The piano thumped but Pinkie did not hear; the shouts, laughter and cries did not reach her that night. Downstairs Muttsy pushed Ma into a corner.

"Looky heah, Ma. Dat girl done played me long enough. Ah pays her room rent, ah pays her boahd an' all ah gets is uh hunk of ice. Now you said you wuz gointer fix things—you tole me so las' night an' heah she done gone tuh bed on me agin."

"Deed, ah kaint do nothin' wid huh. She's thinkin' sho' nuff you goin' git her uh job and she fret so cause tain't come, dat she drunk uh toddy un hits knocked her down jes lak uh log."

"Ada an' all uh them laffin—they say ah done crapped." He felt injured. "Caint ah go talk to her?"

"Lawdy, Muttsy, dat gal ded drunk an' sleepin' lak she's buried."

"Well, caint ah go up an'—an' speak tuh her jus' the same." A yellow backed bill from Muttsy's roll found itself in Ma's hand and put her in such a good humor that she let old man Turner talk all he wanted for the rest of the night.

"Yas, Muttsy, gwan in. Youse *mah* frien'."

Muttsy hurried up to the room indicated. He felt shaky inside there with Pinkie, somehow, but he approached the bed and stood for a while looking down upon her. Her hair in confusion about her face and swinging off the bedside; the brown arms revealed and the soft lips. He blew out the match he had struck and kissed her full on the mouth, kissed her several times and passed his hand down over her neck and throat and then hungrily down upon her breast. But here he drew back.

"Naw," he said sternly to himself, "ah ain't goin' ter play her wid no loaded dice." Then quickly he covered her with the blanket to her chin, kissed her again upon the lips and tipped down into the darkness of the vestibule.

"Ah reckon ah bettah git married." He soliloquized. "B'lieve me, ah will, an' go uptown wid dicties."

He lit a cigar and stood there on the steps puffing and thinking for some time. His name was called inside the sitting room several times but he pretended not to hear. At last he stole back into the room where slept the girl who unwittingly and unwillingly was making him do queer things. He tipped up to the bed again and knelt there holding her hands so fiercely that she groaned without waking. He watched her and he wanted her so that he wished to crush her in his love; crush and crush and hurt her against himself, but somehow he resisted the impulse and merely kissed her lips again, kissed her hands back and front, removed the largest diamond ring from his hand and slipped it on her engagement finger. It was much too large so he closed her hand and tucked it securely beneath the covers.

"She's *mine*!" he said triumphantly. "All mine!"

He switched off the light and softly closed the door as he went out again to the steps. He had gone up to the bed room from the sitting room boldly, caring not who knew that Muttsy Owens took what he wanted. He was stealing forth afraid that someone might *suspect* that he had been there. There is no secret love in those barrens; it is a thing to be approached boisterously and without delay or dalliance. One loves when one wills, and ceases when it palls. There is nothing sacred or hidden—all subject to coarse jokes. So Muttsy re-entered the sitting room from the steps as if he had been into the street.

"Where you been Muttsy?" whined Ada with an awkward attempt at coyness.

"What *you* wanta know for?" he asked roughly.

"Now, Muttsy you know you ain't treatin' me right, honey. How come you runnin' de hawg ovah me lak you do?"

"Git outa mah face 'oman. Keep yo' han's offa me." He clapped on his hat and strode from the house.

Pinkie awoke with a gripping stomach and thumping head.

Ma bustled in. "How yuh feelin' darlin? Youse jes lak a li'l dol baby."

"I got a headache, terrible from that ole whiskey. Thass mah first und las' drink long as I live." She felt the ring.

"Whut's this?" she asked and drew her hand out to the light.

"Dat's Muttsy's ring. Ah seen him wid it fuh two years. How'd y'all make out? He sho is one thur'bred."

"Muttsy? When? I didn't see no Muttsy."

"Dearie, you doan' hafta tell yo' bizniss ef you doan wanta. Ahm a hush-mouf. Thass all right, keep yo' bizniss to you' self." Ma bleared her eyes wisely. "But ah know Muttsy wuz up heah tuh see yuh las' night. Doan' mine *me*, honey, gwan wid 'im. He'll treat yuh right. Ah *knows* he's crazy 'bout yuh. An' all de women is crazy 'bout *him*. Lawd! Lookit dat ring!" Ma regarded it greedily for a long time, but she turned and walked toward the door at last. "Git up darlin'. Ah got fried chickin fuh breckfus' un mush melon."

She went on to the kitchen. Ma's revelation sunk deeper, then there was the ring. Pinkie hurled the ring across the room and leaped out of bed.

"He ain't goin' to make *me* none of his women—I'll die first! I'm goin' outa this house if I starve, lemme starve!"

She got up and plunged her face into the cold water on the washstand in the corner and hurled herself into the shabby clothes, thrust the dollars which she never had occasion to spend, under the pillow where Ma would be sure to find them and slipped noiselessly out of the house and fled down Fifth Avenue toward the Park that marked the beginning of the Barrens. She did not know where she was going, and cared little so long as she removed herself as far as possible from the house where the great evil threatened her.

At ten o'clock that same morning, Muttsy Owens dressed his flashiest best, drove up to Ma's door in a cab, the most luxurious that could be hired. He had gone so far as to stick two one hundred dollar notes to the inside of the windshield. Ma was overcome.

"Muttsy, dearie, what you doin' heah so soon? Pinkie sho has got you goin'. Un in a swell cab too—gee!"

"Ahm gointer git mah'ried tuh de doll baby, thass how come. An' ahm gointer treat her white too."

"Umhumh! Thass how come de ring! You oughtn't never fuhgit me, Muttsy, fuh puttin' y'all together. But ah never thought you'd mah'ry *nobody*—you allus said you wouldn't."

"An' ah wouldn't neither ef ah hadn't of seen *her*. Where she is?"

"In de room dressin'. She never tole me nothin' 'bout dis."

"She doan' know. She wuz sleep when ah made up mah mind an' slipped on de ring. But ah never miss no girl ah wants, you knows me."

"Everybody in this man's town knows you gets whut you wants."

"Naw, ah come tuh take her to brek'fus 'fo we goes tuh de cote-house."

"An' y'all stay heah and eat wid me. You go call her whilst ah set de grub on table."

Muttsy, with a lordly stride, went up to Pinkie's door and rapped and waited and rapped and waited three times. Growing impatient or thinking her still asleep, he flung open the door and entered.

The first thing that struck him was the empty bed; the next was the glitter of his diamond ring upon the floor. He stumbled out to Ma. She was gone, no doubt of that.

"She looked awful funny when ah tole her you wuz in heah,

but ah thought she wuz puttin' on airs," Ma declared finally.

"She thinks ah played her wid a marked deck, but ah didn't. Ef ah could see her she'd love me. Ah know she would. 'Cause ah'd make her," Muttsy lamented.

"I don't know, Muttsy. She ain't no New Yorker, and she thinks gamblin' is awful."

"Zat all she got against me? Ah'll fix that up in a minute. You help me find her and ah'll do anything she says jus' so she marries me." He laughed ruefully. "Looks like ah crapped this time, don't it, Ma?"

The next day Muttsy was foreman of two hundred stevedores. How did he make them work. But oh how cheerfully they did their best for him. The company begrudged not one cent of his pay. He searched diligently, paid money to other searchers, went every night to Ma's to see if by chance the girl had returned or if any clues had turned up.

Two weeks passed this way. Black empty days for Muttsy.

Then he found her. He was coming home from work. When crossing Seventh Avenue at 135th Street they almost collided. He seized her and began pleading before she even had time to recognize him.

He turned and followed her; took the employment office slip from her hand and destroyed it, took her arm and held it. He must have been very convincing for at 125th Street they entered a taxi that headed uptown again. Muttsy was smiling amiably upon the whole round world.

A month later, as Muttsy stood on the dock hustling his men to greater endeavor, Bluefront flashed past with his truck. "Say, Muttsy, you don't know what you missin' since you quit de game. Ah cleaned out de whole bunch las' night." He flashed a roll and laughed. "It don't seem like a month ago you wuz king uh de bones in Harlem." He vanished down the gangplank into the ship's hold.

As he raced back up the gangplank with his loaded truck Muttsy answered him, "And now, I'm King of the Boneheads—which being interpreted means stevedores. Come on over behind dis crate wid yo' roll. Mah wrist ain't got no cramp 'cause ah'm married. You'se gettin' too sassy."

"Thought you wuzn't gointer shoot no mo'!" Bluefront temporized.

"Aw, Hell! Come on back heah," he said impatiently. "Ah'll shoot you any way you wants to—hard or soft roll—you'se trying to stall. You know ah don't crap neither. Come on, mah Pinkie needs a fur coat and you stevedores is got to buy it."

He was on his knees with Bluefront. There was a quick movement of Muttsy's wrist, and the cubes flew out on a piece of burlap spread for the purpose—a perfect seven.

"Hot dog!" he exulted. "Look at dem babies gallop!" His wrist quivered again. "Nine for point!" he gloated. "Ha!" There was another quick shake and nine turned up again. "Shove in, Bluefront, shove in dat roll, dese babies is crying fuh it."

Bluefront laid down two dollars grudgingly. "You said you wuzn't gointer roll no mo' dice after you got married," he grumbled.

But Muttsy had tasted blood. His flexible wrist was already in the midst of the next play.

"Come on, Bluefront, stop bellyachin'. Ah shoots huy for de roll!" He reached for his own pocket and laid down a roll of yellow bills beside Bluefront's. His hand quivered and the cubes skipped out again. "Nine!" He snapped his fingers like a trapdrum and gathered in the money.

"Doxology, Bluefront. Git back in de line wid yo' truck an' send me de others rou' heah one by one. What man can't keep one li'l wife an' two li'l bones? Hurry em up, Blue!"

Sweat

It was eleven o'clock of a Spring night in Florida. It was Sunday. Any other night, Delia Jones would have been in bed for two hours at this time. But she was a washwoman, and Monday morning meant a great deal to her. So she collected the soiled clothes on Saturday when she returned the clean things. Sunday night after church, she sorted them and put the white things to soak. It saved her almost a half day's start. A great hamper in the bedroom held the clothes that she brought home. It was so much neater than a number of bundles lying around.

She squatted in the kitchen floor beside the great pile of clothes, sorting them into small heaps according to color, and humming a song in a mournful key, but wondering through it all where Sykes, her husband, had gone with her horse and buckboard.

Just then something long, round, limp and black fell upon her shoulders and slithered to the floor beside her. A great terror took hold of her. It softened her knees and dried her mouth so that it was a full minute before she could cry out or move. Then she saw that it was the big bull whip her husband liked to carry when he drove.

She lifted her eyes to the door and saw him standing there bent over with laughter at her fright. She screamed at him.

"Sykes, what you throw dat whip on me like dat? You know it would skeer me—looks just like a snake, an' you knows how skeered Ah is of snakes."

"Course Ah knowed it! That's how come Ah done it." He slapped his leg with his hand and almost rolled on the ground in his mirth. "If you such a big fool dat you got to have a fit over a earth worm or a string, Ah don't keer how bad Ah skeer you."

"You aint got no business doing it. Gawd knows it's a sin. Some day Ah'm gointuh drop dead from some of yo' foolishness. 'Nother thing, where you been wid mah rig? Ah feeds dat pony. He aint fuh you to be drivin' wid no bull whip."

"You sho is one aggravatin' nigger woman!" he declared and stepped into the room. She resumed her work and did not answer him at once. "Ah done tole you time and again to keep them white folks' clothes outa dis house."

He picked up the whip and glared down at her. Delia went on with her work. She went out into the yard and returned with a galvanized tub and sit it on the washbench. She saw that Sykes had kicked all of the clothes together again, and now stood in her way truculently, his whole manner hoping, *praying,* for an argument. But she walked calmly around him and commenced to re-sort the things.

"Next time, Ah'm gointer kick 'em outdoors," he threatened as he struck a match along the leg of his corduroy breeches.

Delia never looked up from her work, and her thin, stooped shoulders sagged further.

"Ah aint for no fuss t'night, Sykes. Ah just come from taking sacrament at the church house."

He snorted scornfully. "Yeah, you just come from de church

house on a Sunday night, but heah you is gone to work on them clothes. You aint nothing but a hypocrite. One of them amen-corner Christians—sing, whoop, and shout, then come home and wash white folks' clothes on the Sabbath."

He stepped roughly upon the whitest pile of things, kicking them helter-skelter as he crossed the room. His wife gave a little scream of dismay, and quickly gathered them together again.

"Sykes, you quit grindin' dirt into these clothes! How can Ah git through by Sat'day if Ah don't start on Sunday?"

"Ah don't keer if you never git through. Anyhow, Ah done promised Gawd and a couple of other men, Ah aint gointer have it in mah house. Don't gimme no lip neither, else Ah'll throw 'em out and put mah fist up side yo' head to boot."

Delia's habitual meekness seemed to slip from her shoulders like a blown scarf. She was on her feet; her poor little body, her bare knuckly hands bravely defying the strapping hulk before her.

"Looka heah, Sykes, you done gone too fur. Ah been married to you fur fifteen years, and Ah been takin' in washin' fur fifteen years. Sweat, sweat, sweat! Work and sweat, cry and sweat, pray and sweat!"

"What's that got to do with me?" he asked brutally.

"What's it got to do with you, Sykes? Mah tub of suds is filled yo' belly with vittles more times than yo' hands is filled it. Mah sweat is done paid for this house and Ah reckon Ah kin keep on sweatin' in it."

She seized the iron skillet from the stove and struck a defensive pose, which act surprised him greatly, coming from her. It cowed him and he did not strike her as he usually did.

"Naw you won't," she panted, "that ole snaggle-toothed black woman you runnin' with aint comin' heah to pile up on *mah* sweat and blood. You aint paid for nothin' on this place, and

Ah'm gointer stay right heah till Ah'm toted out foot foremost."

"Well, you better quit gittin' me riled up, else they'll be totin' you out sooner than you expect. Ah'm so tired of you Ah don't know whut to do. Gawd! how Ah hates skinny wimmen!"

A little awed by this new Delia, he sidled out of the door and slammed the back gate after him. He did not say where he had gone, but she knew too well. She knew very well that he would not return until nearly daybreak also. Her work over, she went on to bed but not to sleep at once. Things had come to a pretty pass!

She lay awake, gazing upon the debris that cluttered their matrimonial trail. Not an image left standing along the way. Anything like flowers had long ago been drowned in the salty stream that had been pressed from her heart. Her tears, her sweat, her blood. She had brought love to the union and he had brought a longing after the flesh. Two months after the wedding, he had given her the first brutal beating. She had the memory of his numerous trips to Orlando with all of his wages when he had returned to her penniless, even before the first year had passed. She was young and soft then, but now she thought of her knotty, muscled limbs, her harsh knuckly hands, and drew herself up into an unhappy little ball in the middle of the big feather bed. Too late now to hope for love, even if it were not Bertha it would be someone else. This case differed from the others only in that she was bolder than the others. Too late for everything except her little home. She had built it for her old days, and planted one by one the trees and flowers there. It was lovely to her, lovely.

Somehow, before sleep came, she found herself saying aloud: "Oh well, whatever goes over the Devil's back, is got to come under his belly. Sometime or ruther, Sykes, like everybody else, is gointer reap his sowing." After that she was able to build a spiritual earthworks against her husband. His shells could no longer reach her. *Amen*. She went to sleep and slept until he announced his presence in bed by kicking her feet and rudely snatching the cover away.

"Gimme some kivah heah an' git yo' damn foots over on yo' own side! Ah oughter mash you in yo' mouf fuh drawing dat skillet on me."

Delia went clear to the railing without answering him. A triumphant indifference to all that he was or did.

* * *

THE WEEK WAS AS full of work for Delia as all other weeks, and Saturday found her behind her little pony, collecting and delivering clothes.

It was a hot, hot day near the end of July. The village men on Joe Clarke's porch even chewed cane listlessly. They did not hurl the cane-knots as usual. They let them dribble over the edge of the porch. Even conversation had collapsed under the heat.

"Heah come Delia Jones," Jim Merchant said, as the shaggy pony came 'round the bend of the road toward them. The rusty buckboard was heaped with baskets of crisp, clean laundry.

"Yep," Joe Lindsay agreed. "Hot or col', rain or shine, jes ez reg'lar ez de weeks roll roun' Delia carries 'em an' fetches 'em on Sat'day."

"She better if she wanter eat," said Moss. "Syke Jones aint wuth de shot an' powder hit would tek tuh kill 'em. Not to *huh* he aint."

"He sho' aint," Walter Thomas chimed in. "It's too bad, too, cause she wuz a right pritty lil trick when he got huh. Ah'd uh mah'ied huh mahseff if he hadnter beat me to it."

Delia nodded briefly at the men as she drove past.

"Too much knockin' will ruin *any* 'oman. He done beat huh 'nough tuh kill three women, let 'lone change they looks," said Elijah Mosely. "How Syke kin stommuck dat big black greasy Mogul he's layin' 'round wid, gits me. Ah swear dat eight-rock couldn't kiss a sardine can Ah done thowed out de back do' 'way las' yeah."

"Aw, she's fat, thass how come. He's allus been crazy 'bout fat women," put in Merchant. "He'd a' been tied up wid one long time ago if he could a' found one tuh have him. Did Ah tell yuh 'bout him come sidlin' roun' *mah* wife—bringin' her a basket uh pee-cans outa his yard fuh a present? Yesssir, mah wife! She tol' him tuh take 'em right straight back home, cause Delia works so hard ovah dat washtub she reckon everything on de place taste lak sweat an' soapsuds. Ah jus' wisht Ah'd a' caught 'im 'roun' dere! Ah'd a' made his hips ketch on fiah down dat shell road."

"Ah know he done it, too. Ah sees 'im grinnin' at every 'oman dat passes," Walter Thomas said.

"But even so, he uster eat some mighty big hunks uh humble pie tuh git dat lil' 'oman he got. She wuz ez pritty ez a speckled pup! Dat wuz fifteen yeahs ago. He uster be so skeered uh losin' huh, she could make him do some parts of a husband's duty. Dey never wuz de same in de mind."

"There oughter be a law about him," said Lindsay. "He aint fit tuh carry guts tuh a bear."

Clarke spoke for the first time. "Taint no law on earth dat kin make a man be decent if it aint in 'im. There's plenty men dat takes a wife lak dey do a joint uh sugar-cane. It's round, juicy an' sweet when dey gits it. But dey squeeze an' grind, squeeze an' grind an' wring tell dey wring every drop uh pleasure dat's in 'em out. When dey's satisfied dat dey is wrung dry, dey treats 'em jes lak dey do a cane-chew. Dey throws 'em away. Dey knows whut dey is doin' while dey is at it, an' hates theirselves fuh it but they keeps on hangin' after huh tell she's empty. Den dey hates huh fuh bein' a cane-chew an' in de way."

"We oughter take Syke an' dat stray 'oman uh his'n down in Lake Howell swamp an' lay on de rawhide till they cain't say 'Lawd a' mussy.' He allus wuz uh ovahbearin' niggah, but since dat white 'oman from up north done teached 'im how to run a automobile, he done got too biggety to live—an' we oughter kill 'im," Old Man Anderson advised.

A grunt of approval went around the porch. But the heat was melting their civic virtue and Elijah Moseley began to bait Joe Clarke.

"Come on, Joe, git a melon outa dere an' slice it up for yo' customers. We'se all sufferin' wid de heat. De bear's done got *me*!"

"Thass right, Joe, a watermelon is jes' whut Ah needs tuh cure de eppizudicks," Walter Thomas joined forces with Moseley. "Come on dere, Joe. We all is steady customers an' you aint set us up in a long time. Ah chooses dat long, bowlegged Floridy favorite."

"A god, an' be dough. You all gimme twenty cents and slice away," Clarke retorted. "Ah needs a col' slice m'self. Heah, everybody chip in. Ah'll lend y'll mah meat knife."

The money was quickly subscribed and the huge melon brought forth. At that moment, Sykes and Bertha arrived. A determined silence fell on the porch and the melon was put away again.

Merchant snapped down the blade of his jackknife and moved toward the store door.

"Come on in, Joe, an' gimme a slab uh sow belly an' uh pound uh coffee—almost fuhgot 'twas Sat'day. Got to git on home." Most of the men left also.

Just then Delia drove past on her way home, as Sykes was ordering magnificently for Bertha. It pleased him for Delia to see.

"Git whutsoever yo' heart desires, Honey. Wait a minute, Joe. Give huh two bottles uh strawberry soda-water, uh quart uh parched ground-peas, an' a block uh chewin' gum."

With all this they left the store, with Sykes reminding Bertha that this was his town and she could have it if she wanted it.

The men returned soon after they left, and held their watermelon feast.

"Where did Syke Jones git dat 'oman from nohow?" Lindsay asked.

"Ovah Apopka. Guess dey musta been cleanin' out de town when she lef'. She don't look lak a thing but a hunk uh liver wid hair on it."

"Well, she sho' kin squall," Dave Carter contributed. "When she gits ready tuh laff, she jes' opens huh mouf an' latches it back tuh de las' notch. No ole grandpa alligator down in Lake Bell ain't got nothin' on huh."

* * *

BERTHA HAD BEEN IN town three months now. Sykes was still paying her room rent at Della Lewis'—the only house in town that would have taken her in. Sykes took her frequently to Winter Park to "stomps." He still assured her that he was the swellest man in the state.

"Sho' you kin have dat lil' ole house soon's Ah kin git dat 'oman outa dere. Everything b'longs tuh me an' you sho' kin have it. Ah sho' 'bominates uh skinny 'oman. Lawdy, you sho' is got one portly shape on you! You kin git *anything* you wants. Dis is *mah* town an' you sho' kin have it."

Delia's work-worn knees crawled over the earth in Gethsemane and up the rocks of Calvary many, many times during these months. She avoided the villagers and meeting places in her efforts to be blind and deaf. But Bertha nullified this to a degree, by coming to Delia's house to call Sykes out to her at the gate.

Delia and Sykes fought all the time now with no peaceful interludes. They slept and ate in silence. Two or three times Delia had attempted a timid friendliness, but she was repulsed each time. It was plain that the breaches must remain agape.

* * *

THE SUN HAD BURNED July to August. The heat streamed down like a million hot arrows, smiting all things living upon the earth. Grass withered, leaves browned, snakes went blind in shedding and men and dogs went mad. Dog days!

Delia came home one day and found Sykes there before her. She wondered, but started to go on into the house without speaking, even though he was standing in the kitchen door and she must either stoop under his arm or ask him to move. He made no room for her. She noticed a soap box beside the steps, but paid no particular attention to it, knowing that he must have brought it there. As she was stooping to pass under his outstretched arm, he suddenly pushed her backward, laughingly.

"Look in de box dere Delia, Ah done brung yuh somethin'!"

She nearly fell upon the box in her stumbling, and when she saw what it held, she all but fainted outright.

"Syke! Syke, mah Gawd! You take dat rattlesnake 'way from heah! You *gottuh*. Oh, Jesus, have mussy!"

"Ah aint gut tuh do nothin' uh de kin'—fact is Ah aint got tuh do nothin' but die. Taint no use uh you puttin' on airs makin' out lak you skeered uh dat snake—he's gointer stay right heah tell he die. He wouldn't bite me cause Ah knows how tuh handle 'im. Nohow he wouldn't risk breakin' out his fangs 'gin yo' skinny laigs."

"Naw, now Syke, don't keep dat thing 'roun' heah tuh skeer me tuh death. You knows Ah'm even feared uh earth worms. Thass de biggest snake Ah evah did see. Kill 'im Syke, please."

"Doan ast me tuh do nothin' fuh yuh. Goin' 'roun' tryin' tuh be so damn asterperious. Naw, Ah aint gonna kill it. Ah think uh damn sight mo' uh him dan you! Dat's a nice snake an' anybody doan lak 'im kin jes' hit de grit."

The village soon heard that Sykes had the snake, and came to see and ask questions.

"How de hen-fire did you ketch dat six-foot rattler, Syke?" Thomas asked.

"He's full uh frogs so he cain't hardly move, thass how Ah eased up on 'm. But Ah'm a snake charmer an' knows how tuh handle 'em. Shux, dat aint nothin'. Ah could ketch one eve'day if Ah so wanted tuh."

"Whut he needs is a heavy hick'ry club leaned real heavy on his head. Dat's de bes 'way tuh charm a rattlesnake."

"Naw, Walt, y'll jes' don't understand dese diamon' backs lak Ah do," said Sykes in a superior tone of voice.

The village agreed with Walter, but the snake stayed on. His box remained by the kitchen door with its screen wire covering. Two or three days later it had digested its meal of frogs and literally came to life. It rattled at every movement in the kitchen or the yard. One day as Delia came down the kitchen steps she saw his chalky-white fangs curved like scimitars hung in the wire meshes. This time she did not run away with averted eyes as usual. She stood for a long time in the doorway in a red fury that grew bloodier for every second that she regarded the creature that was her torment.

That night she broached the subject as soon as Sykes sat down to the table.

"Syke, Ah wants you tuh take dat snake 'way fum heah. You done starved me an' Ah put up widcher, you done beat me an Ah took dat, but you done kilt all mah insides bringin' dat varmint heah."

Sykes poured out a saucer full of coffee and drank it deliberately before he answered her.

"A whole lot Ah keer 'bout how you feels inside uh out. Dat snake aint goin' no damn wheah till Ah gits ready fuh 'im tuh go. So fur as beatin' is concerned, yuh aint took near all dat you gointer take ef yuh stay 'roun' *me*."

Delia pushed back her plate and got up from the table. "Ah hates you, Sykes," she said calmly. "Ah hates you tuh de same degree dat Ah uster love yuh. Ah done took an' took till mah belly is full up tuh mah neck. Dat's de reason Ah got mah letter fum de church an' moved mah membership tuh Woodbridge—so Ah don't haftuh take no sacrament wid yuh. Ah don't wantuh see yuh 'roun' me atall. Lay 'roun' wid dat 'oman all yuh wants tuh, but gwan 'way fum me an' mah house. Ah hates yuh lak uh suck-egg dog."

Sykes almost let the huge wad of corn bread and collard greens he was chewing fall out of his mouth in amazement. He had a hard time whipping himself up to the proper fury to try to answer Delia.

"Well, Ah'm glad you does hate me. Ah'm sho' tiahed uh you hangin' ontuh me. Ah don't want yuh. Look at yuh stringy ole neck! Yo' rawbony laigs an' arms is enough tuh cut uh man tuh death. You looks jes' lak de devvul's doll-baby tuh *me*. You cain't hate me no worse dan Ah hates you. Ah been hatin' *you* fuh years."

"Yo' ole black hide don't look lak nothin' tuh me, but uh passle uh wrinkled up rubber, wid yo' big ole yeahs flappin' on each side lak uh paih uh buzzard wings. Don't think Ah'm gointuh be run 'way fum mah house neither. Ah'm goin' tuh de white folks bout *you*, mah young man, de very nex' time you lay yo' han's on me. Mah cup is done run ovah." Delia said this with no signs of fear and Sykes departed from the house, threatening her, but made not the slightest move to carry out any of them.

That night he did not return at all, and the next day being Sunday, Delia was glad that she did not have to quarrel before she hitched up her pony and drove the four miles to Woodbridge.

She stayed to the night service—"Love feast"—which was very warm and full of spirit. In the emotional winds her domestic trials were borne far and wide so that she sang as she drove homeward,

"Jurden water, black an' col'
Chills de body, not de soul
An' Ah wantah cross Jurden in uh calm time."

She came from the barn to the kitchen door and stopped.

"Whut's de mattah, ol' satan, you aint kickin' up yo' racket?" She addressed the snake's box. Complete silence. She went on into the house with a new hope in its birth struggles. Perhaps her threat to go to the white folks had frightened Sykes! Perhaps he was sorry! Fifteen years of misery and suppression had brought Delia to the place where she would hope *anything* that looked towards a way over or through her wall of inhibitions.

She felt in the match safe behind the stove at once for a match. There was only one there.

"Dat niggah wouldn't fetch nothin' heah tuh save his rotten neck, but he kin run thew whut Ah brings quick enough. Now he done toted off nigh on tuh haff uh box uh matches. He done had dat 'oman heah in mah house, too."

Nobody but a woman could tell how she knew this even before she struck the match. But she did and it put her into a new fury.

Presently she brought in the tubs to put the white things to soak. This time she decided she need not bring the hamper out of the bedroom; she would go in there and do the sorting. She picked up the pot-bellied lamp and went in. The room was small and the hamper stood hard by the foot of the white iron bed. She could sit and reach through the bedposts—resting as she worked.

"Ah wantah cross Jurden in uh calm time." She was singing again. The mood of the "love fest" had returned. She threw back the lid of the basket almost gaily. Then, moved by both horror and terror, she sprang back toward the door. *There lay the snake in the basket!* He moved sluggishly at first, but even as she turned round and round, jumped up and down in an insanity of fear, he began to stir vigorously. She saw him pouring his awful beauty from the basket upon the bed, then she seized the lamp and ran as fast as she could to the kitchen. The wind from the open door blew out the light and darkness added to her terror. She sped to the darkness of the yard, slamming the door after her before she thought to set down the lamp. She did not feel safe even on the ground, so she climbed up in the hay barn.

There for an hour or more she lay sprawled upon the hay a gibbering wreck.

Finally she grew quiet, and after that, coherent thought. With this, stalked through her a cold, bloody rage. Hours of this. A period of introspection, a space of retrospection, then a mixture of both. Out of this an awful calm.

"Well, Ah done de bes' Ah could. If things aint right, Gawd knows taint mah fault."

She went to sleep—a twitchy sleep—and woke up to a faint gray sky. There was a loud hollow sound below. She peered out. Sykes was at the wood-pile, demolishing a wire-covered box.

He hurried to the kitchen door, but hung outside there some minutes before he entered, and stood some minutes more inside before he closed it after him.

The gray in the sky was spreading. Delia descended without fear now, and crouched beneath the low bedroom window. The drawn shade shut out the dawn, shut in the night. But the thin walls held back no sound.

"Dat ol' scratch is woke up now!" She mused at the tremendous whirr inside, which every woodsman knows, is one of the sound illusions. The rattler is a ventriloquist. His whirr sounds to the right, to the left, straight ahead, behind, close under foot—everywhere but where it is. Woe to him who guesses wrong unless he is prepared to hold up his end of the argument! Sometimes he strikes without rattling at all.

Inside, Sykes heard nothing until he knocked a pot lid off the stove while trying to reach the match safe in the dark. He had emptied his pockets at Bertha's.

The snake seemed to wake up under the stove and Sykes made a quick leap into the bedroom. In spite of the gin he had had, his head was clearing now.

"Mah Gawd!" he chattered, "ef Ah could on'y strack uh light!"

The rattling ceased for a moment as he stood paralyzed. He waited. It seemed that the snake waited also.

"Oh, fuh de light! Ah thought he'd be too sick"—Sykes was muttering to himself when the whirr began again, closer, right underfoot this time. Long before this, Sykes' ability to think had been flattened down to primitive instinct and he leaped—onto the bed.

Outside Delia heard a cry that might have come from a maddened chimpanzee, a stricken gorilla. All the terror, all the horror, all the rage that man possibly could express, without a recognizable human sound.

A tremendous stir inside there, another series of animal screams, the intermittent whirr of the reptile. The shade torn violently down from the window, letting in the red dawn, a huge brown hand seizing the window stick, great dull blows upon the wooden floor punctuating the gibberish of sound long after the rattle of the snake had abruptly subsided. All this Delia could see and hear from her place beneath the window, and it made her ill. She crept over to the four-o'clocks and stretched herself on the cool earth to recover.

She lay there. "Delia, Delia!" she could hear Sykes calling in a most despairing tone as one who expected no answer. The sun crept on up, and he called. Delia could not move—her legs were gone flabby. She never moved, he called, and the sun kept rising.

"Mah Gawd!" She heard him moan. "Mah Gawd fum Heben!" She heard him stumbling about and got up from her flower-bed. The sun was growing warm. As she approached the door she heard him call out hopefully, "Delia, is dat you Ah heah?"

She saw him on his hands and knees as soon as she reached the door. He crept an inch or two toward her—all that he was able, and she saw his horribly swollen neck and his one open eye shining with hope. A surge of pity too strong to support bore her away from that eye that must, could not, fail to see the tubs. He would see the lamp. Orlando with its doctors was too far. She could scarcely reach the Chinaberry tree, where she waited in the growing heat while inside she knew the cold river was creeping up and up to extinguish that eye which must know by now that she knew.

Under the Bridge

May in the Florida outdoors; May in the open house of Luke Mimms and May in the hearts of the three occupants of the house.

Luke, the father-husband, was glowing. He was fifty-eight and God had granted him a pretty wife one summer less twenty. His son, Artie the beloved, twenty-two, had accepted her at last and was at peace with Luke. The world was bright. Fifty-eight is young after all with love.

Vangie was radiating ecstasy from her black eyes and brown skin. She, the homeless waif, was loved by Luke. She was the mistress of his comfortable household and her big stepson had said he was glad she was there. For three weeks he had sulked in sullen silence. But now—since morning—he had not only permitted her to make up to him, he spent his leisure doing errands for her, or displaying his huge strength for her entertainment.

Artie laughed in his deep baritone. He was at peace again with his beloved father; his new stepmother was not the ogre he had pictured her before he looked at her. She was pretty. She was obliging, and after all she was only a kid, grateful for any little kindness shown her.

"See, Dumplin," Luke gloried, "didn't Ah say Artie'd be all right t'reckly? Yas, mah boy is awful 'fectionate. He wouldn't hurt a flea—he kain't stay 'way f'um his pappy."

Vangie patted Luke's hand, and scolded him prettily.

"It's yo' fault, Honey. You kept callin' Artie 'yo baby' an' Ah thought he wuz a lil' teeny baby chile. Ah never knowed he wuz bigger'n a house. No grown body don't want no step mama. If he wuz a lil' boy Ah figgered Ah'd teach him to love me like he wuz mine."

"Don't mind him," Artie said, "he always calls me 'baby.' Heah Ah is de stronges' man in de country—ain't let nobody th'ow me in a rassle since Ah wuz sixteen—but Ah'm all he's got—Ah mean till you came."

"Kah! Kah!" Luke laughed boisterously. "Ef Ah had a' tol' you Ah had a son twenty-two, you would A' thought Ah wuz ole—Dat Artie boy, he's jealous uh me, dat's whut—we been heah by ourselves since he wuz nine."

"Yeah," Artie added—"It sho' made me good and mad to think we been gettin' 'long all dese years, den w'en Pop gets 'round sixty he got to jump up and get married."

"Ain't but fifty-eight," Luke threw in hastily.

"Whut's the difference? But Ah ain't mad uh nothin' no mo'. If youse happy Ah is. Vangie is a good girl an' Ah'll do all Ah kin to make it nice for her. Ah'm glad not to be foolin' wid the cookin'. Ah got mo' appetite already."

II

Artie did make things nice for Vangie. There was always plenty of stove wood in the wood box and water in the two brass bound pails. He "grubbed" potatoes for her, churned for her, took her fishing with him and even let her go hunting with him when he discovered her enthusiasm for dogs in general, and his pair of "redbone" hounds in particular.

May was burned to June beneath the Florida sun. Berries hung plump and green in clusters among the lacy China-berry trees. The woods were full of color and odors.

June for Luke, for Artie, for Vangie—June in the world.

But Luke was not so happy as he had been. Not that he was jealous—he hated himself at the very thought of such a passion—but Artie and Vangie did seem to have a great deal to talk about in which he had no part. They could enjoy themselves for hours together and did not remember he was alone. Artie never seemed to go out "sparking" on girls anymore—he was forever calling Vangie or she was forever calling him.

Sometimes his great love for the two "young 'uns" would overflow and wash all baser passions from his soul. Then he would assure himself that all was well. He had prayed for peace and harmony between these two, and God had heard him.

"Youse mah wife," Luke said to her one day at the table and closed his gnarled black hand upon her brown one. This was as near as he ever came to betraying the sore on his heart. Artie looked quickly at his father, searchingly. Vangie did not return the caress, but neither did she draw her hand away. So Luke was satisfied.

"Artie baby, don't think cause Ah married, dat you kain't git yo' shear. Youse haff an' haff partners wid me on dis truckin' farm—you kin take over yoh twenty acres whenever you gits ready, an' git married when so evah you please. Pinkie Turk wuz jes' axin 'bout you."

"Thank you, Pop, but Ah reckon the place can stay together lak it tis. No hurry a-tall—Ah ain't in no hurry to jump over de broom-stick wid nobody."

During supper that night the dogs were rather noisy—moonless black night with the alligators booming from Lake Belle whip-poor-will crying in the orange grove—

"Past-Ned old boy, put 'im up!" Artie called out to his "tree" hound. "Go git 'im Beulah," to his "strike." To Vangie he explained: "Them dogs knows it's a good hunting night—b'leeve Ah'll air 'e mout if Ah kin git Pop to go 'long."

"Nope, son. Pop's too tired. Git Dan Carter to go wid you."

"Oh, lemme go wid you, Artie," Vangie begged. "Ah ain't never been in mah life."

"Sure you kin, Vangie."

"Naw, Dumplin', you better not," Luke objected quickly. "You mought git snake-bit."

"Shucks, she kin wear yo' boots," Artie put in.

"Oh, Ah wants to go!" wailed the girl.

"But Honey," Luke contended, "dey mought flush a catamount."

"Aw, we ain't goin' in a hammock," Artie retorted. So Luke, having offered every objection but the real one, gave in.

"You reckon any boogers goin ter git me, Artie? You sho you kin take keer uh me?" she appealed.

"Sho' Ah kin take keer uh you, Vangie, and Ah wouldn't leave you go if Ah couldn't."

So Vangie drew on her husband's boots and followed Artie into the black woods.

Luke crept to bed alone with the dish-rag under his pillow—for that is a powerful charm to keep the marriage bed inviolate.

He heard the deep voices of the hounds "treeing" far away. The late moon hung low and red when the two others returned tired but happy. But Luke could never hear a baying hound again nor look at a low, full moon without that painful heart-contraction he had felt that night in the vastness of his bed alone while his wife strode thru the dark woods, depending upon, looking to someone other than himself, for protection.

By eight o'clock next morning he trod the village road to End-Or. He hurried to the gate of Ned Bickerstaff to get a "hand."

"Does you want dis han' for hate, for to make money come to yuh, for to put yo' enemy on his back, or to keep trouble fum yo' do'?" the old male witch asked.

"Ah—Ah jes' wants to fix it so's nobody kain't git 'tween me and Vangie."

"Does you want him daid, or crippled up fuh life, uh jes' fixed so he kain't stay heah?"

"None of 'em. There ain't no man—now. Ah jes' wants to [be] sure there never ben one."

Bickerstaff made him a small parcel sewed up in red flannel and received ten dollars in return.

"Take dis, Luke Mimms. Long as you got dis, nobody can't never cross you. Wait till sundown, sprinkle wid a drop or two of water and nobody kin git twixt you 'thout water gittin' him. But don't sprinkle it tell youse sho' you wants somethin' done, cause it's bound to come after de sprinklin'. And don't *never* take it off once you put it [on] else it will work the other way."

Luke hurried home to his fields and toiled vigorously all day beside his big brown boy. Like the roots his hands were gnarled; like the soil his skin was brownish black. Dirt of the dirt he appeared to the observer. But like the moist black earth he worked, he held within everything of good and evil. He watched Artie from the corner of his wrinkled eyelids. How he hated that big form that threw its shadow between Vangie and him! How he loved his dear boy, his baby now grown to such splendid manhood! Aha! In his pocket was the little red bag that by its magic made their years equal and enlarged his shrunken old form to that of Artie, the brute magnificent. The dull brown earth-clod was alive and warm with the fire of love and hate. So he sang in his quivering voice:

"There's a balm in Gilead
To make the wounded whole,
There is a balm in Gilead
To heal the sinsick soul."

He trusted to his "hand" and grew cheerful again.

"Artie, les' we all knock off now. Hit's mighty hot an' de bear's bout to git me. Les' put some 'millons tuh cool and drive in to town."

"What fur? Oh, all right, Pop, Ah'll go feed de hauses and change up a bit. You g'wan git dressed—Ah'll hitch up whilst you puts de melons in de spring house."

Vangie waved them off cheerfully and went on with her work.

On the road they laughed, told jokes, commented on timber and crops, fertilizer and stock, laughed and joked some more and finally arrived at Orlando.

Then Luke revealed the object of his trip. He wanted to buy things for Vangie. "Artie, she kin have everything to make a 'oman proud." He stopped, embarrassed, for a moment. "You an' her is the same in mah heart. You know Ah allus tried to give you what yo' lil heart wanted. Ah allus ast Gawd to fit it so's Ah could. To yo' dyin' day Ah wants it to be so. An' now, wid her it's the same. You—you doan' mind, do you Artie boy?"

There was a childish, almost pathetic look in his eyes as he looked up into his son's face, and Artie felt a disturbance in his breast. He put one arm quickly about his father's shoulder, then drew it away and roughly tied the horse to the great oak tree.

"Oh, course Papa. Ah wants you to do for Vangie whutever you so desired. You been a good papa to me. Ah wants you to be jes' as happy as a king. Whut you got in yo' mind to buy her?"

They advanced to the door of the store.

"Well, Ah thought Ah'd buy her a new churn, a store broom, and bolt uh new calliker."

"You reckon she wants dat?" Artie asked skeptically.

"Sho! All women-folks do. Ah uster give yo' ma a bolt uh calliker ev'ry Chris-mas."

He shopped eagerly, giggling like a schoolgirl. Artie shopped also, but his purchase was made without any flourish in another part of the store, and Luke in his excitement asked no questions.

They drove away homeward, but at the last store before leaving town Luke dismounted and bought a large stock of peppermint candy—red and white striped.

"She'll be tickled to death to git dis candy," Luke jubilated.

"You ought to've got dat box kind of candy fuh her," Artie commented gently.

"What! Spen' a whole dallah fuh a teeny lil' box when Ah kin git dis great big stick fuh uh dime?"

At home, Vangie had supper ready and as soon as the horses were unhitched and fed, they gathered about the table. Then the old lover slyly arose and presented his gifts. First the churn, a big brown earthen affair—and Vangie exclaimed happily over it, but there was a little of disappointment in her voice which Luke would have noticed had he not been so consumed by the joy of giving. Then the calico, which she received a little happier, and last the broom and candy, upon which he bumped her mouth awkwardly with his own.

"Oh, you'se mighty good to me, Honey," she told him. "Ah reckon Ah got de bestest husban' in Floridy."

Luke went beaming back to his seat.

Artie nonchalantly tossed a parcel in Vangie's lap.

"Thass a lil' somethin' fum me, too, Vangie. You been waitin' on me and doin' fuh me ever since you been heah an' Ah ain't never give you a cent. Ah'll be buyin' you somethin' all along if you keep on lookin' after me."

It turned out to be a white wool skirt and a pink silk blouse. Poor Vangie was delighted and could not keep the ecstacy out of her eyes and voice.

"Oh, Oh, Artie!" she cried, grasping his hand. "You'se so good to me!"

She held the two garments up to measure and hugged them gleefully.

"Artie, Artie!" she all but wept. "How you know whut mah heart wanted so?"

"Ah, Ah would a bought it fuh you, Vangie, if Ah had a knowed," said Luke miserably and remained silent for the rest of the meal.

That night Luke sprinkled his "hand" and put it on.

The old sun so careless of human woes, shone brightly every day. If Luke wept in his hell of misgivings, the sun came up and sped across the blue, glorying hotly in its strength and power just the same. Old trees rotted at the heart, and the sun nourished young saplings that quickly buried the struggling old forest-monarch in their shadows. The sun went on and on to his sky bed at night, pulling the gray and purple hangings of his couch about him and slept, indifferent to human tears.

Artie and Vangie did nothing that Luke could put his finger upon as unfaithful. It was just their lowered eyes, their happy gazes that hurt him. He did not believe that they had desecrated his hearth, but he could feel their love like a presence occupying the house. It pricked his old skin painfully as soon as he entered.

He could not rage, he could not kill. He loved them both till it all but suffocated him. In this great love he saw they suffered too—that Artie loved him greatly for he laid down his love for his father's sake. But for how much longer? Luke had asked himself.

The sun flung August hotly down upon him.

Vangie dressed every Sunday in the skirt and blouse that Artie had bought her. Luke could only explain this by the fact that Artie had given them. He, of the calico age, could not understand the tastes of the age of silk.

Oh, the house was unbearable! His suspicions had filled every chink and cranny. He began to approach sheltered places stealthily and creep thru the orange grove. Then he would hastily retreat lest he surprise them.

"Tell you whut," he began one evening. "We cain't do nothin' to de crops fuh a week uh mo'—les' we all shut up de house, turn de stock on de pashcher an' go on a-fishin' trip up de rivah!"

"Ooh! Les' we all!" Vangie echoed.

"Ah kin stan' a whole heap uh dat, Papa." Artie laughed and stretched his mighty limbs. "Les' start t'morrer."

III

The awakening sun threw a flaming sword upon the St. John's River the next morning as they embarked.

The camping necessities were piled high in the center of the large rowboat before Artie, who rowed. Vangie was perched in the low stern facing him with Luke at his back in the high prow seat.

Down river they flew under Artie's mighty strokes. The sun lost its redness as it climbed. The hounds with forepaws on the gunwale barked defiances to river alligators, woods, and would not be stilled in their freedom.

"How fur we goin', Artie?" Vangie asked.

"Oh, way past de 'Coast Line' bridge," he answered. "Thass all right, ain't it, Pop?"

"Ah, sho', sho'," the old man answered.

"We been down there heaps uh times on account uh game," Artie went on. "Dere's panthers, catamounts, deers and bears in dem woods 'bout twenty miles off."

"Ooh. Ah'll be skeered," Vangie shuddered.

"No need to be—Ah'm heah," Artie answered quickly. "Ole wile cat 'bout got me when Ah wuz a lil' shaver but Papa kilt him—fought him wid his pocket-knife—ain't he never tole you?"

"Naw, indeedy, please—Luke, tell me."

"Oh, tain't much to tell, Vangie. Hit wuz in dese same woods we gwine to now. Artie allus did love to follow me 'round trapisin' long, holdin' on to mah finger wid his lil' fat han's. His ma useter cry an' say he loved me better'n he done her . . . Well, Ah had some traps set 'round in dem swamps an' he cried to go, so Ah took him. Way down in dat hammock we flushed a wile cat an' she leaped right at mah boy but Ah wuz too quick fur her. Ah got in betwixt an' she landed on me. An' Ah had to fight wid mah han's an' a pocket-knife. Ah kilt her, but she clawed me up so's de doctah had to take a whole heap uh stitches."

He displayed his arms and chest.

Vangie's eyes grew misty.

"An' fuh dat," Artie said flippantly, but with a husky voice, "Ah'm gointer let him be mah papa till Ah die."

They all laughed excessively to hide their feelings.

The sun quieted the dogs, sweated the people, and fried the paint on the boat.

Artie rowed on, his tremendous muscles bunching, stretching, bunching, stretching, as he bent to the oar. As he rowed he sang. The Negro melodies rolled out of his chest in deep baritone and rumbled over the river to be lost among the trees. Deep vibrating tones, high quavering minors. He sang on and on, filling Vangie's ears with his music, her eyes with his body, and her heart with love of him.

Luke saw it all. His son's back was toward him, huge, *huge*, till it swelled and swelled until it blotted out the boat, the river, the woods, the earth, the sun for Luke. The universe held nothing but Artie singing to Vangie and caressing her with his eyes. His old skin pricked and crept uncomfortably.

But, he gloated, the "hand" would hold. They could but bruise themselves against the bars.

Hell? Yes. Fire? No. Just one woman, two men in a boat—two men who love her—two men who love each other.

They suffer from the heat—Artie rowing, most of all. Vangie wets her handkerchief in the river and spreads it over Artie's head under his hat. His arteries swell, her hand trembles. Their faces are close—their lips nearly meet. Involuntarily Luke grasps for his "hand" and all but faints. It was gone. God knows where. String must have worn in two.

The two hours for Luke crawled on up the river and over him with hot brassy feet. The sun was arching toward his bed.

"Ah'm tired," Vangie gasped.

"Not much longer now," Artie comforted her—"We'se gointer camp jes' beyon' de bridge—'bout three miles mo'."

"Luke's 'sleep," Vangie observed.

Artie glanced over his shoulder—

"Guess 'tis pretty hahd on de ole man. We'll camp soon."

But Luke was not asleep. He slumped there with closed eyes lest they see his tears. His first wife had been merely a good worker—he had never loved any woman but Vangie. His whole life had been lived for his boy, so that Artie might know nothing but happiness. And now, that which would give Artie happiness, would at one stroke rob him both of wife and son! His heart contracted so painfully that he gasped and opened his eyes.

The bitterness of life struck him afresh. He blamed them. He didn't. Poor creatures! Designing devils! He closed his eyes again.

The bridge was in sight. And now he noticed the sun was setting. The sky darkened: the fleecy clouds soaked up more color and yet more—magenta, purple, blush, rose with light shafts hurled across the heavens from the west as if the sky monarch on retiring would disperse his train.

With every pull on the oars, Artie leaned nearer to Vangie and she, forgetting, was leaning toward him. He, with the rebirth of the world in his eyes—the eternal torch lighter. She inclining her taper to his light with closed eyes and all consuming love. All who ran might read.

The bridge was at hand. Wide, stone pillared, crouching low over the river. As they shot under, a train rushed screeching overhead.

Here in the darkness, Artie drew in the oars and let the boat drift slowly. His hand touched Vangie's, his feverish lips touched her hungry ones, and lazily, slowly the boat was wafted out again into the light.

They saw at once that Luke was not [asleep]—and both fell a-weeping. Artie forgot about his oars and the boat floated where it would upon the stream.

The indifferent sun, in bed, drew round his purple curtain and slept.

On the river they wept on. The boat drifted on, for Destiny, the grim steersman, had seized the rudder and they were bound—whither?

'Possum or Pig?

Before freedom there was a house slave very much in the confidence of the Master. But young pigs began to disappear, and for good reasons the faithful house slave fell under suspicion.

One night, after his duties at the "big house" were over, he was sitting before his cabin fire. From a pot was seeping the odor of young pig. There was a knock at the door.

"Who dat?" he asked cautiously.

"It's me, John," came the Master's voice.

"Lawd, now, Massa, whut you want way down heah?"

"I'm cold, John. I want to come in."

"Now, Massa, ah jes' lef' a lovely hot fire at de big house. You aughter gwan up dere an' git warm."

"I want to come in, John."

"Massa, whut you wanta come in po' niggah's house an' you got dat fine big house up yander?"

"John, if you don't open this door, I'll have you whipped tomorrow."

John went to the door grumbling about rich white folks hanging around po' niggahs' cabins.

The white man sat down before the blazing fire. The pot boiled and breathed of delicious things within.

After a while he said, "I'm hungry, John. What have you got in that pot?"

"Lawd, now, Massa, whut you wanter eat mah po' vittles fuh and Mistis got roas' chicken an' ham an' chine-bone pie an' everything up to de house? White folks got de funniest ways."

"What's in that pot, John?"

"It's one lil' measly possum, Massa, ah'm bilin' tuh keep fuh a cold snack."

"I want some of it."

"Naw, Massa, you don't want none uh dat dirty lil' possum."

"Yes I do, and if you don't give me some, I'll have you whipped."

John slowly arose and got a plate, knife and fork and opened the pot.

"Well," he said resignedly before dipping in. "Ah put dis heah critter in heah a possum,—if it comes out a pig, 'tain't mah fault."

STEPPED ON A TIN, MAH STORY ENDS.

The Eatonville Anthology

I

THE PLEADING WOMAN

Mrs. Tony Roberts is the pleading woman. She just loves to ask for things. Her husband gives her all he can rake and scrape, which is considerably more than most wives get for their housekeeping, but she goes from door to door begging for things.

She starts at the store. "Mist' Clarke," she sing-songs in a high keening voice, "gimme lil' piece uh meat tuh boil a pot uh greens wid. Lawd knows me an' mah chillen is SO hongry! Hits uh SHAME! Tony don't fee-ee-eee-ed me!"

Mr. Clarke knows that she has money and that her larder is well stocked, for Tony Roberts is the best provider on his list. But her keening annoys him and he arises heavily. The pleader at this shows all the joy of a starving man being seated at a feast.

"Thass right Mist' Clarke. De Lawd loveth de cheerful giver. Gimme jes' a lil' piece 'bout dis big (indicating the width of her hand) an' de Lawd'll bless yuh."

She follows this angel-on-earth to his meat tub and superintends the cutting, crying out in pain when he refuses to move the knife just a teeny bit mo'.

Finally, meat in hand, she departs remarking on the meanness of some people who give a piece of salt meat only two-fingers wide when they were plainly asked for a hand-wide piece. Clarke puts it down to Tony's account and resumes his reading.

With the slab of salt pork as a foundation, she visits various homes until she has collected all she wants for the day. At the Piersons, for instance: "Sister Pierson, plee-ee-ease gimme uh han'ful uh collard greens fuh me an' mah po' chillen! 'Deed, me an' mah chillen is SO hongry. Tony doan' fee-ee-eed me!"

Mrs. Pierson picks a bunch of greens for her, but she springs away from them as if they were poison. "Lawd a mussy, Mis' Pierson, you ain't gonna gimme dat lil' eye-full uh greens fuh me an' mah chillen, is you? Don't be so graspin'; Gawd won't bless yuh. Gimme uh han'full mo'. Lawd, some folks is got everything, an' theys jes' as gripin' an stingy!"

Mrs. Pierson raises the ante, and the pleading woman moves on to the next place, and on and on. The next day, it commences all over.

II

TURPENTINE LOVE

Jim Merchant is always in good humor—even with his wife. He says he fell in love with her at first sight. That was some years ago. She has had all her teeth pulled out, but they still get along splendidly.

He says that first time he called on her he found out that she was subject to fits. This didn't cool his love, however. She had several in his presence.

One Sunday, while he was there, she had one, and her mother

tried to give her a dose of turpentine to stop it. Accidently, she spilled it in her eye and it cured her. She never had another fit, so they got married and have kept each other in good humor ever since.

III

Becky Moore has eleven children of assorted colors and sizes. She has never been married, but that is not her fault. She has never stopped any of the fathers of her children from proposing, so if she has no father for her children it's not her fault. The men round about are entirely to blame.

The other mothers of the town are afraid that it is catching. They won't let their children play with hers.

IV

TIPPY

Sykes Jones' family all shoot craps. The most interesting member of the family—also fond of bones, but of another kind—is Tippy, the Jones' dog.

He is so thin, that it amazes one that he lives at all. He sneaks into village kitchens if the housewives are careless about the doors and steals meats, even off the stoves. He also sucks eggs.

For these offenses he has been sentenced to death dozens of times, and the sentences executed upon him, only they didn't work. He has been fed bluestone, strychnine, nux vomica, even an entire Peruna bottle beaten up. It didn't fatten him, but it didn't kill him. So Eatonville has resigned itself to the plague of Tippy, reflecting that it has erred in certain matters and is being chastened.

In spite of all the attempts upon his life, Tippy is still willing to be friendly with anyone who will let him.

V

THE WAY OF A MAN WITH A TRAIN

Old Man Anderson lived seven or eight miles out in the country from Eatonville. Over by Lake Apopka. He raised feed-corn and cassava and went to market with it two or three times a year. He bought all of his victuals wholesale so he wouldn't have to come to town for several months more.

He was different from us citybred folks. He had never seen a train. Everybody laughed at him for even the smallest child in Eatonville had either been to Maitland or Orlando and watched a train go by. On Sunday afternoons all of the young people of the village would go over to Maitland, a mile away, to see Number 35 whizz southward on its way to Tampa and wave at the passengers. So we looked down on him a little. Even we children felt superior in the presence of a person so lacking in worldly knowledge.

The grown-ups kept telling him he ought to go see a train. He always said he didn't have time to wait so long. Only two trains a day passed through Maitland. But patronage and ridicule finally had its effect and Old Man Anderson drove in one morning early. Number 78 went north to Jacksonville at 10:20. He drove his light wagon over in the woods beside the railroad below Maitland, and sat down to wait. He began to fear that his horse would get frightened and run away with the wagon. So he took him out and led him deeper into the grove and tied him securely. Then he returned to his wagon and waited some more.

Then he remembered that some of the train-wise villagers had said the engine belched fire and smoke. He had better move his wagon out of danger. It might catch afire. He climbed down from the seat and placed himself between the shafts to draw it away. Just then 78 came thundering over the trestle spouting smoke, and suddenly began blowing for Maitland. Old Man Anderson became so frightened he ran away with the wagon through the woods and tore it up worse than the horse ever could have done. He doesn't know yet what a train looks like, and says he doesn't care.

VI

COON TAYLOR

Coon Taylor never did any real stealing. Of course, if he saw a chicken or a watermelon or muskmelon or anything like that that he wanted he'd take it. The people used to get mad but they never could catch him. He took so many melons from Joe Clarke that he set up in the melon patch one night with his shotgun loaded with rock salt. He was going to fix Coon. But he was tired. It is hard work being a mayor, postmaster, storekeeper and everything. He dropped asleep sitting on a stump in the middle of the patch. So he didn't see Coon when he came. Coon didn't see him either, that is, not at first. He knew the stump was there, however. He had opened many of Clarke's juicy Florida Favorite on it. He selected his fruit, walked over to the stump and burst the melon on it. That is, he thought it was the stump until it fell over with a yell. Then he knew it was no stump and departed hastily from those parts. He had cleared the fence when Clarke came to, as it were. So the charge of rock-salt was wasted on the desert air.

During the sugar-cane season, he found he couldn't resist Clarke's soft green cane, but Clarke did not go to sleep this time. So after he had cut six or eight stalks by the moonlight, Clarke rose up out of the cane strippings with his shotgun and made Coon sit right down and chew up the last one of them on the spot. And the next day he made Coon leave his town for three months.

VII

VILLAGE FICTION

Joe Lindsay is said by Lum Boger to be the largest manufacturer of prevarications in Eatonville; Brazzle (late owner of the world's leanest and meanest mule) contends that his business is the largest in the state and his wife holds that he is the biggest liar in the world.

Exhibit A—He claims that while he was in Orlando one day he saw a doctor cut open a woman, remove everything—liver, lights and heart included—clean each of them separately; the doctor then washed out the empty woman, dried her out neatly with a towel and replaced the organs so expertly that she was up and about her work in a couple of weeks.

VIII

Sewell is a man who lives all to himself. He moves a great deal. So often, that 'Lige Moseley says his chickens are so used to moving that every time he comes out into his backyard the chickens lie down and cross their legs, ready to be tied up again.

He is baldheaded; but he says he doesn't mind that, because he wants as little as possible between him and God.

IX

Mrs. Clarke is Joe Clarke's wife. She is a soft-looking, middle-aged woman, whose bust and stomach are always holding a get-together.

She waits on the store sometimes and cries every time he yells at her which he does every time she makes a mistake, which is quite often. She calls her husband "Jody." They say he used to beat her in the store when he was a young man, but he is not so impatient now. He can wait until he goes home.

She shouts in Church every Sunday and shakes the hand of fellowship with everybody in the Church with her eyes closed, but somehow always misses her husband.

X

Mrs. McDuffy goes to Church every Sunday and always shouts and tells her "determination." Her husband always sits in the back row and beats her as soon as they get home. He says there's no sense in her shouting, as big a devil as she is. She just does it to slur him. Elijah Moseley asked her why she didn't stop shouting, seeing she always got a beating out about it. She says she can't "squinch the sperrit." Then Elijah asked Mr. McDuffy to stop beating her, seeing that she was going to shout anyway. He answered that she just did it for spite and that his fist was just as hard as her head. He could last just as long as she. So the village let the matter rest.

XI

DOUBLE-SHUFFLE

Back in the good old days before the World War, things were very simple in Eatonville. People didn't fox-trot. When the town wanted to put on its Sunday clothes and wash behind the ears, it put on a "breakdown." The daring younger set would two-step and waltz, but the good church members and the elders stuck to the grand march. By rural canons dancing is wicked, but one is not held to have danced until the feet have been crossed. Feet don't get crossed when one grand marches.

At elaborate affairs the organ from the Methodist church was moved up to the hall and Lizzimore, the blind man, presided. When informal gatherings were held, he merely played his guitar assisted by any volunteer with mouth organs or accordions.

Among white people the march is as mild as if it had been passed on by Volstead. But it still has a kick in Eatonville. Everybody happy, shining eyes, gleaming teeth. Feet dragged 'shhlap, shhlap! to beat out the time. No orchestra needed. Round and round! Back again, parse-me-la! shlap! shlap! Strut! Strut! Seaboard! Shlap! Shlap! Tiddy bumm! Mr. Clarke in the lead with Mrs. Mosely.

It's too much for some of the young folks. Double shuffling commences. Buck and wing. Lizzimore about to break his guitar. Accordion doing contortions. People fall back against the walls, and let the soloist have it, shouting as they clap the old, old double shuffle songs.

"Me an' mah honey got two mo' days
Two mo' days tuh do de buck"

Sweating bodies, laughing mouths, grotesque faces, feet drumming fiercely. Deacons clapping as hard as the rest.

"Great big nigger, black as tar
Trying tuh git tuh hebben on uh 'lectric car."

"Some love cabbage, some love kale
But I love a gal wid a short skirt tail."

"Long tall angel—steppin' down.
Long white robe an' starry crown."

"'Ah would not marry uh black gal (bumm bumm!)
Tell yuh de reason why
Every time she comb her hair
She make de goo-goo eye.

Would you not marry a yaller gal (bumm bumm!)
Tell yuh de reason why
Her neck so long an' stringy
Ahm 'fraid she'd never die.

Would you not marry uh preacher
Tell yuh de reason why
Every time he comes tuh town
He makes de chicken fly."

When the buck dance was over, the boys would give the floor to the girls and they would parse-me-la with a sly eye out of the corner to see if anybody was looking who might "have them up in church" on conference night. Then there would be more dancing. Then Mr. Clarke would call for everybody's best attention and announce that *'freshments was served! Every gent'man would please take his lady by the arm and scorch her right up to de table fur a treat!*

Then the men would stick their arms out with a flourish and ask their ladies: "You lak chicken? Well, then, take a wing." And the ladies would take the proffered "wings" and parade up to the long table and be served. Of course most of them had brought baskets in which were heaps of jointed and fried chicken, two or three kinds of pies, cakes, potato pone and chicken purlo. The hall would separate into happy groups about the baskets until time for more dancing.

But the boys and girls got scattered about during the war, and now they dance the fox-trot by a brand new piano. They do waltz and two-step still, but no one now considers it good form to lock his chin over his partner's shoulder and stick out behind. One night just for fun and to humor the old folks, they danced, that is, they grand marched, but everyone picked up their feet. *Bah!!*

XII

THE HEAD OF THE NAIL

Daisy Taylor was the town vamp. Not that she was pretty. But sirens were all but non-existent in the town. Perhaps she was forced to it by circumstances. She was quite dark, with little brushy patches of hair squatting over her head. These were held down by shingle-nails often. No one knows whether she did this for artistic effect or for lack of hair-pins, but there they were shining in the little patches of hair when she got all dressed for the afternoon and came up to Clarke's store to see if there was any mail for her.

It was seldom that anyone wrote to Daisy, but she knew that

the men of the town would be assembled there by five o'clock, and some one could usually be induced to buy her some soda-water or peanuts.

Daisy flirted with married men. There were only two single men in town. Lum Boger, who was engaged to the assistant school-teacher, and Hiram Lester, who had been off to school at Tuskegee and wouldn't look at a person like Daisy. In addition to other drawbacks, she was pigeon-toed and her petticoat was always showing so perhaps he was justified. There was nothing else to do except flirt with married men.

This went on for a long time. First one wife then another complained of her, or drove her from the preserves by threat.

But the affair with Crooms was the most prolonged and serious. He was even known to have bought her a pair of shoes.

Mrs. Laura Crooms was a meek little woman who took all of her troubles crying, and talked a great deal of leaving things in the hands of God.

The affair came to a head one night in orange picking time. Crooms was over at Oneido picking oranges. Many fruit pickers move from one town to the other during the season.

The *town* was collected at the store-postoffice as is customary on Saturday nights. The *town* has had its bath and with its week's pay in pocket fares forth to be merry. The men tell stories and treat the ladies to soda-water, peanuts and peppermint candy.

Daisy was trying to get treats, but the porch was cold to her that night.

"Ah don't keer if you don't treat me. What's a dirty lil nickel?" She flung this at Walter Thomas. "The ever-loving Mister Crooms will gimme anything atall Ah wants."

"You better shet up yo' mouf talking 'bout Albert Crooms. Heah his wife comes right now."

Daisy went akimbo. "Who? Me! Ah don't keer whut Laura Crooms think. If she ain't a heavy hip-ted Mama enough to keep him, she don't need to come crying to me."

She stood making goo-goo eyes as Mrs. Crooms walked upon the porch. Daisy laughed loud, made several references to Albert Crooms, and when she saw the mail-bag come in from Maitland she said, "Ah better go in an' see if Ah ain't got a letter from Oneido."

The more Daisy played the game of getting Mrs. Crooms' goat, the better she liked it. She ran in and out of the store laughing until she could scarcely stand. Some of the people present began to talk to Mrs. Crooms—to egg her on to halt Daisy's boasting, but she was for leaving it all in the hands of God. Walter Thomas kept on after Mrs. Crooms until she stiffened and resolved to fight. Daisy was inside when she came to this resolve and never dreamed anything of the kind could happen. She had gotten hold of an envelope and came laughing and shouting, "Oh, Ah can't stand to see Oneido lose!"

There was a box of ax-handles on display on the porch, propped up against the door jamb. As Daisy stepped upon the porch, Mrs. Crooms leaned the heavy end of one of those handles heavily upon her head. She staggered from the porch to the ground and the timid Laura, fearful of a counter-attack, struck her again and Daisy toppled into the town ditch. There was not enough water in there to do more than muss her up. Every time she tried to rise, down would come that ax-handle again. Laura was fighting a sacred fight. With Daisy thoroughly licked, she retired to the store porch and left her fallen enemy in the ditch. None of the men helped Daisy—even to get out of the ditch. But Elijah Moseley, who was some distance down the street when the trouble began, arrived as the victor was withdrawing. He rushed up and picked Daisy out of the mud and began feeling her head.

"Is she hurt much?" Joe Clarke asked from the doorway.

"I don't know," Elijah answered. "I was just looking to see if Laura had been lucky enough to hit one of those nails on the head and drive it in."

Before a week was up, Daisy moved to Orlando. There in a wider sphere, perhaps, her talents as a vamp were appreciated.

XIII

PANTS AND CAL'LINE

Sister Cal'line Potts was a silent woman. Did all of her laughing down inside, but did the thing that kept the town in an uproar of laughter. It was the general opinion of the village that Cal'line would do anything she had a mind to. And she had a mind to do several things.

Mitchell Potts, her husband, had a weakness for women. No one ever believed that she was jealous. She did things to the women, surely. But most any townsman would have said that she did them because she liked the novel situation and the queer things she could bring out of it.

Once he took up with Delphine—called Mis' Pheeny by the town. She lived on the outskirts on the edge of the piney woods. The town winked and talked. People don't make secrets of such things in the village. Cal'line went about her business with her thin black lips pursed tight as ever, and her shiny black eyes unchanged.

"Dat devil of a Cal'line's got somethin' up her sleeve!" The town smiled in anticipation.

"Delphine is too big a cigar for her to smoke. She ain't crazy," said some as the weeks went on and nothing happened. Even

Pheeny herself would give an extra flirt to her over-starched petticoats as she rustled into church past her of Sundays.

Mitch Potts said furthermore, that he was tired of Cal'line's foolishness. She had to stay where he put her. His African soup-bone (arm) was too strong to let a woman run over him. 'Nough was 'nough. And he did some fancy cussing, and he was the fanciest cusser in the county.

So the town waited and the longer it waited, the odds changed slowly from the wife to the husband.

One Saturday, Mitch knocked off work at two o'clock and went over to Maitland. He came back with a rectangular box under his arm and kept straight on out to the barn and put it away. He ducked around the corner of the house quickly, but even so, his wife glimpsed the package. Very much like a shoe-box. So!

He put on the kettle and took a bath. She stood in her bare feet at the ironing board and kept on ironing. He dressed. It was about five o'clock but still very light. He fiddled around outside. She kept on with her ironing. As soon as the sun got red, he sauntered out to the barn, got the parcel and walked away down the road, past the store and into the piney woods. As soon as he left the house, Cal'line slipped on her shoes without taking time to don stockings, put on one of her husband's old Stetsons, worn and floppy, slung the axe over her shoulder and followed in his wake. He was hailed cheerily as he passed the sitters on the store porch and answered smiling sheepishly and passed on. Two minutes later passed his wife, silently, unsmilingly, and set the porch to giggling and betting.

An hour passed perhaps. It was dark. Clarke had long ago lighted the swinging kerosene lamp inside.

[XIV]

Once 'way back yonder before the stars fell all the animals used to talk just like people. In them days dogs and rabbits was the best of friends—even tho both of them was stuck on the same gal—which was Miss Nancy Coon. She had the sweetest smile and the prettiest striped and bushy tail to be found anywhere.

They both run their legs nigh off trying to win her for themselves—fetching nice ripe persimmons and such. But she never give one or the other no satisfaction.

Finally one night Mr. Dog popped the question right out. "Miss Coon," he says, "Ma'am, also Ma'am, which would you ruther be—a lark flyin' or a dove a settin'?"

Course Miss Nancy blushed and laughed a little and hid her face behind her bushy tail for a spell. Then she said sorter shy like, "I does love yo' sweet voice, brother dawg—but—but I ain't jes' exactly set in my mind yit."

Her and Mr. Dog set on a spell, when up comes hopping Mr. Rabbit wid his tail fresh washed and his whiskers shining. He got right down to business and asked Miss Coon to marry him, too.

"Oh, Miss Nancy," he says, "Ma'am, also Ma'am, if you'd see me settin' straddle of a mud-cut leadin' a minnow, what would you think? Ma'am also Ma'am?" which is a out and out proposal as everybody knows.

"Youse awful nice, Brother Rabbit and a beautiful dancer, but you cannot sing like Brother Dog. Both you uns come back next week to gimme time for to decide."

They both left arm-in-arm. Finally Mr. Rabbit says to Mr. Dog, "Taint no use in me going back—she ain't gwinter have me. So I mought as well give up. She loves singing, and I ain't got nothing but a squeak."

"Oh, don't talk that a' way," says Mr. Dog, tho' he is glad Mr. Rabbit can't sing none.

"Thass all right, Brer Dog. But if I had a sweet voice like you got, I'd have it worked on and make it sweeter."

"How! How! How!" Mr. Dog cried, jumping up and down.

"Lemme fix it for you, like I do for Sister Lark and Sister Mocking-bird."

"When? Where?" asked Mr. Dog, all excited. He was figuring that if he could sing just a little better Miss Coon would be bound to have him.

"Just you meet me t'morrer in de huckleberry patch," says the rabbit and off they both goes to bed.

The dog is there on time next day and after a while the rabbit comes loping up.

"Mawnin', Brer Dawg," he says kinder chippy like. "Ready to git yo' voice sweetened?"

"Sholy, sholy, Brer Rabbit. Let's we all hurry about it. I wants tuh serenade Miss Nancy from de piney woods tuh night."

"Well, den, open yo' mouf and poke out yo' tongue," says the rabbit.

No sooner did Mr. Dog poke out his tongue than Mr. Rabbit split it with a knife and ran for all he was worth to a hollow stump and hid hisself.

The dog has been mad at the rabbit ever since.

Anybody who don't believe it happened, just look at the dog's tongue and he can see for himself where the rabbit slit it right up the middle.

STEPPED ON A TIN, MAH STORY ENDS.

Book of Harlem

1. A pestilence visiteth the land of Hokum, and the people cry out. 4. Toothsome, a son of Georgia, returns from Babylon, and stirreth up the Hamites. 10. Mandolin heareth him and resolveth to see Babylon. 11. He convinceth his father and departs for Babylon. 21. A red-cap toteth his bag, and utterth blasphemy against Mandolin. 26. He lodgeth with Toothsome, and trieth to make the females of Harlem, but is scorned by them. 28. One frail biddeth him sit upon a tack. 29. He taketh council with Toothsome and is comforted. 33. He goeth to an hall of dancing, and meeting a damsel there, shaketh vehemently with her. 42. He discloseth himself to her and she telleth him what to read. 46. He becometh Panic, and quoteth poetry. 51. Toothsome cometh to him with a question, and is satisfied.

1. And in those days when King Volstead sat upon the throne in Hokum, then came a mighty drought upon his land, and many cried out in agony thereof.

2. Then did the throat parch and the tongue was thrust into the cheek of many voters.

3. And men grew restless and went up and down in the land saying, "We are verily the dry-bones of which the prophet Ezekiel prophesied."

4. Then returned one called Toothsome unto his town of Standard Bottom, which is in the province of Georgia. And he was of the tribe of Ham.

5. And his raiment was very glad, for he had sojourned in the city of Babylon, which is ruled by the tribe of Tammany. And his garments putteth out the street lamps, and the Vaseline upon his head, yea verily the slickness thereof did outshine the sun at noonday.

6. And the maidens looked upon him and were glad, but the men gnasheth together their bridgework at [the] sight of him. But they drew near to him and listened to his accounts of the doings of Babylon, for they all yearned unto that city.

7. And the mouth of Toothsome flapped loudly and fluently in the marketplace, and the envy of his hearers increased an hundredfold.

8. Then stood one youth before him, and his name was called Mandolin. And he questioned Toothsome eagerly, asking 'how come,' and 'wherefore' many times.

9. And Toothsome answered him according to his wit. Moreover he said unto the youth, "Come thou also to the city as unto the ant, and consider her ways and be wise."

10. And the heart of Mandolin was inflamed, and he stood before his father and said, "I beseech thee now, papa, to give unto me my portion that I may go hence to great Babylon and see life."

11. But his father's heart yearned towards him, and he said, "Nay, my son, for Babylon is full of wickedness, and thou art but a youth."

12. But Mandolin answered him saying, "I crave to gaze upon its sins. What do you think I go to see, an prayer-meeting?"

13. But his father strove with him and said, "Why dost thou crave Babylon when Gussie Smith, the daughter of our neighbor, will make thee a good wife? Tarry now and take her to wife, for verily she is a mighty biscuit cooker before the Lord."

14. Then snorted Mandolin with scorn and said, "What care I for biscuit-cookers when there be Shebas of high voltage on every street in Harlem? For verily man liveth not on bread alone, but by every drop of banana oil that drippeth from the tongue of the lovely."

15. Then strove they together all night. But at daybreak did Mandolin touch the old man on the hip, yea verily upon the pocket-bearing joint, and triumphed.

16. So the father gave him his blessing, and he departed out of Standard Bottom on his journey to Babylon.

17. And he carried with him of dreams of forty-and-four thousand, and of wishes of ten thousands, and of hopes ten thousands.

18. But of tears or sorrows carried he none out of all that land. Neither bore he any fears away with him.

19. And journeyed he many days upon the caravan of steel, and came at last unto the city of Babylon, and got him down within the place.

20. Then rushed there many upon him who wore scarlet caps upon the head, saying, "Porter? Shall I tote thy bags for thee?"

21. And he marvelled greatly within himself, saying, "How charitably are the Babylonians, seeing they permit no stranger to tote his own bag! With what great kindness am I met!"

22. And he suffered one to prevail and tote his bag for him. Moreover he questioned him concerning the way to Harlem which is a city of Ham in Babylonia.

23. And when he of the scarlet cap had conducted Mandolin unto a bus, then did Mandolin shake hands with him and thank him greatly for his kindness, and stepped upon the chariot as it rolled away, and took his way unto Harlem.

24. Then did the bag-toter blaspheme greatly, saying, "Oh, the cock-eyed son of a wood louse! Oh, the hawg! Oh, the sea-buzzard! Oh, the splay-footed son of a doodle bug and cock-roach! What does he take me for? The mule's daddy! The clod-hopper! If only I might lay my hands upon him, verily would I smite him, yea, until he smelt like onions!"

25. But Mandolin journeyed on to Harlem, knowing none of these things.

26. And when he came unto the place, he lodged himself with Toothsome, and was glad.

27. And each evening stood he before the Lafayette Theatre and a-hemmed at the knees that passed, but none took notice of him. Moreover flashed he the chicken feed which he possessed, but none turned the head except to snigger at him.

28. Moreover, one frail of exceeding sassiness bade him go to and cook an radish, and seat himself upon an tack, which being interpreted is slander.

29. Then went he unto his roommate and saith, "How now doth the damsel think me? Have I not a smiling countenance, and coin in my jeans? My heart is heavy for I sojourned in Harlem for many weeks, but as yet I have spoken to no female."

30. Then spoke Toothsome, and answered him saying, "Seek not swell Shebas in mail-order britches. Go thou into the marketplace and get thee Oxford bags and jacket thyself likewise. Procure thee shoes and socks. Yea, anoint thy head with oil until it runneth over so that thou not dare hurl thyself into bed unless thou wear weed chains upon the head, lest thou skid out again.

31. Moreover lubricate thy tongue with banana oil, for from the oily lips proceedth the breath of love."

32. And Mandolin hastened to do all that his counselor bade him.

33. Then hied him to the hall of dancing where many leaped with the cymbal, and shook with the drums.

34. And his belly was moved, for he saw young men seize upon damsels and they stood upon the floor and "messed around" meanly. Moreover many "bumped" them vehemently. Yea, there were those among him who shook with many shakings.

35. And when he saw all of these things, Mandolin yearned within his heart to do likewise, but as yet he had spoken to no maiden.

36. But one damsel of scarlet lips smiled broadly upon him, and encouraged him with her eyes, and the water of his knees turned to bone, and he drew nigh unto her.

37. And his mouth flew open and he said, "See now how the others do dance with the cymbal and the harp, yea even the saxophone? Come thou and let us do likewise."

38. And he drew her and they stood upon the floor. Now this maiden was a mighty dancer before the Lord; yea of the mightiest of all the tribe of Ham. And the shakings of the others was as one stricken with paralysis beside a bowl of gelatine. And the heart of the youth leaped for joy.

39. And he was emboldened, and his mouth flew open and the banana oil did drip from his lips, yea even down to the floor, and the maiden was moved.

40. And he said, "Thou sure art propaganda! Yea, verily thou shakest a wicked ankle."

41. And she being pleased, answered him, "Thou art some sheik thyself. I do shoot a little pizen to de ankle if I do say so myself. Where hast thou been all my life that I have not seen thee?"

42. Then did his mouth fly open, and he told her everything of Standard Bottom, Georgia, and of Babylon, and of all those things which touched him.

43. And her heart yearned towards him, and she resolved to take him unto herself and to make him wise.

44. And she said unto him, "Go thou and buy the books and writings of certain scribes and Pharisees which I shall name

unto you, and thou shalt learn everything of good and evil. Yea, thou shalt learn as much as the Chief of Niggerati, who is called Carl Van Vetchen."

45. And Mandolin diligently sought all these books and writings that he was bidden, and read them.

46. Then he was sought for all feasts, and stomps, and shakings, and none was complete without him. Both on 139th street and on Lenox avenue he was sought, and his fame was great.

47. And his name became Panic, for they asked one or the other, "Is he not a riot in all that he doeth?"

48. Then did he devise poetry, and played it upon the piano, saying,

"Skirt by skirt on every flirt
They're getting higher and higher
Day by day in every way
There's more to admire
Sock by sock and knee by knee
The more they show, the more we see
The skirts run up, the socks run down
Jingling bells run round and round
Oh week by week, and day by day
Let's hope that things keep on this way
Let's kneel right down and pray."

49. And the women all sought him, the damsels and the matrons and the grandmothers and all those who wear the skirt, and with them his name was continually Panic.

50. And all the men sought him because his raiment was such that all knew from them the styles which would come to pass.

51. And he roomed no more with Toothsome, but had unto himself swell lodgings. But one day Toothsome sought him and asked,

52. "How now dost thou come to Harlem and become Panic unto the virgin, and the matron, and the grandmatron, and unto the sheik and the Niggerati (which being interpreted means Negro literati) and unto all those above 125th street? In all my years in Babylon none has called me thus."

53. And Mandolin, who is called Panic, answered him, "In my early days in Babylon was I taught to subscribe to *Vanity Fair*, and to read it diligently, for no man may know his way about Babylon without it."

54. Then did a great light dawn upon him called Toothsome, and he rushed forth to subscribe to the perfect magazine.

55. And of his doings and success after that, is it not written in the Book of Harlem?

The Book of Harlem

CHAPTER I.

1. Jazzbo counteth the shekels of his father and resolveth to depart for Harlem. 10. Whamm blesseth him. 14. He cometh to Harlem. 18. He learneth modern ways and disporteth himself.

1. Now in those days did one who had travelled far return unto his native land, even Waycross, Georgia, and say unto the youths thereof: hearken and behold for I have travelled much, even to great Babylon, and to a division of that city called Harlem, and beheld there many browns of exceeding sharpness, yea even pink mamas of beauty that maketh the heart glad.

2. Thus spake he, and moreover told them many things that made their hearts burn within them with envy of him.

3. And many yearned to go forth as he did to the great Babylon, but they lacked shekels of silver and the greens of sufficient length to provide transportation thereto.

4. But came one called Jazzbo, the son of Whamm, and hearkened unto the one who spake unto them and he said in his heart that he would go, for Whamm had many shekels.

5. Then spake he to his father thus: "lo, I am become a man. Shall I not go forth and seek my fortune, and perchance find a maiden of exceeding virtue that I may take her to wife?"

6. "Perhaps," saith his father, "but wherefore goeth thou to a far city to seek a wife among Jezebels, when there be Cora, thy neighbor's daughter, a damsel of great piety, who wilt bear thee many sons, and moreover, she is a mighty biscuit-cooker before the Lord."

7. Then did Jazzbo stand before his father and snort with scorn, saying, "Wherefore must I wed a cooker of biscuits when I crave not bread? Behold, man was not made to live by bread alone, but upon every thrill that proceedeth from life. Go to, now, wherefore should I marry that drink of boiled water, when in great Babylon there are females that are as a cocktail to the tonsils?"

8. When Whamm heard all this, then did he rend his garments, for he was greatly troubled.

9. Then when he had yielded, did Jazzbo ask of him a mighty check, saying that the squabs and chickens of Harlem would require corn. But Whamm understood none of these sayings and puzzled greatly.

10. But the next morning he arose and gave Jazzbo the check and sent him away.

11. Then hastened the young man to Babylon, and descended at a great meeting place of trains called Pennsylvania Station, and there fell many porters upon him, even those who wear the cap of scarlet upon the head, crying, "Porter? Gimme

that bag that I may bear it for thee." And they strove among themselves, but one prevailed and bore his baggage for him.

12. And when they had come outside the station to the chariot called the bus, then did Jazzbo shake the extended hand of the porter and thank him earnestly, for his great kindness, and he marveled at the great attention and favor shown the comer to Babylon, and seeing that the chariot moved away, he mounted himself with all his upon it and rode away, leaving naught of tips behind him.

13. Then did the porter grow full of wrath and utter many blasphemies concerning Jazzbo, saying, "The low-down son of a cockroach! What does the splay-footed son of a woodlouse take me for? The bastard!" And many other blasphemies did he utter, but Jazzbo heard none of these things for he was on his route to the great Harlem.

14. And when he had sojourned among the Harlemites for a space, he went forth upon the streets of the city and gazed upon the damsels, and behold, they were fair, and Jazzbo's heart was glad within him that he had come.

15. And he smiled upon many as they passed, for verily the green of his father, yea, even his shekels, burned his pockets, and he said 'ahem' and cleared his throat at many but none smiled upon him. But one maiden of great sassiness turned upon him and bade him go and cook a radish and he went home with his heart heavy within him.

16. Then spake he to his room-mate and said, "Alas I have journeyed to rejoice with the maidens, but as yet none have smiled

upon me. Have I not shekels in my pockets? Am I not young? Have I the face of a monkey that none wilt flirt with me[?] O sleeper on the bed next to mine, tell me how come!"

17. Then did his room-mate enlighten him, saying, "Seek not a swell sheba in mail-order britches. Go to, get thyself Oxford bags of exceeding bagginess, and procure thyself much haberdashery. Moreover, seek out the shop of hair cutting and those that do massage and manicure, and see that thy hair is of such slickness that thou dare not hurl thyself into the bed lest thou wear weed chains, for verily thou shalt skid out again. Then hie thee to the halls of dancing, even the tabernacles of jazz, and there learn to wiggle thy ankles, meanly. Moreover oil thy tongue with bananas, and gargle thy throat with flapdoodle so that verily a line shall proceed from thy mouth every time thou come into the presence of females. Then shall the damsels prize thee mightily and fawn upon thee, and shall say thou art sharp as a tack. Then take thou thy choice, for thou art young and full of manly beauty."

18. Jazzbo did all these things that his friend counseled him and when he gazed upon himself in the glass, he leaped for joy.

19. Then came he to the hall of dancing, and heard there many horns that hooted and wailed, and the snort of drums and the clang of cymbals. And his foot awoke and patted the floor unceasingly and he beat upon his breast because he knew not how to dance.

20. There came to him waiters, even those who serve upon the table, and angered him with their overcharging and impudence, for their heads are made of wood, but verily their tongues are made of brass.

21. Now, when the trumpets sounded, even the saxophones, then the multitude arose, two by two and stood upon the floor and shook with many shakings.

22. And some there were who jigg-walked with spirit, and some among them who performed the mess-around with great vehemence, and yet others who bumped-the-bump meanly with beautiful maidens and bumped them even to the Baltimore bump and were glad.

23. Then did Jazzbo yearn within his liver and tear his hair because he knew not how to do thus.

24. But a maiden with pomegranate lips called to him with her eyes and they said, 'come let us also stand upon the floor and do thus,' but he was afraid. Nevertheless went he over and stood before her and said, "Wilt thou forgive thy servant for being so brash as to speak to thee without an introduction?"

25. But the maiden's lips brushed aside his murmurings and they stood upon the floor and she taught him many dances and they bumped meanly together with great accord, yea, messed around.

26. And the maiden parked her head upon his shoulder and his mouth flew open and he told her all about his father's shekels, and she loved him. Then did he oil his jaws with banana oil and delight her ears so that she dreamed of coats of the fur of mink and sedans of twelve cylinders, and fine jewels and costly raiment. But he sheiked her thus to air out his line of stuff, and when he saw that it worked, he was glad. So they both returned to their abode and were satisfied.

27. Then he thought no more of her and when the night came again, went to another tabernacle of joy and did the same. Thus did he for many nights.

28. Then when he had dwelt in the land of the Harlemites for many months and had learned many things, even to wise-cracking, then did he forget that he was a hick (which being interpreted, means dweller-in-the-tall-grass), and he read diligently the chronicles of his fathers, and they were full of begats, and resolved within his heart to take unto himself a wife and begat sons and daughters to inherit his shekels after him.

29. Then he opened his mouth and said unto his room-mate, even he who slept on the next bed, "Tell me how I shall find a maiden, one of exceeding virtue, that I may take her to wife? And how shall the Lord reveal to me that she is an virgin, that I may know?"

30. "Ha! Ask the maiden herself, and she shall tell thee." Thus spake his friend without laughter and Jazzbo was satisfied. For he knew, now, many beautiful maidens who pleased him and he said, "Truly man lives not by bread alone, but by every drop of banana oil that falls from the lips of the lovely."

31. And it came to pass that that very night he called upon a damsel of great beauty and he asked her if she be a virgin and she answered him yes, and so they were married and he bought her fur of the mink, and much fine raiment and a sedan of twelve cylinders, and for many years they kept a cat and a poodle.

SELAH

The Back Room

Lilya Barkman, born Lillie Barker, stood in the little alcove just off her luxurious parlor. She was looking at a large oil painting of herself, and a man stood beside her, looking and admiring.

"You always were a peach, Lilya, and Porter David has you on the canvas as you are. When you grow old, if you ever do, you can take pleasure in showing the world that you had the world in a jug once."

"Bill Cameron, I ask you with my feet turned out if that is nice. You know how I hate discussing age. I'm going to be young till I'm ninety, then I'm going to turn to something good to eat—never going to be old. That is why I haven't married, it ages a woman so—worrying with a house and husband at the same time."

Dr. Cameron looked at her roguishly and laughed. "Still you have a house and you seem to manage several men pretty well without leaving any traces of the wear and tear on your face. You haven't changed a bit in the ten or twelve years that I have known you."

"There you go at it again! Next thing you will say is that you can remember proposing to me when I was a girl."

"I did propose, some years ago, and you turned me down flat.

Everybody in Harlem knew that. It took me a long time to live down all the loving I had saved up for you. Say, when are you going to get married? Are you still kidding Bob Magee along? God, he hangs on well."

"Well, to tell you the truth, I don't know whether I love him or not. Seriously, now I guess I will marry him some day, if some man that I like better doesn't take me." She looked coyly out of the corner of her long eyes at the man beside her. "Then I'll retire, as it were, and use this back room for entertaining instead of the parlor. You know, Bill, I am secretly sentimental. This room is a shrine, dedicated to youth and beauty. I have this splendid portrait of myself wearing both, and when I cease to have it, I'll no longer need the big parlor anyway, so I won't stay on the battlefield to be trampled on by the new ones. I'll retire with all the honors of war to this little stronghold and live over my triumphs with someone who loves me. Doesn't that sound nice and peaceful?"

"Yes, it does. By the way, who is taking you to the Brooks' tonight?"

"Oh, er, well why don't you take me?"

"I'll be glad to—just like old times, eh, Lilya?"

"You bet. I never realized how much I enjoyed you until that other one grabbed you."

"But you had turned me down, Lilya, don't be spiteful."

"Yes, but she never waited till my tracks got cold before she had on the wedding ring."

"Dog in the manger! Well, she's dead now, so let's don't talk about it. I'll be here for you at nine—how's that."

"All rightie, Bill."

She sent him away with one of her warmest smiles and began laying out gowns. It was only six o'clock, but she always made a careful toilet, and tonight she meant to be killing.

She started the water to running in the tub and thrust back her well groomed hair under a stocking cap, peering at herself in the mirror as she did so. My she looked tired! And she had not been out at night for three days. She couldn't be getting old, surely! She took her long-handled mirror and rushed into the alcove and alternately studied the portrait and herself. From the canvas a pair of long, full-lashed eyes, a little mystic a little glowing, looked everywhere and nowhere out of a creamy face with a metallic glow beneath the soft downiness. Europe and Africa warred in her face, a Grecian nose about a full, luscious mouth with a blue-black cloud of curly hair falling well below the waist.

Her own face showed tiny lines that seemed to crowd up and shrink the eyes, the lips losing some of the bursting cherry freshness, a line or two from [the] corner of the mouth, hair a little tarnished, a figure growing just the tiniest bit fullish.

She all but screamed. God had been good to send Dr. Cameron back to her a wealthy widower when she needed him most. She was telling the truth when she said that she had really wanted him after she had lost him eight years before. Well, she had had her fun and she was glad that she had not let Bob Magee worry her into marriage. He had stuck to his guns well, though, nine years. Whew! He must be about forty and she was thirty-eight, though she never declared a day over twenty-five. A few people knew she was more, but never put her past thirty. If she didn't land Cameron, then Magee's law practice was good, and he was attractive enough, simply couldn't stir a thing inside her. She shut off the bath and went to the telephone.

"Morningside 0000 * * * Yes, Bob, this is Lilya * * * Yes, how did you know? * * * What's that? Ha! Ha! Be your age, Bob * * * Nonsense, I—I just can't see you tonight. Oh, we'll let the old party go. I don't care so much about the Brooks' anyway, and I have a toothache * * * Oh, just a little, don't bother. No, you can't come over. NO! Now I must run and see about [my] bath, yes water running, g'bye, oh, shucks, Goodbye."

There! That left her a clear field for the evening so that she could concentrate on Bill. If she landed him, of course she would, what was he back from Pittsburgh for if not to see her? It would make no difference if Bob did hear she was at the party, if she didn't, she could explain anything to him. People of Harlem said that she could show him a lump of coal and make him see pink. She laughed to herself. "Heads I win, tails I grab it."

West 139th Street at ten p.m. Rich fur wraps tripping up the steps of the well furnished home in the 200 block. Sedans, coaches, coupes, roadsters. Inside fine gowns and tuxedos, marcel waves and glitter. People who seemed to belong to every race on earth—Harlem's upper class had gathered there her beauty and chivalry.

And Lilya Barkman shone and glittered with the rest. A careful massage had thrown back the clock for the moment. Dr. Cameron was very courteous. People raised the brow on seeing them together and wagged the head. As soon as she came down from the cloakroom he led her to a beautiful girl who looked about seventeen and introduced them.

"Lilya, this is my little niece, and I have come over here to see if I couldn't get her in Barnard. Mary Ann, this is Miss Barkman, an old friend of mine."

So that was the thing that had brought him to New York! She took her cue—she would be nice to Mary Ann. What a name! But she told her that she loved it and the child warmed up to her at once.

At eleven Bob walked in. He was furious, she could see that at once. Looked as if he would stride over and beat her with his fists. But he was too polished to be other than polite. He looked wonderful in his dinner jacket. As soon as she could do so with ease, she went to him and tried to smooth him down and succeeded, partially.

"I saw through your toothache right away," he told her under his breath, "I had seen Bill Cameron, you know." She laughed like a child, and he almost forgave her.

"Stop growling, big, good looking bear, Lilya's big caveman. You make poor little me terribly afraid of you. He dragged me up here to meet his little niece, there she is over there by the piano, she's cute and I'll let you dance with her if you stop frowning."

She introduced them and flew back to Dr. Cameron, just in time to see him dance off with someone else. Bob and Mary Ann passed her doing a stiff and chaste fox-trot, she refused to dance and sat out the number. Bill came to her after the third dance and they got on well.

Twelve o'clock. Formality had been rubbed off, everybody was being their own age or under. Everybody being modern. Cigarettes burning like fireflies on a summer night. A Charleston contest with a great laundry show. Hey! Hey! Powder gone, but a lively prettiness taking its place. A wealthy woman in the foolish forties giggling on the shoulder of a twenty-year-old. He is amusing himself by giving her what he calls a good sheiking as they dance around. They are bumping and she is panting a laugh at every bump. Businessman near fifty dancing with a sweet young thing with a short dress and her knees rouged.

"You are dancing too close," she protests.

"No I'm not, you little devil! G'wan and let my knees get a little sociable with yours."

Hey, Hey, Flinging the Charleston high and wide. A well known singer begins doing the black bottom by spanking the can.

"What makes you hold me so close? I won't dance with you if you don't behave," the bare-kneed girl threatens.

"It's not my fault. Every time my feet see pretty pink knees, they get social inclinations and bring me on the run. Can't be helped, girlie. S'too bad."

Dr. Cameron continues to rush Lilya. Bob sticks to Mary Ann out of pique and glowers at Lilya occasionally.

Crowd grows noisier. Cocktails aplenty. Punch bowl always full. Good food, good liquor, pretty women, good-looking men, and Lilya was in the center of it all with Bill, laughing like the rest, doing like the rest, and keeping what she had seen that evening in the looking glass hidden way down beneath her laughter. She played this game, that meant so much to her, faultlessly. But then she had always played a compelling hand at love. She always won, people expected it.

One o'clock. Somebody said cabaret. Scrambling into wraps and on to Smalls. All but Lilya and Cameron.

"No, Lilya, don't go there. Let's go to your house—I want to talk over something with you."

"Oh, all right, Bill. What about Mary Ann? What a delightful name for a pretty girl!"

"Er—er, can she spend the night with you? I had thought of leaving her where she is, but I'd feel better if she was with you."

That was arranged just as Mary came running up, dragging Bob after her. "OOH, Unkie, can I go to the cabaret with everyone else and Mr. Magee?"

"No, I 'er—Oh, he doesn't want to be bothered with you. Come on, you're going to spend the night with Miss Barkman."

"Oh, I'd love to take her, Bill, she's doing me a favor."

Lilya smiled down in her fur collar at his tone. Trying to punish her, eh? Wait till the bomb she was slipping under him went off! She spoke up game as he—"Oh, let her go, Bill. Bob will look after her." Served him right! She'd make a nurse maid out of him for trying to be smart.

So Bob was dragged away by the screamingly happy Mary Ann and Dr. Cameron and Lilya went home.

She lit the gas logs and made cocoa and they sat down to talk.

"You know, Lilya, I am so happy that you took to Mary. I want her to enjoy her school life here in New York, and you can be a sort of big sister to her. Would you have her here with you in case I can't get her into the dormitories?"

"I'd just love it, Bill."

"Gee, I'm glad that's settled. The other thing may seem sorter silly to you, but I don't know. We live by our hearts after all, don't we?"

"Surely, Bill."

"Well, I'm thinking of getting married again and I have had Mary Ann since her mother died three years ago, and, er, the woman I am going to marry doesn't get on with Mary very well. Oh, she's a lovely creature otherwise—just seems to strike fire out of Mary everytime they meet. Funny isn't it?"

Lilya agreed that it was and laughed a little to prove that she was amused. She had a bad time of it. All she could do was to set her face in a laughing grimace and keep it that way until Bill bade her a grateful goodbye.

As soon as the door closed after him, she flung herself upon the couch in the alcove, beneath the lovely portrait of her as she had been. A marvelous piece of work by a painter who never became known, but would have been if he had not met Lilya Barkman just after she had fled the boredom of a small South Carolina town. Her beauty not only captured his brush, he willingly laid down his palette before the altar of love and died two deaths.

It was a long time before the bell rang flippantly, as if the ringer was unmindful [of] all emotion save his own. She went to the front door slowly and saw dimly through the ground glass, a double shadow. Surely Bob wasn't kissing Mary! She opened the door softly, not to spy, but because in her present mood she didn't want to talk. Tomorrow, she would get Bob on the wire and straighten things up, and get married right away, so people wouldn't think too much of seeing her and Bill together.

She need not have tipped, for they never heard her. Bob was kissing Mary Ann in a full blown fashion and she was kissing back with all herself. Lilya went back to her couch and turned her eyes up to the fresh, young face on the canvas. "Well, what are you going to do about it?" she asked the pictured one belligerently. But the face seemed to mock her and say, "I am youth, and beauty. I know nothing, feel nothing, except the things that belong to me."

She heard them tiptoe into the parlor. Sorter muffled giggles of ecstasy. She heard Bob's big, booming voice trying to whisper. That voice that was so magnificent, that swayed so many juries, saying, "I kiss one 'ittle finger, two 'ittle finger, three 'ittle finger, and put on the ring. Say, I'll have to tie this big thing of mine on until tomorrow, then Tiffany is going to fix one for papa's kitten. Baby, tell Bobby when you found out you loved him."

"The very first minute you came in the door, big, brave stupid. I was trembling 'cause I was scared you'd never see me."

"A big fool, I was looking somewhere else. I found out while I was helping you out of the cab at Smalls. Gee, it's late, darling, I think you had better call Lilya, er, Miss Barkman so I can say goodnight. Tiffany's at two, now don't forget."

Lilya called out from the couch, "I won't come in, Bob, goodnight."

Monkey Junk

1. And it came to pass in those days that one dwelt in the land of Harlemites who thought that he knew all the law and the prophets.

* * *

2. Also when he arose in the morning and at noonday his mouth flew open and he said, "Verily, I am a wise guy. I knoweth all about women."

* * *

3. And in the cool of the evening he saith and uttereth, "I know all there is about the females. Verily I shall not let myself be married."

* * *

4. Thus he counselled within his liver for he was persuaded that merry maidens were like unto death for love of him.

* * *

5. But none desired him.

* * *

6. And in that same year a maiden gazeth upon his checkbook and she coveted it.

* * *

7. Then became she coy and sweet with flattery and he swalloweth the bait.

* * *

8. And in that same month they became man and wife.

* * *

9. Then did he make a joyful noise, saying, "Behold, I have chosen a wife, yea verily a maiden I have exalted above all others, for see I have wed her."

* * *

10. And he gave praises loudly unto the Lord, saying, "I thank you that I am not as other men—stupid and blind and imposed by every female that listeth. Behold how diligently I have sought and winnowed out the chaff from the wheat! Verily have I chosen well, and she shalt be rewarded for her virtue, for I shall approve and honor her."

* * *

11. And for an year did he wooed her with his shekels and comfort her with his checkbook and she endured him.

* * *

12. Then did his hand grow weary of check signing and he slackened his speed.

* * *

13. Then did his pearl of great price form the acquaintance of many men and they prospered her.

* * *

14. Then did he wax wrathful in his heart because other men posed the tongue in the cheek and snickered behind the hand as he passed, saying, "Verily his head is decorated with the horns, he that is so wise and knoweth all the law and the prophets."

* * *

16. And he chided his wife saying, "How now dost thou let others less worthy bite thy husband in the back? Verily now I am sore and I meaneth not maybe."

* * *

17. But she answered him laughingly saying, "Speak not out of turn. Thou wast made to sign checks, not to make love signs. Go now, and broil thyself an raddish."

* * *

18. Then answered he, "Thy tongue doth drip sassiness and thy tongue impudence, no ye not that I shall leave thee?"

* * *

19. But she answered him with much gall, "Thou canst not do better than to go—but see that thou leave behind thee many signed checks."

* * *

20. And, when he heard these things, did he gnash his teeth and sweat great hunks of sweat.

* * *

21. And he answered, "Verily I am through with thee—thou canst NOT snore in my ear no more."

* * *

22. Then placeth she her hands upon the hip and sayeth, "Let not that lie get out, for thou art NOT through with me."

* * *

23. And he answered her saying, "Thou hast flirted copiously and surely the back-biters shall sign thy checks henceforth—for I am through with thee."

* * *

24. But she answered him, "Nay, thou art not through with me—for I am a darned sweet woman and thou knowest it.

Don't let that lie get out. Thou shalt never be through with me as long as thou hath bucks."

* * *

25. "Thou are very dumb for now that I, thy husband, knoweth that thou art a flirt, making glad the heart of back-biters, I shall support thee no more—for verily I know ALL the law and the prophets thereof."

* * *

26. Then answered she with a great sassiness of tongue, "Neither shalt not deny me thy shekels for I shall seek them in law, yea shall I lift up my voice and the lawyers and judges shall hear my plea and thou shalt pay dearly. For verily they permit no turpitudinous mama to suffer. Selah and amen."

* * *

27. But he laughed at her saying hey! hey! hey! many times for verily he considered with his kidneys that he knew his rights.

* * *

28. Then went she forth to the market place and sought the places that deal in fine raiment and bought silken linen, yea lingerie and hosiery of fine silk, for she knew in her heart that she must sit in the seat and witness and hear testimony to things lest she get no alimony.

* * *

29. Even of French garters bought she the finest.

* * *

30. Then hastened she away to the houses where sat Pharisees and Sadducees and those who know the law and the prophets and one among them was named Miles Paige, him being a young man of fair countenance.

* * *

31. And she wore her fine raiment and wept mightily as she told of her wrongs.

* * *

32. But he said unto her, "Thou has not much of a case, but I shall try it for thee. But practice not upon me neither with tears nor with hosiery—for verily I be not a doty juryman. Save thy raiment for the courts."

* * *

33. But her husband sought no counsel for he said, "Surely she hath sinned against me—even cheated most vehemently. Shall not the court rebuke her when I shall tell of it. For verily I know also the law."

* * *

34. Then came the office of the court and said, "Though shalt give thy wife temporary alimony of fifty shekels until the trial cometh."

* * *

35. And he was wrathful but he wagged the head and said, "I pay now, but after the trial I shall pay no more. He that laughest last is worth two in the bush."

* * *

36. And entered he boldly into the courts of law and sat down at the trial. And his wife and her lawyer came also.

* * *

37. But he looked upon the young man and laughed, for Miles Paige had yet no beard and the husband looked upon him with scorn, even as Goliath looked upon David.

* * *

38. And the judge sat upon the high seat and the jury sat in the box and many came to see and to hear, and the husband rejoiced within his heart for the multitude would hear him speak and confound the learned doctors.

* * *

39. Then called he witnesses and they did testify that the wife was an flirt. And they sat upon the stand again and the young Pharisee, even Paige questioned them, and verily they were steadfast.

* * *

40. Then did the husband rejoice exceedingly and ascended the stand and testified to his great goodness unto his spouse.

* * *

41. And when the young lawyer asked no questions he waxed stiff necked for he divined that he was afraid.

* * *

42. And the young man led the wife upon the stand and she sat upon the chair of witnesses and bear testimony.

* * *

43. And she gladdened the eyes of the jury and the judge leaned down from his high seat and beamed upon her for verily she was some brown.

* * *

44. And she turned soulful eyes about her and all men yearned to fight for her.

* * *

45. Then did she testify and cross the knees, even the silk covered joints, and weep. For verily she spoke of great evils visited upon her.

* * *

46. And the young Pharisee questioned her gently and the jury leaneth forward to catch every word which fell from her lips.

* * *

47. For verily her lips were worth it.

* * *

48. Then did they all glare upon the husband; yea the judge and jury frowned upon the wretch, and would have choked him.

* * *

49. And when the testimony was finished and she had descended from the stand, did the young man, even Miles Paige, stand before the jury and exhort them.

* * *

50. Saying, "When in the course of human events, Romeo, Romeo, wherefore art thou and how come what for?" And many other sayings of exceeding wiseness.

* * *

51. Then began the jury to foam at the mouth and went the judge into centrance. Moreover made the lawyer many gestures which confounded the multitude, and many cried, "Amen" to his sayings.

* * *

52. And when he had left off speaking then did the jury cry out "Alimony (which being interpreted means all his jack) aplently!"

* * *

53. And the judge was pleased and said, "An hundred shekels per month."

* * *

54. Moreover did he fine the husband heavily for his cruelties and abuses and his witnesses for perjury.

* * *

55. Then did the multitude rejoice and say, "Great is Miles Paige, and mighty is the judge and jury."

* * *

56. And then did the husband rend his garments and cover his head with ashes for he was undone.

* * *

57. But privately he went to her and said, "Surely, thou hast tricked me and I am undone by thy guile. Wherefore, now should I not smite thee, even mash thee in the mouth with my fist?"

* * *

58. And she answered him haughtily saying, "Did I not say that thou wast a dumb cluck? Go to, now, thou had better not touch this good brown skin."

* * *

59. And he full of anger spoke unto her, "But I shall surely smite thee in the nose—how doth old heavy hitting papa talk?"

* * *

60. And she made answer unto him, "Thou shalt surely go to the cooler if thou stick thy rusty fist in my face, for I shall holler like a pretty white woman."

* * *

61. And he desisted. And after many days did he recieve a letter saying, "Go to the monkeys, thou hunk of mud, and learn things and be wise."

* * *

62. And he returned unto Alabama to pick cotton.

SELAH

The Country in the Woman

Looka heah Cal'line, you oughta stop dis heah foolishness you got. Youse in New Yawk now—you aint down in Florida. Thaas just what Ah say—you kin git a woman out de country, but you can't git a country out de woman."

The woman, Caroline Potts, in sloppy clothes and run-down shoes, was standing arrogantly akimbo at Seventh Avenue and 134th Street. She was standing between her husband, Mitchell Potts, and a woman, heavy built and stylish in a Lenox Avenue way.

The woman was easing on down 134th Street away from the threatening black eyes of Caroline. Mitchell wanted to vanish, too, but his wife was blocking his way. He didn't know whether to run, to fight or to cajole, for Caroline was as temperamental as Mercury. Nobody ever knew how she would take things. Back in the Florida village from which they had migrated, Caroline Potts and her doings were the chief topics of conversation. Whatever she did was original. Mitchell was always having a side gal and Caroline was always catching him. No one besides her husband believed that she was jealous. She had an uncultivated sense of humor. She enjoyed the situation. Men and women behave so queerly when caught red-handed at anything. Sometimes when they expected fight she laughed and passed on. Sometimes she thought out ingenious embarrassing situations and engineered the two into them, with all the cruelty of the rural.

Her body was wiry and tough as nails and she could hold up her end of the argument anytime in a rough and tumble with her husband, so he couldn't hope to settle things that way. All these things were in Mitchell's mind as he faced her on Seventh Avenue. He saw a number of people crowding around them and he was eager to be going.

"Les us g'wan home, Cal'line."

"You wuznt headed dat way when ah met you."

"Yes, ah wuz, too. Ah just walked a piece of de way wid Lucy Taylor."

"You done walked enough 'pieces' wid dat 'oman to carry you back down home."

Mitchell caught her arm cajolingly. "Aw come on, dese heah folks is all standin' round trying to git into mine and yo' bizness."

She permitted herself to be led, but before she moved she let out: "Maybe dat hussy think she's a big hen's biddy but she don't lay no gobbler eggs. She might be a big cigar, but I sho kin smoke her. The very next time she gits in my way, I'll kick her clothes up round her neck like a horse collar. She'll think lightnin' struck her all right, now."

All of which was very delectable to the ears of the crowd on the street but "pizen" to Mitchell. He led her away to their flat in the "Caribbean Forties" with as much anxiety as if she had been so much trinitrotoluol.

There she grew as calm as if nothing had happened and cooked him a fine dinner which they still spoke of as supper.

After which he felt encouraged to read her a lecture on getting the country out of the woman.

"Lissen, Cal'line, you oughten ack lak you did today. Folks up heah don't run after they husbands and carry on cause they sees him swappin' a few jokes wid another woman. You aint down in de basement no more—youse in New Yawk."

"Swappin' JOKES! So you tryin' to jerk de wool over MY eyes? New Yawk! Humph! Youse the same guy you wuz down home. You aint one bit different—aint nothin' changed but you clothes."

"How come YOU don't git YO'SELF some more? Ah sho is tired uh dat 'way-down-in-Dixie' look you totes."

"Who, me? Humph! Ah aint studying about all dese all-front-and-no-back colored folks up in Harlem. Ah totes de cash on MAH hip. Don't try to git 'way from de subjick. You better gimme dat 'oman if you don't want trouble outa me. Ah aint nobody's fool."

Mitchell jumped to his feet. "You aint going to show off on me in Harlem like you useder down home. Carryin' on and cuttin de fool! I'll take my fist to you."

"Yas, and if you do, ah'll up wid MAH fist and lamm you so hard you'll lay an egg. Don't you git ME mad, Mitchell Potts."

"Well, then you stop running down women like Lucy Taylor. She's a NICE woman. You just keep her name out yo' mouth. Fack is, you oughter be made to beg her pardon."

Caroline turned from the dishpan very cooly. That was just it—NOTHING seemed to stir her up. Even her anger seemed unemotional—a pretense the effort of a good performer.

"Ah let Lucy Taylor g'wan home today, an' didn't lay de weight of mah hand on her, so her egg-bag oughter rest easy. But don't you nor her try to bull-doze me; cause if you do, you'll meet your mammy drunk. Ah ain't gointer talk no mo."

They went to bed that night full of feelings. No one could know what the paradoxical Caroline had stewing inside her, but all who ran might read the heart of Mitchell.

His body was warm for Lucy Taylor with all the ardor of a new affair. Caroline's encounter had aroused his protective instinct too. Moreover he was mad clear through because his vanity was injured—all by this dark brown lump of country contrariness that was lying beside him in a yellow homespun nightgown. He wanted to feel his fist crashing against her jaw and forehead and see her hitting the floor time after time. But he knew he couldn't win that way. She was too tough. Every one of their battles had ended in a draw.

He thought too of the side gals he had had down in Florida and how his wife had not only worsted them, but had made them all—and HIM—low foolish.

1. Daisy Miller—he had bought her shoes—that which all rural ladies of pleasure crave—and Caroline had found out and had come out to a picnic where Daisy was fluttering triumphantly and had forced her to remove the shoes before everybody and walk back to town barefoot, while Caroline rode comfortably along in her buckboard with a rawhide whip dangling significantly from her masculine fist. Daisy was laughed out of town.

2. Delphine Hicks—Caroline had waited for her beside the church steps one First Sunday (big meeting day) and had thrown her to the ground and robbed the abashed vampire of her underthings. Billowy underclothes were the fashion and in addition Delphine was large. Caroline had seen fit to have her pony make the homeward trip with its hindquarters thrust into Delphine's ravished clothes.

3. She had removed a hat from the head of Della Clarke and had cleared her throat raucously and spat into it. She had then forced Della to put it back upon her head and wear it all during the big Odd Fellows barbecue and log-rolling.

Mitchell thought and his heart hardened. Everybody in the country cut the fool over husbands and wives—violence was the rule. But he was in New Yawk and—and—just let her start something!

Mitchell had changed. He loved Caroline in a way, but he wanted his fling, too. The country had cramped his style, but Harlem was big—Caroline couldn't keep up with him here. He looked the big town and tried hard to act it. After work, he affected Seventh Avenue corners and a man about town air. Silk Shebas, too; no cotton underwear for him.

Time went past in weekly chunks and Caroline said nothing more, and so Mitchell decided she had forgotten. He told the men at work about it and they all laughed and confessed the same sort of affairs, but they all added that their wives paid no attention.

"Man, you oughter make her stop that foolishness; she's up North now. Make her know it."

Mitchell felt vindicated and saw Lucy Taylor with greater frequency. Much silk underwear passed under the bridge and there was talk of a fur coat for Thanksgiving. But he had ceased to meet her in 134th Street. They switched to 132nd, between Seventh and Lenox.

Whenever they passed his friends before the poolroom at 132nd and Seventh, the men acted wisely, unknowing Caroline would never find out thru them, surely.

One Saturday near the middle of November, late in the afternoon, Mitchell strolled into the poolroom in the Lafayette building, with a natural muskrat coat over his arm.

"Hi, Mitch," a friend hailed him; "I see you got de herbs with you. Must be putting it over on your lifetime loud speaker."

"You talking outa turn, big boy. Come on outside."

They went out on the sidewalk.

"Say, Mitch, I didn't know you had it in you—you're a real big-timer! Whuts become of your wife lately?"

Mitchell couldn't resist a little swagger after the admiration in his friend's voice. He held up the coat for inspection.

"Smoke it over, kid. What you think of it? Set me back one hundred smackers—dat."

"Boy! It's there! Wife or your sweet-stuff?"

"You KNOW it's for Lucy. Dat wife of mine don't need no coat like dis. But, man, ah sho done tamed her. She don't dare stick her paddle in my boat no mo—done got some of dat country out of her."

"I'm glad to hear dat 'cause there aint no more like her no-wheres. Naw sir! Folks like her comes one at a time—like lawyer going to Heaven."

"Well, any of 'em will cool down after I massage their jaw wid mah African soup-bone, yessir! I knocks 'em into a good humor," Mitchell lied boldly. "Heah come Lucy, now. Oh boy! She sho is propaganda!"

"I'll say she's red hot—she just want don't for the red light!"

She came up smiling coyly as she noticed, in the order of their importance to her, the new fur coat, Mitchell's nifty suit and Mitchell.

"Well, so long Tweety, see you in the funny papers."

"So long, Mitch, I'll pick you up off the junk pile."

Lucy and the fur-bearing Mitchell strolled off down 132nd Street. It was nearly sundown and the sidewalk was becoming crowded.

About twenty minutes later the loungers were amazed to see a woman on Seventh Avenue strolling leisurely along with an axe over her shoulder. Tweety recognized Caroline and grew cold. Somehow she had found out and was in pursuit—with an axe! He grew cold with fear for Mitchell, but he hadn't the least idea which of the brownstone fronts hid the lovers. He tried to stop Caroline with conversation.

"Howdy do, Mrs. Potts; going to chop some wood?"

Very unemotionally, "Ah speck so."

"Ha, ha! You forgot you aint back down South don't you?"

"Nope. Theys wood to be chopped up North too," and she passed on, leaving the corner agog.

"Somebody ought to have stopped her. That female clod-hopper is going to split Mitch's head—and he's a good scout."

"We ought to call the police."

"Somebody ought to overtake her and take that axe away."

"Who for instance?"

So it rested there. No one felt like trying to take an axe from Caroline. She went on and they waited, full of anxiety.

A few minutes later they saw her returning just as leisurely, her wiry frame wrapped in the loose folds of a natural muskrat coat. Over her shoulder like a Roman lictor, she bore the axe, and from the head of it hung the trousers of Mitchell's natty suit, the belt buckle clacking a little in the breeze.

It was nearly five weeks—long after Thanksgiving—before the corner saw Mitchell again, and then he seemed a bit shy and diffident.

"Say, Mitch, where you been so long? And how's your sweet-stuff making it?"

"Oh Lucy? Aint seen her since the last time."

"How come—Y'all aint mad?"

"Naw, it's dat wife of mine. Ah caint git de country out dat woman. Lets go somewhere and get a drink."

The Gilded Six-Bits

It was a Negro yard around a Negro house in a Negro settlement that looked to the payroll of the G. and G. Fertilizer works for its support.

But there was something happy about the place. The front yard was parted in the middle by a sidewalk from gate to door-step, a sidewalk edged on either side by quart bottles driven neck down into the ground on a slant. A mess of homey flowers planted without a plan but blooming cheerily from their helter-skelter places. The fence and house were whitewashed. The porch and steps scrubbed white.

The front door stood open to the sunshine so that the floor of the front room could finish drying after its weekly scouring. It was Saturday. Everything clean from the front gate to the privy house. Yard raked so that the strokes of the rake would make a pattern. Fresh newspaper cut in fancy edge on the kitchen shelves.

Missie May was bathing herself in the galvanized washtub in the bedroom. Her dark-brown skin glistened under the soapsuds that skittered down from her wash rag. Her stiff young breasts thrust forward aggressively like broad-based cones with the tips lacquered in black.

She heard men's voices in the distance and glanced at the dollar clock on the dresser.

"Humph! Ah'm way behind time t'day! Joe gointer be heah 'fore Ah git mah clothes on if Ah don't make haste."

She grabbed the clean meal sack at hand and dried herself hurriedly and began to dress. But before she could tie her slippers, there came the ring of singing metal on wood. Nine times.

Missie May grinned with delight. She had not seen the big tall man come stealing in the gate and creep up the walk grinning happily at the joyful mischief he was about to commit. But she knew that it was her husband throwing silver dollars in the door for her to pick up and pile beside her plate at dinner. It was this way every Saturday afternoon. The nine dollars hurled into the open door, he scurried to a hiding place behind the cape jasmine bush and waited.

Missie May promptly appeared at the door in mock alarm.

"Who dat chunkin' money in mah do'way?" she demanded. No answer from the yard. She leaped off the porch and began to search the shrubbery. She peeped under the porch and hung over the gate to look up and down the road. While she did this, the man behind the jasmine darted to the china berry tree. She spied him and gave chase.

"Nobody ain't gointer be chunkin' money at me and Ah not do 'em nothin'," she shouted in mock anger. He ran around the house with Missie May at his heels. She overtook him at the kitchen door. He ran inside but could not close it after him before she crowded in and locked with him in a rough and tumble. For several minutes the two were a furious mass of male and female energy. Shouting, laughing, twisting, turning, tussling, tickling each other in the ribs; Missie May clutching onto Joe and Joe trying, but not too hard, to get away.

"Missie May, take yo' hand out mah pocket!" Joe shouted out between laughs.

"Ah ain't, Joe, not lessen you gwine gimme whateve' it is good you got in yo' pocket. Turn it go, Joe, do Ah'll tear yo' clothes."

"Go on tear 'em. You de one dat pushes de needles round heah. Move yo' hand Missie May."

"Lemme git dat paper sack out yo' pocket. Ah bet it's candy kisses."

"Tain't. Move yo' hand. Woman ain't got no business in a man's clothes nohow. Go way."

Missie May gouged way down and gave an upward jerk and triumphed.

"Unhhunh! Ah got it. It 'tis so candy kisses. Ah knowed you had somethin' for me in yo' clothes. Now Ah got to see whut's in every pocket you got."

Joe smiled indulgently and let his wife go through all of his pockets and take out the things that he had hidden there for her to find. She bore off the chewing gum, the cake of sweet soap, the pocket handkerchief as if she had wrested them from him, as if they had not been bought for the sake of this friendly battle.

"Whew! dat play-fight done got me all warmed up," Joe exclaimed. "Got me some water in de kittle?"

"Yo' water is on de fire and yo' clean things is cross de bed. Hurry up and wash yo'self and git changed so we kin eat. Ah'm hongry." As Missie said this, she bore the steaming kettle into the bedroom.

"You ain't hongry, sugar," Joe contradicted her. "Youse jes' a little empty. Ah'm de one whut's hongry. Ah could eat up camp meetin', back off 'ssociation, and drink Jurdan dry. Have it on de table when Ah git out de tub."

"Don't you mess wid mah business, man. You git in yo' clothes. Ah'm a real wife, not no dress and breath. Ah might not look lak one, but if you burn me, you won't git a thing but wife ashes."

Joe splashed in the bedroom and Missie May fanned around in the kitchen. A fresh red and white checked cloth on the table. Big pitcher of buttermilk beaded with pale drops of butter from the churn. Hot fried mullet, crackling bread, ham hock atop a mound of string beans and new potatoes, and perched on the window-sill a pone of spicy potato pudding.

Very little talk during the meal but that little consisted of banter that pretended to deny affection but in reality flaunted it. Like when Missie May reached for a second helping of the tater pone, Joe snatched it out of her reach.

After Missie May had made two or three unsuccessful grabs at the pan, she begged, "Aw, Joe gimme some mo' dat tater pone."

"Nope, sweetenin' is for us men-folks. Y'all pritty lil frail eels don't need nothin' lak dis. You too sweet already."

"Please, Joe."

"Naw, naw. Ah don't want you to git no sweeter than whut you is already. We goin' down de road a lil piece t'night so you go put on yo' Sunday-go-to-meetin' things."

Missie May looked at her husband to see if he was playing some prank. "Sho' nuff, Joe?"

"Yeah. We goin' to de ice cream parlor."

"Where de ice cream parlor at, Joe?"

"A new man done come heah from Chicago and he done got a place and took and opened it up for a ice cream parlor, and bein' as it's real swell, Ah wants you to be one de first ladies to walk in dere and have some set down."

"Do Jesus, Ah ain't knowed nothin' 'bout it. Who de man done it?"

"Mister Otis D. Slemmons, of spots and places—Memphis, Chicago, Jacksonville, Philadelphia and so on."

"Dat heavy-set man wid his mouth full of gold teethes?"

"Yeah. Where did you see 'im at?"

"Ah went down to de sto' tuh git a box of lye and Ah seen 'im standin' on de corner talkin' to some of de mens, and Ah come on back and went to scrubbin' de floor, and he passed and tipped his hat whilst Ah was scourin' de steps. Ah thought Ah never seen *him* befo'."

Joe smiled pleasantly. "Yeah, he's up to date. He got de finest clothes Ah ever seen on a colored man's back."

"Aw, he don't look no better in his clothes than you do in yourn. He got a puzzlegut on 'im and he so chuckle-headed, he got a pone behind his neck."

Joe looked down at his own abdomen and said wistfully, "Wisht Ah had a build on me lak he got. He ain't puzzle-gutted, honey. He jes' got a corperation. Dat make 'm look lak a rich white man. All rich mens is got some belly on 'em."

"Ah seen de pitchers of Henry Ford and he's a spare-built man and Rockefeller look lak he ain't got but one gut. But Ford and Rockefeller and dis Slemmons and all de rest kin be as many-gutted as dey please, Ah'm satisfied wid you jes' lak you is, baby. God took pattern after a pine tree and built you noble. Youse a pritty man, and if Ah knowed any way to make you mo' pritty still Ah'd take and do it."

Joe reached over gently and toyed with Missie May's ear. "You jes' say dat cause you love me, but Ah know Ah can't hold no light to Otis D. Slemmons. Ah ain't never been nowhere and Ah ain't got nothin' but you."

Missie May got on his lap and kissed him and he kissed back in kind. Then he went on. "All de womens is crazy 'bout 'im everywhere he go."

"How you know dat, Joe?"

"He tole us so hisself."

"Dat don't make it so. His mouf is cut cross-ways, ain't it? Well, he kin lie jes' lak anybody else."

"Good Lawd, Missie! You womens sho is hard to sense into things. He's got a five-dollar gold piece for a stick-pin and he got a ten-dollar gold piece on his watch chain and his mouf is jes' crammed full of gold teethes. Sho wisht it wuz mine. And whut make it so cool, he got money 'cumulated. And womens give it all to 'im."

"Ah don't see whut de womens see on 'im. Ah wouldn't give 'im a wink if de sheriff wuz after 'im."

"Well, he tole us how de white womens in Chicago give 'im all dat gold money. So he don't 'low nobody to touch it at all. Not even put dey finger on it. Dey tole 'im not to. You kin make 'miration at it, but don't tetch it."

"Whyn't he stay up dere where dey so crazy 'bout 'im?"

"Ah reckon dey done made 'im vast-rich and he wants to travel some. He say dey wouldn't leave 'im hit a lick of work. He got mo' lady people crazy 'bout him than he kin shake a stick at."

"Joe, Ah hates to see you so dumb. Dat stray nigger jes' tell y'all anything and y'all b'lieve it."

"Go 'head on now, honey and put on yo' clothes. He talkin' 'bout his pritty womens—Ah want 'im to see *mine*."

Missie May went off to dress and Joe spent the time trying to make his stomach punch out like Slemmons' middle. He tried the rolling swagger of the stranger, but found that his tall bone-and-muscle stride fitted ill with it. He just had time to drop back into his seat before Missie May came in dressed to go.

On the way home that night Joe was exultant. "Didn't Ah say ole Otis was swell? Can't he talk Chicago talk? Wuzn't dat funny whut he said when great big fat ole Ida Armstrong come in? He asted me, 'Who is dat broad wid de forte shake?' Dat's a new word. Us always thought forty wuz a set of figgers but he showed us where it means a whole heap of things. Sometimes he don't say forty, he jes' say thirty-eight and two and dat mean de same thing. Know whut he tole me when Ah wuz payin' for our ice cream? He say, 'Ah have to hand it to you, Joe. Dat wife of yours is jes' thirty-eight and two. Yessuh, she's forte!' Ain't he killin'?"

"He'll do in case of a rush. But he sho is got uh heap uh gold on 'im. Dat's de first time Ah ever seed gold money. It lookted good on him sho nuff, but it'd look a whole heap better on you."

"Who, me? Missie May youse crazy! Where would a po' man lak me git gold money from?"

Missie May was silent for a minute, then she said, "Us might find some goin' long de road some time. Us could."

"Who would be losin' gold money round heah? We ain't even seen none dese white folks wearin' no gold money on dey watch chain. You must be figgerin' Mister Packard or Mister Cadillac goin' pass through heah."

"You don't know whut been lost 'round heah. Maybe somebody way back in memorial times lost they gold money and went on off and it ain't never been found. And then if we wuz to find it, you could wear some 'thout havin' no gang of womens lak dat Slemmons say he got."

Joe laughed and hugged her. "Don't be wishful 'bout me. Ah'm satisfied de way Ah is. So long as Ah be yo' husband, Ah don't keer 'bout nothin' else. Ah'd ruther all de other womens in de world to be dead than for you to have de toothache. Less we go to bed and git our night rest."

It was Saturday night once more before Joe could parade his wife in Slemmons' ice cream parlor again. He worked the night shift and Saturday was his only night off. Every other evening around six o'clock he left home, and dying dawn saw him hustling home around the lake where the challenging sun flung a flaming sword from east to west across the trembling water.

That was the best part of life—going home to Missie May. Their white-washed house, the mock battle on Saturday, the dinner and ice cream parlor afterwards, church on Sunday nights when Missie out-dressed any woman in town—all, everything was right.

One night around eleven the acid ran out at the G. and G. The foreman knocked off the crew and let the steam die down. As Joe rounded the lake on his way home, a lean moon rode the lake in a silver boat. If anybody had asked Joe about the moon on the lake, he would have said he hadn't paid it any attention. But he saw it with his feelings. It made him yearn painfully for Missie. Creation obsessed him. He thought about children. They had been married more than a year now. They had money put away. They ought to be making little feet for shoes. A little boy child would be about right.

He saw a dim light in the bedroom and decided to come in through the kitchen door. He could wash the fertilizer dust off himself before presenting himself to Missie May. It would be nice for her not to know that he was there until he slipped into his place in bed and hugged her back. She always liked that.

He eased the kitchen door open slowly and silently, but when he went to set his dinner bucket on the table he bumped into a pile of dishes, and something crashed to the floor. He heard his wife gasp in fright and hurried to reassure her.

"Iss me, honey. Don't git skeered."

There was a quick, large movement in the bedroom. A rustle, a thud, and a stealthy silence. The light went out.

What? Robbers? Murderers? Some varmint attacking his helpless wife, perhaps. He struck a match, threw himself on guard and stepped over the door-sill into the bedroom.

The great belt on the wheel of Time slipped and eternity stood still. By the match light he could see the man's legs fighting with his breeches in his frantic desire to get them on. He had both chance and time to kill the intruder in his helpless condition—half in and half out of his pants—but he was too weak to take action. The shapeless enemies of humanity that lived in the hours of Time had waylaid Joe. He was assaulted in his weakness. Like Samson awakening after his haircut. So he just opened his mouth and laughed.

The match went out and he struck another and lit the lamp. A howling wind raced across his heart, but underneath its fury he heard his wife sobbing and Slemmons pleading for his life. Offering to buy it with all that he had. "Please, suh, don't kill me. Sixty-two dollars at de sto'. Gold money."

Joe just stood. Slemmons looked at the window, but it was screened. Joe stood out like a rough-backed mountain between him and the door. Barring him from escape, from sunrise, from life.

He considered a surprise attack upon the big clown that stood there laughing like a chessy cat. But before his fist could travel an inch, Joe's own rushed out to crush him like a battering ram. Then Joe stood over him.

"Git into yo' damn rags, Slemmons, and dat quick."

Slemmons scrambled to his feet and into his vest and coat. As he grabbed his hat, Joe's fury overrode his intentions and he grabbed at Slemmons with his left hand and struck at him with his right. The right landed. The left grazed the front of his vest. Slemmons was knocked a somersault into the kitchen and fled through the open door. Joe found himself alone with Missie May, with the golden watch charm clutched in his left fist. A short bit of broken chain dangled between his fingers.

Missie May was sobbing. Wails of weeping without words. Joe stood, and after awhile he found out that he had something in his hand. And then he stood and felt without thinking and without seeing with his natural eyes. Missie May kept on crying and Joe kept on feeling so much and not knowing what to do with all his feelings, he put Slemmons' watch charm in his pants pocket and took a good laugh and went to bed.

"Missie May, whut you cryin' for?"

"Cause Ah love you so hard and Ah know you don't love *me* no mo'."

Joe sank his face into the pillow for a spell then he said huskily, "You don't know de feelings of dat yet, Missie May."

"Oh Joe, honey, he said he wuz gointer give me dat gold money and he jes' kept on after me— —"

Joe was very still and silent for a long time. Then he said, "Well, don't cry no mo', Missie May. Ah got yo' gold piece for you."

The hours went past on their rusty ankles. Joe still and quiet on one bed-rail and Missie May wrung dry of sobs on the other. Finally the sun's tide crept upon the shore of night and drowned all its hours. Missie May with her face stiff and streaked towards the window saw the dawn come into her yard. It was day. Nothing more. Joe wouldn't be coming home as usual. No need to fling open the front door and sweep off the porch, making it nice for Joe. Never no more breakfast to cook; no more washing and starching of Joe's jumper-jackets and pants. No more nothing. So why get up?

With this strange man in her bed, she felt embarrassed to get up and dress. She decided to wait till he had dressed and gone. Then she would get up, dress quickly and be gone forever beyond reach of Joe's looks and laughs. But he never moved. Red light turned to yellow, then white.

From beyond the no-man's land between them came a voice. A strange voice that yesterday had been Joe's.

"Missie May, ain't you gonna fix me no breakfus'?"

She sprang out of bed. "Yeah, Joe. Ah didn't reckon you wuz hongry."

No need to die today. Joe needed her for a few more minutes anyhow.

Soon there was a roaring fire in the cook stove. Water bucket full and two chickens killed. Joe loved fried chicken and rice. She didn't deserve a thing and good Joe was letting her cook him some breakfast. She rushed hot biscuits to the table as Joe took his seat.

He ate with his eyes in his plate. No laughter, no banter.

"Missie May, you ain't eatin' yo' breakfus'."

"Ah don't choose none, Ah thank yuh."

His coffee cup was empty. She sprang to refill it. When she turned from the stove and bent to set the cup beside Joe's plate, she saw the yellow coin on the table between them.

She slumped into her seat and wept into her arms.

Presently Joe said calmly, "Missie May, you cry too much. Don't look back lak Lot's wife and turn to salt."

The sun, the hero of every day, the impersonal old man that beams as brightly on death as on birth, came up every morning and raced across the blue dome and dipped into the sea of fire every evening. Water ran down hill and birds nested.

Missie knew why she didn't leave Joe. She couldn't. She loved him too much, but she could not understand why Joe didn't leave her. He was polite, even kind at times, but aloof.

There were no more Saturday romps. No ringing silver dollars to stack beside her plate. No pockets to rifle. In fact the yellow coin in his trousers was like a monster hiding in the cave of his pockets to destroy her.

She often wondered if he still had it, but nothing could have induced her to ask nor yet to explore his pockets to see for herself. Its shadow was in the house whether or no.

One night Joe came home around midnight and complained of pains in the back. He asked Missie to rub him down with liniment. It had been three months since Missie had touched his body and it all seemed strange. But she rubbed him. Grateful for the chance. Before morning, youth triumphed and Missie exulted. But the next day, as she joyfully made up their bed, beneath her pillow she found the piece of money with the bit of chain attached.

Alone to herself, she looked at the thing with loathing, but look she must. She took it into her hands with trembling and saw first thing that it was no gold piece. It was a gilded half dollar. Then she knew why Slemmons had forbidden anyone to touch his gold. He trusted village eyes at a distance not to recognize his stick-pin as a gilded quarter, and his watch charm as a four-bit piece.

She was glad at first that Joe had left it there. Perhaps he was through with her punishment. They were man and wife again. Then another thought came clawing at her. He had come home to buy from her as if she were any woman in the long house. Fifty cents for her love. As if to say that he could pay as well as Slemmons. She slid the coin into his Sunday pants pocket and dressed herself and left his house.

Half way between her house and the quarters she met her husband's mother, and after a short talk she turned and went back home. Never would she admit defeat to that woman who prayed for it nightly. If she had not the substance of marriage she had the outside show. Joe must leave *her*. She let him see she didn't want his old gold four-bits too.

She saw no more of the coin for some time though she knew that Joe could not help finding it in his pocket. But his health kept poor, and he came home at least every ten days to be rubbed.

The sun swept around the horizon, trailing its robes of weeks and days. One morning as Joe came in from work, he found Missie May chopping wood. Without a word he took the ax and chopped a huge pile before he stopped.

"You ain't got no business choppin' wood, and you know it."

"How come? Ah been choppin' it for de last longest."

"Ah ain't blind. You makin' feet for shoes."

"Won't you be glad to have a lil baby chile, Joe?"

"You know dat 'thout astin' me."

"Iss gointer be a boy chile and de very spit of you."

"You reckon, Missie May?"

"Who else could it look lak?"

Joe said nothing, but he thrust his hand deep into his pocket and fingered something there.

It was almost six months later Missie May took to bed and Joe went and got his mother to come wait on the house.

Missie May was delivered of a fine boy. Her travail was over when Joe came in from work one morning. His mother and the old women were drinking great bowls of coffee around the fire in the kitchen.

The minute Joe came into the room his mother called him aside.

"How did Missie May make out?" he asked quickly.

"Who, dat gal? She strong as a ox. She gointer have plenty mo'. We done fixed her wid de sugar and lard to sweeten her for de nex' one."

Joe stood silent awhile.

"You ain't ast 'bout de baby, Joe. You oughter be mighty proud cause he sho is de spittin' image of yuh, son. Dat's yourn all right, if you never git another one, dat un is yourn. And you know Ah'm mighty proud too, son, cause Ah never thought well of you marryin' Missie May cause her ma used tuh fan her foot round right smart and Ah been mighty skeered dat Missie May wuz gointer git misput on her road."

Joe said nothing. He fooled around the house till late in the day then just before he went to work, he went and stood at the front of the bed and asked his wife how she felt. He did this every day during the week.

On Saturday he went to Orlando to make his market. It had been a long time since he had done that.

Meat and lard, meal and flour, soap and starch. Cans of corn and tomatoes. All the staples. He fooled around town for awhile and bought bananas and apples. Way after while he went around to the candy store.

"Hello, Joe," the clerk greeted him. "Ain't seen you in a long time."

"Nope, Ah ain't been heah. Been round in spots and places."

"Want some of them molasses kisses you always buy?"

"Yessuh." He threw the gilded half dollar on the counter. "Will dat spend?"

"Whut is it, Joe? Well, I'll be doggone! A gold-plated four-bit piece. Where'd you git it, Joe?"

"Offen a stray nigger dat come through Eatonville. He had

it on his watch chain for a charm—goin' round making out iss gold money. Ha ha! He had a quarter on his tie pin and it wuz all golded up too. Tryin' to fool people. Makin' out he so rich and everything. Ha! Ha! Tryin' to tole off folkses wives from home."

"How did you git it, Joe? Did he fool you, too?"

"Who, me? Naw suh! He ain't fooled me none. Know whut Ah done? He come round me wid his smart talk. Ah hauled off and knocked 'im down and took his old four-bits way from 'im. Gointer buy my wife some good ole lasses kisses wid it. Gimme fifty cents worth of dem candy kisses."

"Fifty cents buys a mighty lot of candy kisses, Joe. Why don't you split it up and take some chocolate bars, too. They eat good, too."

"Yessuh, dey do, but Ah wants all dat in kisses. Ah got a lil boy chile home now. Tain't a week old yet, but he kin suck a sugar tit and maybe eat one them kisses hisself."

Joe got his candy and left the store. The clerk turned to the next customer. "Wisht I could be like those darkies. Laughin' all the time. Nothin' worries 'em."

Back in Eatonville, Joe reached his own front door. There was the ring of singing metal on wood. Fifteen times. Missie May couldn't run to the door, but she crept there as quickly as she could.

"Joe Banks, Ah hear you chunkin' money in mah do'way. You wait till Ah got mah strength back and Ah'm gointer fix you for dat."

She Rock

1. Hiram offereth Oscar a job in Harlem and 7. Oscar answereth him and complaineth that his wife is strong of mind and arm. 14. Hiram showeth Oscar a way of escape and Oscar accepteth it. 19. Cal'line casteth down their plan and goeth to Babylon with them. 26. Hiram comforteth Oscar. 28. Oscar goeth hot cha-cha. 30. Ethel Waters prophesieth in Babylon and Oscar harkeneth unto her. 34. He meeteth a damsel who changeth his name to "Gang." He pranceth with her and is glad. 36. Cal'line saith nothing and Oscar singeth of his triumph. 38. Oscar buyeth his Sheba a fur coat. 40. Cal'line findeth mouth paint and accuseth Oscar. 42. He bawleth her out and departeth to the feast of Thanksgiving. 46. Cal'line cometh with an axe and breaketh up the party. 57. Oscar resolveth to return to Sanford. 59. Hiram enquireth of him and is answered.

* * *

1. The word came to Hiram, son of Mimms, in Sanford which lieth near Orlando in Florida, saying,

2. Arise, hitch up thy britches and go unto thy brother, the same which is called Oscar, and dwelleth nigh thee.

3. And when thou comest to his house thou shalt say unto him, thus saith Mister Charlie, the same which hireth me and many others, behold he hath covenanted with Kings and Princes in Great Babylon, that mother of the Empire State building and divers other towers.

4. And he hath made writings with them that he shall do thus and thus that they may pay him many sheckels and the Princes of Babylon hath answered him yea.

5. Now therefore requireth he many men of weak brains and strong backs such as thou art that he may perform his vows unto the Princes that sit in Wall Street.

6. If thou wilt go with us open thy mouth and speak so shall he enter thy name upon the scroll of them that toteth brick and beareth the hod upon the shoulder.

7. Then did Oscar the brother of Hiram speak and answer him saying, "Yea, verily my soul cleaveth to that city upon the Hudson and my feet yearneth to journey thither, but lo, thou knowest that I be married unto a woman called Cal'line.

8. Yea, likewise thou knowest that she beeth an oppressive female that lifteth her voice in all things and prevaileth against me.

9. Behold how she crieth not like unto other women when I strive against her with mine fists. Nay, she weepeth not, but verily taketh stove-wood in the left hand and weighteth the right hand with iron and smiteth me hip and thigh."

10. Then spake Hiram and answered. "All these things have been revealed unto me. Did I not behold thee fleeing before her in the evenings, and humbling thyself in the mornings?

11. Know thou not that thou hast divorce in thy heel? Who shall find thee in Great Babylon? Who shall discover thy hiding place in Harlem?"

12. But Oscar was afraid and said, "even so, she shall find me. It hath become a saying in the streets of Sanford, Oscar loveth many women but Cal'line findeth him ever and lifteth up her mighty hand.

13. Therefore have I likened her unto iron and compared her unto a stone; saying, lo I am married unto an she-rock. It hath become a saying in the streets of Sanford and a mockery in the high places thereof."

14. Then strove Hiram with Oscar mightily for he would that his brother depart from his wife unknowing unto her and sojourn in the city of Babylon. Saying thus shalt thou escape her and love women as thy heart wills, seeing she is opposed to thy desires.

15. So he prevailed over his brother Oscar and Oscar said him yea. Thus drank he many fingers of moonshine and swallowed much coon-dick. For it is written that corn giveth courage to the soul but coon-dick maketh glad the heart.

16. Therefore on the sixth day departed Oscar with all his goods, yea verily his belts and britches with the shirts of many colors, and cometh to the dwelling of Hiram that they might set out upon the journey together.

17. Then rejoiced they among themselves and said God is with us. Now shall Oscar rejoice in his singleness upon the railroad and dance without Cal'line in Harlem. Yea verily, the she-rock is swallowed up in loneliness, the immovable woman shall be desolate.

18. Let it not be sung in the streets of Sanford that Cal'line prevailed over Oscar forever, for he shall cherish divers women in Harlem. While she of great strength waileth in Sanford. Selah.

19. But when they cometh to [the] railroad station where meeteth the great behemoths of steel, that bloweth out smoke from the nostrils; whose belly is full of steam,

20. There sitteth Cal'line there before them. She hath also borne with her baggage for a great journey.

21. Then would Oscar have fled, but he was sore afraid neither asked he of her, "woman what doest thou here?"

22. Likewise said she nothing to anyone, for she be a woman of exceedingly few words, but she sat before her baggage and chewed mightily upon the gum that was between her jaws. Yea, verily she smacked vehemently upon it and gazed upon Oscar as upon a stone, and his liver turned to water within him.

23. And when approached he that was called Cap'n and enquireth of them, saying "what woman is that sitteth with thee? Behold, her name is not upon the scroll."

24. Then answereth Oscar, "The same is my wife. She goeth with us also or else."

25. "Else what?" Cap'n enquired of him, but he shook his head sadly and answered him not.

26. But Hiram cometh to him on the train and saith, be of good cheer for tho she goeth with thee to Babylon, even she cannot keep check upon thee in Harlem, verily the houses beeth too many. The streets also are numerous and of great length. Thou shalt find great multitudes of damsels; yea frail eels of great beauty and they shall gladden thy heart. She shall see thee only at thy comings in from labor and goings out to pleasures.

27. And Oscar answered him, Amen.

28. When cometh they unto the city called Babylon by some and by other Bagdad upon the subway, then stood Oscar in the highway continually and many knew him and taught him saying,

29. "Put off thy ways of Sanford, Florida, and hearken unto Harlem," and he hearkened.

30. And in those days came the voice of the prophetess Ethel Waters, who prophesied in Harlem and in Philadelphia and in divers other cities crying hear, oh ye sons and daughters of Ham and Hagar, shake that thing. Yea verily I grow sick and wearing of advising you to shake that thing. How long must I yet say up, the hour is upon you shake that thing. Yea behold it is shaken in Georgia, and shivered exceedingly in Memphis. Yet, already hath Uncle John, who is full of years and reigneth over jelly roll, hath he a hump in his back occasioned by exceeding great number of shakings go thou and do likewise.

31. And the multitudes hearkened unto the voice of the prophetess and arose as one man and shook with many shakings.

32. Yea, shook the fat with the lean, the rich with the poor; the aged with the young, verily was there not a shaking like unto this before nor after it.

33. And Oscar hastened from one place unto another hearkening unto the words of the prophetess.

34. Cometh he to one female who beheld him smiting the pocket book grievously and saith unto him, "verily thou are Caliente," which being interpreted meaneth "hot" and the saying pleased Oscar.

35. Also saith she, "thy prowess is like unto the prowess of ten men," and henceforth thy name shall be "Gang" and this also made glad the heart of Oscar and she smote upon his pocket as David smote upon the harp. Then she said unto Oscar "truly thy name shall be Daddy also," which being interpreted meaneth "gimme" and it was so.

36. And to all the goings out and comings in saith Cal'line not one word. Thus was it said by Oscar unto his brother.

37. Surely Babylon hath confounded the mighty and laid waste the strength of the rock. Therefore will I smite the ukulele and sing a song of triumph. The heart of Oscar is made glad—the son of Mimms.

For lo, he would have fled from before the she-rock, but she pursued and overthrew him.

His heart was as dust.

His soul yearned [for] softness yet was he yoked unto a stone.

But Babylon hath made humble the smiting woman of Sanford.

Yea, its towers and its hot mamas hath undone the haughty. She is silent and her mind made broad.

The anointed of the Lord hath waited his hour.

For wisdom hath said.

Five years are not too long for a Condar to wear a ruffled shirt.

Her strength is departed.

If the frog hath wings so that he no longer bumpeth his hips upon the ground;

If the frog hath hip pockets, then would he tote a pistol that the snakes dare not eat him, then shall the strength of Cal'line return. Go to, Oscar, son of Mimms and buy thy mamma [a] seal skin coat as she hath begged of thee. The mind of Cal'line is made broad. The way is made straight.

38. Therefore in August did Oscar put up a coat for her that calleth him daddy that it might be fully paid when the feast of Thanksgiving drew nigh and it was so.

39. Thanksgiving was fully come did Oscar take the coat from the merchant and bear it to the house of his brother saying, three days hence we celebrate the feast. Then shall I give unto my slick sheba the gift. Let it abide with thee until then.

40. Cal'line knoweth all these things from signs and revelations but she held her peace. Also many days had she followed the steps of her husband and knew where he wenteth and what he did there.

41. And behold he sat with her the day before the feast whilest she washeth his shirts. And she saith unto him "Oscar, thou hast another woman besides me." Then he arose in his place and rebuked her saying,

42. "Thou art untruthful thou woman with the pepper patch upon thy head."

43. But she strove with him saying, "surely it is so. Behold here is mouth-paint upon thy collar, and if she be so nigh unto thee as to wipe her mouth upon the collar of thy shirt, she knoweth thee well."

44. Then he grew wrath and departed saying, "This be great Babylon, not Sanford, moreover thou art no tea for my fever, neither are thou a B. C. for my headache, go to, cook thyself radish. Behold and see thou are still Sanford while I am Harlem."

45. Then straightaway he [de]parted and took the coat of sealslander and bore it unto whom it was promised, and they made merry with corn and with chicken, both the bosom and the hip thereof.

46. And in the midst of their rejoicing there cometh blows upon the door, yea, great smitings upon the lock thereof like the grumbling of thunder.

47. And the people who were in the apartment with them fled saying "surely the law desireth admittance." So they departed by the fire escape.

48. But Oscar abode in the place with her who called him daddy saying "If such knocking should come upon a door in San-

ford wherein I tarried, I would arise and flee even in these pajamas for my soul would say it is Cal'line."

49. But no woman beareth the axe in Babylon. Let us feast yet more before we journey to the show.

50. Then cometh yet other blows that breaketh the lock and shattereth the door in pieces, and Oscar poketh his head out of the bedroom door and behold Cal'line standeth before him.

51. And when he would have withdrawn his head into the bedroom and shut tight the door, Cal'line thrust forth the axe and prevented him.

52. And when she had fully come into the room, he fled out by the window and took his way home by taxi chariot that the people in the streets might not mock him.

53. Then did Cal'line stand before the sweet mamma and smack her cheek and thigh. Yea verily she smote her exceeding with the fist and mocked her, saying,

54. Tell it not on Seventh Avenue and speak it not before the Lafayette that thou knoweth not why I socketh thee. A smart gal of Babylon like unto thee will be bound to know.

55. So saying she collected the coat and pants of her husband with the shoes and shirt thereof and added also the new coat of furs upon the axe-handle and departed out of that house and took her away.

56. Then did the people laugh and say he fled away in pajamas but his wife bringeth home the bacon with the axe.

57. And when many days had passed and Oscar smiled not at his labors nor made merry with his mamma, did Hiram question him, saying, "Oscar, son of my mother, what grieveth thee?"

58. And Oscar answered him, "I go and return unto Sanford, yea."

59. Then Hiram enquired again, "dost thou not love Babylon and the frails thereof? Why returnest thou to Sanford?" Oscar answered him

60. Verily love I the city of Babylon and all the women therein, but it is written a man shall possess a wife of exceeding broad-mindedness, else he cannot come at the essence of the thing. Then Hiram enquired of him

61. "Didst thou not say unto me at divers times that thou had taught wisdom to the heathen and made broad the mind of Cal'line?"

62. Then did Oscar answer him sorrowfully and say, yea in my folly did I open my mouth and boast that I had made wise the simple and made broad the mind of her that was narrow.

63. But hearken unto my voice and give ear to my teaching.

64. She that toteth the axe in Babylon is narrow of mind, and she that smiteth locks is of little faith.

65. Therefore what profiteth a man if he stand among a multitude of sweet ones if it be forbidden that he possess even one?

66. For lo, the mind of Cal'line hath not been broadened and her head hath not learned a darned thing.

SELAH!

The Fire and the Cloud

Moses sat upon his new-made grave on Mount Nebo. His back stooped wearily, but his strong gaze leaped the Jordan and travelled over the land of Canaan.

A lizard popped out of a hole under a rock directly before Moses.

"Good morning, O brother-of-insufficient-walking-legs. I find you at waking where I left you at sun-rest." So the reptile greeted Moses.

With his eyes still in Canaan, Moses answered. "Ah yes, little kin who-uses-all-his-legs-for-walking, the labor has been long. This is the thirtieth day that I have sojourned upon this mountain." He waved at the mound of stone. "Behold, friend, it is finished."

From the top of a low bush near the left foot of Moses the lizard studied the work. "It is good. But you have been a long time in the building of your nest. Your female must be near death from retaining her eggs."

"No fecund female awaits this labor."

"A male alone?"

"A male alone."

"Perhaps you are a widower also. It is very sad, but you must know that fat lizards have many sudden-striking enemies." A tear dewed the leaf beneath him.

"I am alone, O lizard, because I am alone."

The lizard felt that Moses' answer lacked reason and he would have taught him how to make answer as do the great ones in the council of lizards, but when he lifted his head to speak, he beheld the head of Moses enveloped in a dense white cloud. "The gods have borne away the head of the rock-lifter," he thought aloud, and scurried to his hole in quivering awe. He slept and memory fled away. So soon he emerged and looked into the benign eyes of the nation-maker from the same bush.

"The lizard says that the present hour is much hotter than the tender ones of morning," he began abruptly.

"The lizard is wise," Moses answered casually.

"The words of lizards are full of truth," the reptile went on cunningly. "But even so, O friend-who-digs-his-hole-above-ground, the greatest among us has no rod that can summon fly-swarms at will." The lizard said this and looked at Moses under-eyed.

"That is true," Moses agreed with his thoughts at a distance.

"All your works accumulate praise. Twenty and nine days you have been with me upon this mountain, and each day you have called forth a swarm of flies at the hour when I am most hungry."

"Pardon me, friend," Moses said humbly. "The thirtieth day shall be as the twenty-nine." He lifted his rod ever so slightly and flies swarmed over the bush upon which the lizard rested. "Sup."

The lizard ate. The last fly of the swarm was just enough. Every day it had been so. He looked at Moses in admiration.

"Whence do you come, O Master?"

Moses pointed to the plain of Moab where the tents of Israel crowded the horizon.

"How do you say that you are alone if of your kind such hosts of multitudes be at hand?"

"I am that I am and so I am alone. I am Moses, The-drawn-out. It is given me to call God by his power-compelling names. I bear his rod. The blind and the mute have companionship, but I am a leader."

"I see that your leadership has galled your shoulders. Why then did you go before?"

"I went because I was sent. In my agony I cried into nothingness and enquired 'Why am I called?' There was no answer. Only the voice that again said 'Go!'"

"How long, O mighty Moses, have you led?"

"Forty years and more. From the mountain of God I returned to Egypt, and with my stretched-out arm I confounded the Pharaoh, and led my people forth with a mighty hand. From the Nile, where we were bondsmen, to beyond the Jordan, where they shall rule."

"Ah Moses, because you have so exalted your kind and kindred, their love for you must exceed this great mountain in thickness and the height would not be less."

"Lizard, love is not created by service to mankind. But if the good be deemed sufficiently great, man sometimes erects little mountains of stone to the doer called monuments. They do this so that in the enjoyment of this benefit they forget not the benefactor. The heart of man is an ever empty abyss into which the whole world shall fall and be swallowed up."

"Do none of the hosts love their deliverer?"

"Who shall know? However, Joshua is strong in soul and body. He shall follow me. He gives thought to me. If I do not return to my tent before another day begins, he will ascend this mountain in search of me."

"Your labors have brought little joy."

"Lizard, forty years ago I led a horde of slaves out of Egyptian bondage and held them in the wilderness until I grew men. Look now upon the plain of Moab. A great people! They shall rule over nations and dwell in cities they have not builded. Yet they have rebelled against me ever. A stiff-necked race of people. They murmur against me anew because I have held them before the Jordan for forty days. Their taste would humble them before the armies of Canaan. They must wait yet another thirty days. I have not striven with God, with the wilderness, with rebellion and my own soul for forty years to bring them to a new bondage in the land beyond the Jordan. They shall wait for strength."

"How then, Moses, will you hold your horde of murmurers on the brink of the Jordan when their eyes already feast on the good land?"

"If a leader dies in Israel, the hosts mourn thirty days."

Again the head of Moses disappeared in cloud and a sleep fell upon the lizard. But the cloud-splitting eye of Moses carried to the silver gilt hills of Canaan lying half in the late night, and half in shadows of the setting sun, and his soul wandered beyond the Jordan for the space of half an hour. When it returned to him upon Nebo he gazed down upon the tented nation beneath him, and the nation-maker sorrowing, wept over Israel. But Israel, unknowing, sang and danced, hammered its swords, milked its cows, got born and died.

"Ah Moses," the lizard observed on waking. "You shall yet rejoice. Soon your hosts will triumph beyond the Jordan, and you shall be called king of kings."

"I have already known the palaces of the Pharaohs, lizard, but I was not happy in the midst of them."

"You were an alien in the Egyptian palaces, but the mansions in Canaan shall be of your kindred."

"When the Israelites shall erect palaces, God shall raise up abundant palace-dwellers to fill them. I have taught them statutes and judgements fit for the guidance of kings and shepherds alike."

"But will they remember your laws?"

"If I tarry within this that I have erected on Nebo, then shall they remember my laws in Canaan. People value monuments above men, and signs above works."

The lizard travelled around the tomb and studied its contours.

"But Moses, your splendid new dwelling has no hole by which you may enter. A queer dwelling. A hole above ground—no entrance."

"This is no dwelling, lizard. It is a place of burial."

"I am no longer young, Moses, perhaps, I nodded. What buried yon there?"

"No, you did not witness it, but here is interred the voice of Sinai, the stretched-out arm of Moses, the law-giver, the nation-maker."

"Those are your words, but I behold you sitting as you sat at sunrise."

"Those are your thoughts, but you see the old man of the wilderness sitting upon the tomb of Moses."

Whereupon Moses arose and took one long look at the tented nation in the valley, and his face shone as it had done at Sinai when even Aaron had feared to look upon it. He took one dragging look beyond the Jordan, then wrapped his mantle closely about him.

"Sun is set," he said in low rumbles. "I depart."

He laid his rod upon the new-made tomb, set his face sternly towards the wilderness and walked away, leaning lightly on a new-cut staff.

"But wait, O Moses!" the lizard squeaked after him. "You have left your rod behind."

"Oh, Joshua will pick it up," he called back and strode on.

ACKNOWLEDGMENTS

The seeds of this project were planted nearly a decade ago. So while it may seem pro forma to say that this project is deeply indebted to the kindness and generosity of many people, it is, nevertheless, quite true. My debts, professional and personal, are numerous, and I apologize in advance for any omissions.

I am indebted to Tracy Sherrod, my editor at Amistad Press, for her thoughtful feedback on drafts as I navigated the needs of the diverse readers we hope will find this volume. Nate Muscato and David Kuhn at Aevitas Creative have shared their wisdom and insights through a tangled process. Joy Harris and her team at the Joy Harris Literary Agency have been a pleasure to work with. I also wish to thank the Zora Neale Hurston Trust for entrusting me with a project that I dreamed of as a graduate student. I am grateful for the opportunity. It has been a labor of love.

My friend and mentor Henry Louis Gates Jr. laid the foundation for this volume in two distinctive ways. He was the first to collect Hurston's stories for contemporary readers. In addition, his pioneering efforts to make important black periodicals accessible to scholars in the Black Literature Index brought together six of the undocumented stories that appear here, as well as numerous other recovered texts that continue to help scholars document and study African American literary history. Always ready to share his insights, his wise counsel has made this collection better. Likewise, the important work of Glenda R. Carpio and Werner Sollors helped Hurston's uncollected *Pittsburgh Courier* stories find a new audience. Their beautifully edited issue of *Amerikastudien / American Studies* made five of Hurston's "lost" stories available to academics around the world and drew much-needed attention to a body of work that had been overlooked. To Paul Lucas at Janklow & Nesbit Associates I am indebted for his commitment to seeing these stories collected.

One of my ambitions for this project was to return to the first printings of Hurston's stories for fresh transcriptions. Most of the stories here do not exist in typescript and none in Hurston's hand. My efforts to look anew at Hurston's stories in their original contexts would not have been possible without the assistance of librarians and archivists around the nation. For their support and encouragement, I am indebted to JoEllen ElBashir, curator at the Moorland-Spingarn Research Center at Howard University; Delisa Minor Harris, Special Collections librarian at the John Hope and Aurelia E. Franklin Library at Fisk University; June Can and Adrienne Leigh Sharp, in access services for the Beinecke Rare Book and Manuscript Library at Yale University; and Florence M. Turcotte, literary manuscripts archivist, and Steven Hersh, public and support services assistant, at the George A. Smathers Libraries at the University of Florida. In addition, Abby Wolf, executive director; Kevin M. Burke, director of research; and Rob W. Heinrich, non-resident fellow, at the Hutchins Center for African & African American Research at

Harvard University, led by Professor Gates, generously helped me obtain copies of rare publications not available to me elsewhere.

In every way imaginable, Texas Woman's University, my academic home, has offered its support as I have balanced the demands of teaching and administrative work with the need to complete this project. Abigail Tilton, dean of the College of Arts and Sciences; my generous departmental colleagues; and my graduate students have been unwavering in their support for my endeavors. Susan Whitmer, Amanda Zerangue, and Julie Reed Sullivan, three of our gracious and talented librarians at Blagg-Huey Library, along with Erik Martin, systems engineer, offered spectacular technological support as I experimented with using OCR software to create initial transcriptions of stories.

In its infancy, and again as it took its current form, this project benefited from the contributions of three graduate research assistants at Texas Woman's University. Aaron Cassidy and Allyson Hibdon both helped me transcribe and collate for accuracy all of the stories included here. Allyson, who worked intensively on the project, contributed broadly to the volume and to my good humor on long days of collation work. Allyson's role in the project was facilitated by a 2018 Creative Arts and Humanities research grant from Texas Woman's University, which proved invaluable. Daniel Stefanelli, funded by a 2019 Creative Arts and Humanities grant, served as a sharp-eyed proofreader. I am grateful for the support. The new transcriptions presented here would not have been possible without it.

Finally, I want to thank my family and friends, some of whom have patiently listened to me talk about Zora for more than two decades now. To my parents, Carole and Lee Fager, I owe my first archival research trip. While still a graduate student, my love of archival work and Hurston merged at the Moorland-Spingarn Research Center at Howard University on a trip financed by them. My brother, Evan Fager, and my nephews, Lee and Seth, sacrificed our time together so that I could focus on this project. For laughter, generosity of spirit, and encouragement I have always been able to depend on my chosen family and Texas support system: Lou Thompson, Jennifer Phillips-Denny, Lisa Grimaldo, Claire Sahlin, Amanda Oswalt, and Rhonda Redfearn. My husband, Rex West, has always supported my pursuit of professional goals, encouraged me to persist when I thought I could not, and served as my ballast and anchor in seas so rough that I thought they might sink me. Without these people, the volume you hold in your hands would likely not exist.

Saying *thank you* is hardly enough. There are no words.

NOTES

Editor's Note

1. Glenda R. Carpio and Werner Sollors, "The Newly Complicated Zora Neale Hurston," *The Chronicle Review* (January 7, 2011): B6–10.

Introduction

1. Mary Helen Washington, "Zora Neale Hurston: A Woman Half in Shadow," in *I Love Myself When I Am Laughing . . . and Then Again When I Am Looking Mean and Impressive: A Zora Neale Hurston Reader*, ed. Alice Walker (Old Westbury, NY: Feminist Press, 1979).
2. Robert Hemenway, *Zora Neale Hurston: A Literary Biography* (Urbana: Univ. of Illinois Press, 1977), 19.
3. Zora Neale Hurston, *Dust Tracks on a Road: An Autobiography* (1942; repr., New York: HarperCollins, 1991), 1; and "High John de Conquer," in *Folklore, Memoirs, and Other Writings*, ed. Cheryl A. Wall (New York: Library of America, 1995), 923. Hurston also uses a variant of the phrase in a letter dated 8 September 1944 (see Zora Neale Hurston, *Zora Neale Hurston: A Life in Letters*, ed. Carla Kaplan [New York: Doubleday, 2001], 500). For other scholars' use of the phrase, see Claudia Tate, "Hitting 'A Straight Lick with a Crooked Stick': *Seraph on the Suwanee*, Zora Neale Hurston's Whiteface Novel," *Discourse:*

Journal for Theoretical Studies in Media and Culture 19, no. 2 (1997): 72–87; and Susan Meisenhelder, *Hitting a Straight Lick with a Crooked Stick: Race and Gender in the Work of Zora Neale Hurston* (Tuscaloosa: Univ. of Alabama Press, 1999), 1–13.

4. Sarah-Jane (Saje) Mathieu, "The African American Great Migration Reconsidered," *OAH Magazine of History* 23, no. 4 (October 2009): 20.

5. For a discussion of the religious disputes between migrants and long-time residents, see Curtis J. Evans, *The Burden of Black Religion* (New York: Oxford Univ. Press, 2008), chapters 4–6. Judith Weisenfeld's *Hollywood Be Thy Name: African American Religion in American Film, 1929–1949* (Berkeley: Univ. of California Press, 2007) provides an excellent discussion of the tensions between the sacred and secular. Erin Chapman's *Prove It on Me: New Negroes, Sex, and Popular Culture in the 1920s* (New York: Oxford Univ. Press, 2012) offers an insightful examination of gender roles and sexuality in the period. Cherene Sherrard-Johnson's *Portraits of the New Negro Woman: Visual and Literary Culture in the Harlem Renaissance* (New Brunswick, NJ: Rutgers Univ. Press, 2007) offers an excellent examination of the middle-class norms female migrants encountered. For Farah Jasmine Griffin's treatment of migration narratives, see *"Who Set You Flowin'?": The African-American Migration Narrative* (New York: Oxford Univ. Press, 1995).

6. Hazel V. Carby, "The Politics of Fiction, Anthropology, and the Folk: Zora Neale Hurston," in *New Essays on "Their Eyes Were Watching God,"* ed. Michael Awkward (New York: Cambridge Univ. Press, 1990), 76–77.

7. Hurston, *Dust Tracks*, 19 and 1.

8. Cheryl A. Wall was the first to document Hurston's birth date through US Census records. See her *Women of the Harlem Renaissance* (Bloomington: Indiana Univ. Press, 1995), 143.

9. Valerie Boyd, *Wrapped in Rainbows: The Life of Zora Neale Hurston* (New York: Scribner, 2003), 72.

10. For Hurston's description of Howard, see her *Dust Tracks*, 113. Valerie Boyd documents this period of Zora's life in *Wrapped in Rainbows*, 75–81. Hurston supported herself by working as a manicurist at George Robinson's 1410 G Street shop, a "whites only" barbershop

frequented by Washington's powerful and elite. Robinson, himself an African American with six shops in the city, served only a white clientele in this shop, and Hurston found working there educational, as she enjoyed interacting with reporters and staffers from the Hill. The whites-only policy in the shop also forced her to wrestle with the moral and financial realities of Jim Crow practices. While she opposed Jim Crow, she also understood that serving blacks in the shop posed a serious threat to her livelihood and that of everyone else who worked in the shop. It was a complex, deeply personal reality she acknowledges in *Dust Tracks* without offering a solution or a judgment on the matter. See her recollections in *Dust Tracks,* 115–20.

11. Elizabeth McHenry, *Forgotten Readers: Recovering the Lost History of African American Literary Societies* (Durham, NC: Duke Univ. Press, 2002), 297.
12. Ronald M. Johnson, "Those Who Stayed: Washington Black Writers of the 1920's," *Records of the Columbia Historical Society, Washington, D.C.* 50 (1980): 494. Owen Dodson explains that the salon hostess "took in stray people, artists who were out of money like Zora Neale Hurston for long periods." For this quote and a larger discussion of the group see David Krasner, "Dark Tower and the Saturday Nighters: Salons as Themes in African American Drama," *American Studies* 49, no. 1/2 (Spring/Summer 2008): 81–95.
13. Boyd, *Wrapped in Rainbows,* 93.
14. In the fiction category, Hurston's "Spunk" won second place, while "Black Death" won honorable mention. Her play *Color Struck* won second place, while *Spears* won honorable mention in the category for drama. See Boyd's discussion of the award dinner, in *Wrapped in Rainbows,* 97. Hemenway provides a more substantive discussion in *Zora Neale Hurston: A Literary Biography,* 20–21.
15. Hurston, *Dust Tracks,* 121–22; Hurston, *Zora Neale Hurston: A Life in Letters,* 55; Boyd, *Wrapped in Rainbows,* 101.
16. Alain Locke, ed., *The New Negro: An Interpretation* (1925; repr., New York: Atheneum, 1992), 1–16.
17. While we often think of authenticity as a good or desirable quality, the term can also be used to limit what counts as valuable, meaning-

ful, or "real." In book reviews of Hurston's work, white reviewers often describe her work as "authentic," but those same reviewers also often reveal (inadvertently, of course) their racist conceptions of what constitutes authentic depictions of black life. Put another way, if Hurston's folk characters are authentic, then what does that mean for the characters of her fellow writers Jessie Fauset and Nella Larsen, who wrote about middle-class characters? Or for Hurston's own Lilya Barkman? Are those middle-class characters inauthentic because they are not folk characters?

18. Locke called this the process of "class differentiation." See his essay "The New Negro," 6.
19. James Weldon Johnson, ed., *The Book of American Negro Poetry* (1922; repr., New York: Harcourt Brace Jovanovich, 1969), 41.
20. Zora Neale Hurston, "Race Cannot Become Great Until It Recognizes Its Talent," *Washington Tribune*, December 29, 1934.
21. Hurston, "Race Cannot Become Great."
22. Zora Neale Hurston, "Art and Such," in *Folklore, Memoirs, and Other Writings*, ed. Cheryl A. Wall (New York: Library of America, 1995), 910.
23. Langston Hughes, "The Negro Artist and the Racial Mountain" (1926), in *Within the Circle*, ed. Angelyn Mitchell (Durham, NC: Duke Univ. Press, 1994), 56; Hurston, "Art and Such," 910.
24. Ann duCille, *The Coupling Convention: Sex, Text, and Tradition in Black Women's Fiction* (New York: Oxford Univ. Press, 1993), 3–4.
25. See Kimberle Crenshaw's foundational essay "Demarginalizing the Intersection of Race and Sex: A Black Feminist Critique of Antidiscrimination Doctrine, Feminist Theory and Antiracist Politics," *University of Chicago Legal Forum*, no. 1 (1989): 139–67.
26. Zora Neale Hurston, "A Bit of Our Harlem," *Negro World*, April 8, 1922, 6. The story was first reprinted in *African Fundamentalism: A Literary and Cultural Anthology of Garvey's Harlem Renaissance*, ed. Tony Martin (Dover, MA: Majority Press, 1991), 287–89. It also appears in *Black Literature 1827–1940*, ed. Henry Louis Gates Jr. (1987–1996): Fiche1217.10.

27. "Jordan, Lawrence Victor," *Who's Who in Colored America 1938–1940* (Brooklyn: T. Yenser, 1940), 306.
28. Adele S. Newson, ed., *Zora Neale Hurston: A Reference Guide* (Boston: G. K. Hall, 1987); John Lowe, *Jump at the Sun: Zora Neale Hurston's Cosmic Comedy* (Champaign, IL: Univ. of Illinois Press, 1994), 20.
29. For classic migration tales that end tragically, see Rudolph Fisher, "The City of Refuge," in *The City of Refuge: The Collected Stories of Rudolph Fisher*, ed. John McCluskey (Columbia, MO: Univ. of Missouri Press, 2008), 35–47; and Marita Bonner, "The Whipping," in *Frye Street and Environs*, ed. Joyce Flynn and Joyce Occomy Stricklin (Boston: Beacon Press, 1987), 185–94.
30. Cheryl Wall has dated "Book of Harlem" to approximately 1921, but it seems more likely that Hurston wrote it during the mid-1920s and that it is an earlier incarnation of the story the *Courier* published. The address on the typescript of "Book of Harlem" on deposit at Yale University indicates Hurston was already living in New York when she wrote it, and the typescript was part of Carl Van Vechten's personal collection, which would also suggest that she wrote it after relocating to Harlem in 1925. Finally, the story mentions Van Vechten by name, just as the other stories Hurston published in 1927 mention famous personages, such as the singer and actress Ethel Waters and the attorney Myles Paige. It was her generation's version of a cameo appearance. For Wall's dating of the story, see her "Note on the Text," in *Hurston: Novels and Stories* (New York: Library of America, 1995), 1034.
31. See Wyatt Houston Day, ed., *American Visions* (December/January 1997): 14–19.
32. The story first appeared in the December 1926 (vol. 1, no. 3) issue of *The X-Ray*, an "Official Organ of Zeta Phi Beta Sorority."
33. Unpublished essay; quoted by permission of the author.
34. For a discussion of this gap in Hurston's biography, see Boyd, *Wrapped in Rainbows*, 68–69.
35. The characters discussed here share similarities with "toxic masculinity," but readers see so little of the characters' emotional lives that I cannot apply the term here.
36. Meisenhelder, *Hitting a Straight Lick with a Crooked Stick*, 5–7.

37. In 2005 I documented "Monkey Junk," "The Back Room," "She Rock," and "The Country in the Woman" in *Zora Neale Hurston and American Literary Culture*. I uncovered them in Henry Louis Gates's landmark microfiche collection *Black Literature 1827–1940*. Then in 2010, Glenda S. Carpio and Werner Sollors also chanced upon the stories while perusing microfilm of the newspaper. Through their efforts, the *Courier* stories became front-page news. A short time later, Carpio and Sollors gathered all five of the *Courier* stories as the centerpiece of a special issue of an academic journal, *Amerikastudien / American Studies*.
38. For further discussion of Porter's art, see Glenda R. Carpio and Werner Sollors, "Part One: 'The Book of Harlem,' 'Monkey Junk,' and 'The Back Room,'" *Amerikastudien / American Studies* 55, no. 4 (2010): 564. It seems likely that Hurston and Porter crossed paths in the relatively small world of New Negro artists and the still smaller world of black artists in the nation's capital. For a biography of Porter, see Donald F. Davis, "James Porter of Howard: Artist, Writer," *Journal of Negro History* 70, no. 3–4 (Summer–Fall 1985): 89–91. After studying abroad, Porter returned to Howard as a faculty member and wrote what his biographer Donald F. Davis calls "the fundamental book for those who delve into black art history." James A. Porter's "Woman Holding a Jug" is reproduced in *Amerikastudien / American Studies* 55, no. 4 (2010): 576.
39. Alona Sagee, "Bessie Smith: 'Down Hearted Blues' and 'Gulf Coast Blues' Revisited," *Popular Music* 26, no. 1 (2006): 121. A reference to the song also appears in Rudolph Fisher's "The City of Refuge," 14.
40. Sagee, "Bessie Smith," 121.
41. Carpio and Sollors, "Part One: 'The Book of Harlem,' 'Monkey Junk,' and 'The Back Room,'" 563.
42. For further discussion of gender in these stories, see my essay "'Youse in New Yawk': The Gender Politics of Zora Neale Hurston's 'Lost' Caroline Stories," *African American Review* 47, no. 4 (Winter 2014): 477–93.
43. See Hugh Davis, "'She Rock': A 'New' Story by Zora Neale Hurston," *The Zora Neale Hurston Forum* 18 (2004): 14–20.

44. Details about how Davis uncovered the story were provided in an email to the author.
45. West, "'Youse in New Yawk': The Gender Politics of Zora Neale Hurston's 'Lost' Caroline Stories," 489.
46. For a discussion of Wright's response to Hurston's work see my *Zora Neale Hurston and American Literary Culture* (Gainesville: Univ. Press of Florida, 2005), 109–26.
47. Hemenway, *Zora Neale Hurston,* 74.
48. Hemenway, *Zora Neale Hurston,* 77.
49. Julius Lester, *Black Folktales* (New York: Grove Press, 1991), ix; Hemenway, *Zora Neale Hurston,* 79.
50. Boyd, *Wrapped in Rainbows,* 218–35.
51. Hurston, *Dust Tracks,* 188–89.
52. For a discussion of the reception of *Their Eyes Were Watching God,* see my *Zora Neale Hurston and American Literary Culture,* 91–126. A discussion of Hurston's recovery and canonization follows on pages 229–48.

BIBLIOGRAPHY

Bonner, Marita. "The Whipping." In *Frye Street and Environs*, edited by Joyce Flynn and Joyce Occomy Stricklin, 185–94. Boston: Beacon Press, 1987.

Boyd, Valerie. *Wrapped in Rainbows: The Life of Zora Neale Hurston*. New York: Scribner, 2003.

Cameron, Christopher. "Zora Neale Hurston, Freethought, and African American Religion." *Journal of Africana Religions* 4, no. 2 (2016): 236–44. muse.jhu.edu/article/621873.

Carby, Hazel V. "The Politics of Fiction, Anthropology, and the Folk: Zora Neale Hurston." In *New Essays on "Their Eyes Were Watching God,"* edited by Michael Awkward, 71–93. Cambridge: Univ. of Cambridge Press, 1990.

Carpio, Glenda R., and Werner Sollors, eds. *African American Literary Studies: New Texts, New Approaches, New Challenges*. Special issue of *Amerikastudien / American Studies* 55, no. 4 (2010): 551–780.

Carpio and Sollors. "The Newly Complicated Zora Neale Hurston." *The Chronicle Review* (January 7, 2011): B6–10.

Chapman, Erin D. *Prove It on Me: New Negroes, Sex, and Popular Culture in the 1920s*. New York: Oxford Univ. Press, 2012.

Crenshaw, Kimberle. "Demarginalizing the Intersection of Race and Sex: A Black Feminist Critique of Antidiscrimination Doctrine, Feminist Theory, and Antiracist Politics." In *Feminism and Politics*, edited by Anne Phillips, 314–43. New York: Oxford Univ. Press, 1998.

Davis, Donald F. "James Porter of Howard: Artist, Writer." *The Journal of Negro History* 70, no. 3–4: 89–91.

Davis, Hugh. "'She Rock': A 'New' Story by Zora Neale Hurston." *Zora Neale Hurston Forum* 18 (2004): 14–20.

duCille, Ann. *The Coupling Convention: Sex, Text, and Tradition in Black Women's Fiction*. New York: Oxford Univ. Press, 1993.

Evans, Curtis J. *The Burden of Black Religion*. Oxford: Oxford Univ. Press, 2008.

Fisher, Rudolph. "The City of Refuge." In *The City of Refuge: The Collected Stories of Rudolph Fisher*. Edited by John McCluskey. Columbia, MO: Univ. of Missouri Press, 2008.

Gates, Henry Louis Jr., ed. *Black Literature, 1827–1940*. Alexandria, VA: Chadwyck-Healey, 1987–1996.

Griffin, Farah Jasmine. *"Who Set You Flowin'?": The African-American Migration Narrative*. New York: Oxford Univ. Press, 1996.

Harold, Claudrena N. "Marcus Garvey." In *Harlem Speaks: A Living History of the Harlem Renaissance*, edited by Cary D. Wintz, 389–410. Naperville, IL: Sourcebooks, 2007.

Harriss, M. Cooper. "Preacherly Texts: Zora Neale Hurston and the Homiletics of Literature." *Journal of Africana Religions* 4, no. 2 (2016): 278–90.

Hemenway, Robert E. *Zora Neale Hurston: A Literary Biography*. Urbana: Univ. of Illinois Press, 1977.

Hughes, Langston. "The Negro Artist and the Racial Mountain." In *Within the Circle*, edited by Angelyn Mitchell, 55–59. Durham, NC: Duke Univ. Press, 1994.

Hughes, Langston, and Zora Neale Hurston. *Mule Bone: A Comedy of Negro Life*. Edited by George Houston Bass and Henry Louis Gates Jr. New York: Harper Perennial, 1991.

Hurston, Zora Neale. "Art and Such." In *Folklore, Memoirs, and Other Writings*. Edited by Cheryl A. Wall, 905–11. New York: Library of America, 1995.

———. "The Back Room." *Pittsburgh Courier*, February 19, 1927, sec. 2, p. 1. *Black Literature 1827–1940* (1987–1996): fiche 1627.05.

———. *Barracoon: The Story of the Last "Black Cargo."* Edited by Deborah Plant. New York: Amistad, 2018.

———. "A Bit of Our Harlem." *Negro World*, April 8, 1922, 6. *Black Literature 1827–1940* (1987–1996): fiche 1217.10.

———. "Book of Harlem." Typescript, Zora Neale Hurston Collection. James Weldon Johnson Collection in the Yale Collection of American Literature, Beinecke Rare Book and Manuscript Library.

———. "The Book of Harlem." *Pittsburgh Courier*, February 12, 1927, sec. 2, p. 1. *Black Literature 1827–1940* (1987–1996): fiche 1626.11.

———. *Color Struck*. 1926. In *Zora Neale Hurston: Collected Plays*. Edited by Jean Lee Cole and Charles Mitchell, 33–50. New Brunswick, NJ: Rutgers Univ. Press, 2008.

———. *The Complete Stories of Zora Neale Hurston*. New York: HarperCollins, 1995.

———. "The Conversion of Sam" [listed as "Conversion of Man"]. Typescript. Zora Neale Hurston Collection, 1919–1945. Schomburg Center for Research in Black Culture.

———. "The Country in the Woman." *Pittsburgh Courier*, March 26, 1927, sec. 2, p. 1. *Black Literature 1827–1940* (1987–1996): fiche 1628.05.

———. *Dust Tracks on a Road: An Autobiography*. 1942. Reprint, New York: HarperCollins, 1991.

———. "The Emperor Effaces Himself." In *Call and Response: Key Debates in African American Studies*, edited by Henry Louis Gates Jr. and Jennifer Burton, 267–71. New York: W. W. Norton, 2011.

———. *Every Tongue Got to Confess: Negro Folk-tales from the Gulf States*. New York: HarperCollins, 2001.

———. "High John de Conquer." In *Folklore, Memoirs, and Other Writings*. Edited by Cheryl A. Wall, 922–31. New York: Library of America, 1995.

———. "Monkey Junk." *Pittsburgh Courier*, March 5, 1927, sec. 2, p. 1. *Black Literature 1827–1940* (1987–1996): fiche 1627.09.

———. "Race Cannot Become Great Until It Recognizes Its Talent." *Washington Tribune*, December 29, 1934. n.p.

———. "She Rock." *Pittsburgh Courier*, August 5, 1933, sec. 2, p. 3. *Black Literature 1827–1940* (1987–1996): fiche 1740.10.

———. *Spears* (1926). In *Zora Neale Hurston: Collected Plays*. Edited by Jean Lee Cole and Charles Mitchell, 51–62. New Brunswick, NJ: Rutgers Univ. Press, 2008.

———. *Their Eyes Were Watching God*. 1937. Reprint, New York: Harper Perennial, 2013.

———. "Under the Bridge." *X-Ray* 1, no. 3 (1925): 9–12. Reprinted in *American Visions* (December/January 1997), edited by Wyatt Houston Day: 14–19.

———. *Zora Neale Hurston: A Life in Letters*. Edited by Carla Kaplan. New York: Doubleday, 2001.

Hyest, Jenny. "'Born with God in the House': Feminist Vision and Religious Revision in the Works of Zora Neale Hurston." *Legacy: A Journal of American Women Writers* 35, no. 1 (2018): 25–47. https://www.muse.jhu.edu/article/696339.

Johnson, Charles S. *Ebony and Topaz: A Collectenea*. 1927. Reprint, Freeport, NY: Black Heritage Library Collection, 1971.

Johnson, James Weldon, ed. *The Book of American Negro Poetry*. 1922. Reprint, New York: Harcourt Brace Jovanovich, 1969.

Johnson, Ronald M. "Those Who Stayed: Washington's Black Writers in the 1920's," *Records of the Columbia Historical Society, Washington, D.C.* 50 (1980): 484–99.

"Jordan, Lawrence Victor." *Who's Who in Colored America 1938–1940*. Brooklyn: T. Yenser, 1940: 306.

Joseph, Philip. "The Verdict from the Porch: Zora Neale Hurston and Reparative Justice." *American Literature* 74, no. 3 (2002): 455–83. https://www.muse.jhu.edu/article/1844.

Krasner, David. "Dark Tower and the Saturday Nighters: Salons as Themes in African American Drama." *African American Studies* 49, no. 1/2 (Spring/Summer 2008): 81–95.

Larsen, Nella. *Quicksand and Passing*. Edited by Deborah E. McDowell. New Brunswick, NJ: Rutgers Univ. Press, 1986.

Lester, Julius. *Black Folktales*. New York: Grove Press, 1991.

Locke, Alain. "The New Negro." In *The New Negro*. 1925. pp. 1–16. Reprint, New York: Atheneum, 1992.

"Myles Anderson Paige." *Who's Who in Colored America 1941–44*. Brooklyn: T. Yenser, n.d.: 392.

Lawless, Elaine J. "What Zora Knew: A Crossroads, a Bargain with the Devil, and a Late Witness." *The Journal of American Folklore* 126, no. 500: 152–73. www.jstor.org/stable/10.5406/jamerfolk.126.500.0152.

Lowe, John. *Jump at the Sun: Zora Neale Hurston's Cosmic Comedy*. Urbana: Univ. of Illinois Press, 1994.

Manigault-Bryant, James A., and Lerhonda S. Manigault-Bryant. "Conjuring Pasts and Ethnographic Presents in Zora Neale Hurston's Modernity." *Journal of Africana Religions* 4, no. 2 (2016): 225–35.

Martin, Tony. *African Fundamentalism: A Literary and Cultural Anthology of Garvey's Harlem Renaissance*. Dover, MA: Majority Press, 1983.

———. *Literary Garveyism: Garvey, Black Arts, and the Harlem Renaissance*. Dover, MA: Majority Press, 1983.

Mathieu, Sarah-Jane (Saje). "The African American Great Migration Reconsidered." *OAH Magazine of History* 23, no. 4 (October 2009): 19–23.

McHenry, Elizabeth. *Forgotten Readers: Recovering the Lost History of African American Literary Societies*. Durham, NC: Duke Univ. Press, 2002.

Meisenhelder, Susan Edwards. *Hitting a Straight Lick with a Crooked Stick*. Tuscaloosa, AL: Univ. of Alabama Press, 1999.

Moylan, Virginia Lynn. *Zora Neale Hurston's Final Decade*. Gainesville, FL: Univ. Press of Florida, 2011.

Newson, Adele S. *Zora Neale Hurston: A Reference Guide*. Boston: G. K. Hall, 1987.

Rosenberg, Rachel A. "Looking for Zora's Mule Bone: The Battle for Artistic Authority in the Hurston-Hughes Collaboration." *Modernism/modernity* 6, no. 2 (April 1999): 79–105. doi: 10.1353/mod.1999.0021.

Ryan, Barbara. "In/visible Men: Hurston, 'Sweat' and Laundry Icons." *American Studies* 51, no. 1/2 (Spring/Summer 2010): 69–88.

Sherrard-Johnson, Cherene. *Portraits of the New Negro Woman: Visual and Literary Culture in the Harlem Renaissance*. New Brunswick, NJ: Rutgers Univ. Press, 2007.

Spagnuolo, Daniel. "Paraphernalia of Conjure: Hurston and the Black Folk Preacher." Unpublished paper, 2009.

Tate, Claudia. "Hitting 'A Straight Lick with a Crooked Stick': *Seraph on the Sewanee*, Zora Neale Hurston's Whiteface Novel." In *The Psychoanalysis of Race*, edited by Christopher Lane, 380–94. New York: Columbia Univ. Press, 1998.

Toomer, Jean. *Cane*. 1923. Reprint, New York: W. W. Norton, 2011.

Walker, Alice. "Looking for Zora." In *I Love Myself When I Am Laughing . . . And Then Again When I Am Looking Mean and Impressive: A Zora Neale Hurston Reader*, edited by Alice Walker, 297–313. New York: Feminist Press, 1979.

———. "On Refusing to Be Humbled by Second Place in a Contest You Did Not Design: A Tradition by Now." In *I Love Myself When I Am Laughing . . . And Then Again When I Am Looking Mean and Impressive: A Zora Neale Hurston Reader*, edited by Alice Walker, 1–4. New York: Feminist Press, 1979.

Wall, Cheryl A. *Women of the Harlem Renaissance*. Bloomington, IN: Univ. of Indiana Press, 1995.

Weisenfeld, Judith. *Hollywood Be Thy Name: African American Religion in American Film, 1929–1949*. Berkeley: Univ. of California Press, 2007.

West, M. Genevieve. "'Youse in New Yawk': The Gender Politics of Zora Neale Hurston's 'Lost' Caroline Stories." *African American Review* 47, no. 4 (Winter 2014): 477–93.

———. *Zora Neale Hurston and American Literary Culture*. Gainesville, FL: Univ. Press of Florida, 2005.

CREDITS

"John Redding Goes to Sea" was originally published in *Stylus*, May 1921, and was reprinted in *Opportunity*, January 1926.

"A Bit of Our Harlem" was originally published in *Negro World*, April 8, 1922.

"Drenched in Light" was originally published in *Opportunity*, December 1924.

"The Bone of Contention" was first published posthumously in *Mule Bone: A Comedy of Negro Life*, collected and edited by George Houston Bass and Henry Louis Gates Jr. by Harper Perennial, 1991.

"Magnolia Flower" was originally published in *The Spokesman*, July 1925.

"Muttsy" was originally published in *Opportunity*, June 1925.

"Black Death" was first published posthumously in *The Complete Stories of Zora Neale Hurston*, collected and edited by Henry Louis Gates Jr. and Sieglinde Lemke by Harper Perennial, 1995.

"Spunk" was originally published in *Opportunity*, August 1926.

"'Possum or Pig?" was originally published in *The Forum*, September 1926.

"The Eatonville Anthology" was originally published serially in *The Messenger*, September–November 1926.

"Sweat" was originally published in *Fire*, November 1926.

"Under the Bridge" was originally published in *The X-Ray*, December 1926.

"Book of Harlem" was first published posthumously in *Zora Neale Hurston: Novels and Stories*, collected and edited by Cheryl A. Wall by Library of America, 1995.

"The Book of Harlem" was originally published in *The Pittsburgh Courier*, February 12, 1927.

"The Back Room" was originally published in *The Pittsburgh Courier*, February 19, 1927.

"Monkey Junk" was originally published in *The Pittsburgh Courier*, March 5, 1927.

"The Country in the Woman" was originally published in *The Pittsburgh Courier*, March 26, 1927.

"The Gilded Six-Bits" was originally published in *Story*, August 1933.

"She Rock" was originally published in *The Pittsburgh Courier*, August 5, 1933.

"The Fire and the Cloud" was originally published in *Challenge*, September 1934.

ABOUT THE AUTHOR

ZORA NEALE HURSTON was a novelist, folklorist, and anthropologist. She was the author of four novels (*Jonah's Gourd Vine*, 1934; *Their Eyes Were Watching God*, 1937; *Moses, Man of the Mountain*, 1939; and *Seraph on the Suwanee*, 1948); three books of folklore (*Mules and Men*, 1935; *Tell My Horse*, 1938; and *Every Tongue Got to Confess*, 2001); an autobiography (*Dust Tracks on a Road*, 1942); an ethnography (*Barracoon*, 2018); and more than fifty short stories, essays, and plays. She attended Howard University, Barnard College, and Columbia University, and graduated from Barnard College in 1928. She was born on January 7, 1891, in Notasulga, Alabama, and grew up in Eatonville, Florida. She died in Fort Pierce, Florida, in 1960. In 1973, Alice Walker had a headstone placed at her grave site with this epitaph: ZORA NEALE HURSTON: "A GENIUS OF THE SOUTH."